Lyrical Darkness

*11 dark fiction stories inspired by
the music that rocks your soul.*

*A.T.Reid ~ Sharon Love Cook ~ Niki Danforth ~ Ann Fields
Donnie Light ~ Connor Millard ~ Terri Reid
David McAfee ~ Ophelia Julien ~ Andrea Jones*

SHE LOVES YOU

by

Ophelia Julien

"You know who I ran into yesterday?" David Chase pitched the question in the most casual tone possible, seeking to startle his companion into an uncomfortable and thus greatly satisfying reaction.

Eric LaMark looked bored as he speared a bite of steak. "Who?" he asked, voice nearly expressionless to convey his disdain.

"Emmy. Emmy Cosgrove."

The reaction was better than he hoped. Eric choked on his mouthful of sirloin, gulped a large swallow of ice water, and stared at his tablemate with shocked if watery eyes. *"Who?"*

"Emily Cosgrove. Emmy. You know. The girl you proposed to three years ago that turned you down flat and went back to England?" He paused a moment. "She never even said goodbye," he added in a soft voice, more to himself than as a comment.

Eric stared at him, struck into silence, a fact David noted with a quiet glee.

* * *

David had been looking for Emmy, seeking her unconsciously, for those three years, but when she turned up again he was still shocked. The first time he saw her was at the intersection down the block from his office. She was kitty-corner to him, waiting to cross to his side of the street, but she didn't see him wave at her when they passed on opposite sides of the through street, and the lunch crowd was so big that he lost sight of her as she continued on her way.

Emily Cosgrove. She had been the major heartbreak of his college life, a sweet-smiled, sweet-faced biology major with dark hair, exotic eyes, and the surprising accent of a girl born and bred somewhere in England. She had told him where, but it hadn't meant much to an Indiana boy. All he knew was that her accent made her that much more attractive. When they talked, her conversational prompt wasn't "uh-huh" and "go on" but a quick "yeah, yeah, yeah" uttered so softly and so politely that he was both charmed and flattered that she found him so interesting. Well, maybe she didn't, but if not, she never let on. He lost his heart to her the very first time they spoke in the student union.

And of course she fell completely ass-over-elbows for Eric LaMark, childhood annoyance grown to a rich, good-looking, charming, self-centered jerk of a pre-law major who was somehow irresistible to women in a way that both baffled and irritated David. He had known—hadn't he?—that as soon as Emmy and Eric saw each other, he, David, would achieve instant invisible man status. This was nothing new, but this time he minded. Emily was the world to him.

So when he ran into her again in the here and now, this time as he lingered over one last cup of coffee at the sidewalk shop before getting himself back behind his desk, his life took on that amazing rainbow sheen it had when she was around. He had missed her when she fled back to England, but the edge had worn away with time. Now as he stared up at her smiling face he felt his heart give a painful leap even as he was smiling back. "Emmy," he had whispered, and stumbled to his feet. "Please," he said aloud. "Please, sit down."

And she had, edging around the chair beside him before he could pull it out, and settling herself into it, flipping her long black hair over her shoulder in that familiar gesture. "David Chase," she said. "All dressed up in his suit and tie. Aren't you the best sight ever?" Her accent washed over him like sun-warmed honey.

"How are you? What are you up to? How've you been? Where did you go?"

She held up her hands to stop him, laughing. "Stop, stop!" She looked him over and smiled with approval. "Do you even have time for this? Have I caught you during your lunch break?"

"Yes and yes. I'm nearly done with lunch, but I have time to catch up, at least a little." He gazed into her dark brown eyes and was rewarded with warmth and affection. "And if I run out of time, maybe we can continue over drinks? Say, five-thirty?"

She smiled at him again. "Oh, why not? We can chat for a bit. It's taken me forever to find my way back here." She sat back in the chair and folded her hands in her lap. "Where should we start?"

"You, of course." David couldn't stop staring at her. He had missed everything about her, the sheen of her hair in sunlight, the liveliness in her every expression. She was even wearing an outfit he remembered from several years back, the simple black skirt paired with a brightly flowered blouse that turned her skin to spun caramel. "Where did you go? I know Eric planned to propose to you." She glanced down for a moment and David feared he had put his foot in it. "I'm sorry, Em. We don't have to go into that—"

She waved his concern away with her hand. "No, it's all right. It was a long time ago. "You and I talked about that, right? That Eric was going to propose? Truth is, he didn't."

"He what?" David was appalled. "But I thought…"

"You and me both." She made a wry face at him. "We didn't end well," she admitted.

"That bastard. That son of a—" David was spluttering in near fury.

"Never mind," she said, voice soft. "I should have realized. Eric always was the womanizer, wasn't he? So handsome. So smooth. A right lady-killer, that one."

"He's a lot of things," David said bitterly. "If I'd known, well." He looked at her and found the courage to say it. "I always loved you. You knew that, right?"

Her smile was sad. "I picked the wrong guy, huh?"

He swallowed. "It's not like it's too late," he said.

She looked down again, her hair swinging down across her face, and was silent for a moment. David reached out to touch her shoulder but she raised her head to look at him, leaning back against the chair, and once more gave him her sunniest smile. "Want to hear something really funny?" she said. "I still think about him all the time. And I still love him. Do you believe that?"

He shook his head. "No. I don't."

A bitterness twisted her mouth but it was gone in a second. "He hurt me really badly, David. You have no idea. Now," she said with a shrug, "I don't think that he meant to, but there it is. But if you ever see him…" She broke off and looked at him. "Do you?"

He couldn't lie to her. "Yes."

She grinned. "Tell him I love him." Then she laughed. "And don't even ask me. Yes, you have to do this."

He sighed loudly. "All right. I'll tell him."

"And you? What about you?" she asked.

"Pretty boring," he answered. "I finished school. I'm still working at the first place that hired me."

"Really? What are you doing?"

"Remember how I wanted to go into computers?"

"Yeah, yeah, yeah," she said, her accent coloring the simple prompt. "Did you?"

"No, I wound up in communications." He made a face at her laugh. "I work for an advertising agency."

"That's good, David. Really good."

"It'll do for now. What about you?"

"What about me?" She glanced at her watch. "Oh, wow, is that the time already? David, I need to go, I'm sorry. Maybe catch up another time?"

"Drinks at five-thirty?" Her expression told him no. "Okay, then tell me where and when," he said, rising from his chair with her.

"Can I find you here most days?"

"Here or very close. Usually around lunch time."

"Marvelous." Emmy could say that without sounding like an upper-crust matron. "I'll find you, promise."

"I'll hold you to that!" he called after her as she blew him an air kiss and hurried away down the sidewalk, disappearing into the crowd.

* * *

David ended his tale and smiled faintly at the memory. "And just like that, she was off and running."

Eric had stopped eating. "This is a joke, right? That you saw her?"

"What? No. No joke. Why would I do that?"

But Eric didn't answer the question. Instead, "She said that she still loves me?" His voice was hollow.

"Yup. I have no idea why." David glanced at his friend, smirking, and was startled by the expression on Eric's face. "I'd have given my right arm for her to say that about me. I can't believe you didn't propose to her."

"She told you that, too? That I didn't propose?"

"Yeah, she said that. And she told me I should tell you that she still thinks about you. I don't know why." He looked at Eric. "Why didn't you marry her?"

"Why didn't you?" Eric snapped back.

"You were in the way."

They stared at each other and then Eric pushed back from the table. "I'll see you another time," he said and turned away.

"That's what Emmy and I said to each other, too." As soon as he said it, David saw Eric's back stiffen mid-step, and he gloated.

* * *

Dinner that night consisted of a microwave meal, a cold beer, and a long conversation with Maggie Brooke, ex-lover and good friend. "The thing is," David said, pulling the film from his pasta primavera and wishing that he still had some garlic bread in his freezer, "I haven't seen her in three years and it was like no time had passed at all."

"Meaning what?" Maggie had eaten already at her own apartment and answered David's invitation to come over with her characteristic amiability. Maggie rarely got excited about anything, a trait that made her a great friend but somewhat lacking for a love relationship. Still, once they realized they were better platonically than otherwise, they enjoyed a connection that was open, honest, and relaxed. David knew he could tell Maggie just about anything.

"I'm not sure. I think it means that I'm still in love with her."

"Oh, Lord."

"No, seriously."

"David, you fall in love every time you turn around. Remember the hostess at that seafood restaurant? And then there was that teacher you met when you joined the health club. And after that—" She caught the expression on his face and relented. "I think if you could do it, you'd have gone after the weather girl on Channel 8."

"She's not my type."

"She's exactly your type."

"Not when she has a fiancé who's an ex-NFL linebacker."

Maggie grinned at him. "Okay, that's valid. But to get back to…Emma, was it?"

"Emmy. Short for Emily." He grabbed a fork from the drawer beside the stove and came to sit at the table with her. "I don't know, Mags. It was amazing to see her. And then I found out she's still in love with Eric." His voice was dark around a mouthful of pasta.

"Eric? The guy you've known since junior high?"

"That would be him. Jerk," David grumbled, half-joking. Being envious of Eric was a fact of life.

"You always say that about him."

"You've met him. You said the same thing."

"True. He does like himself quite a lot."

"Here's the thing. Three years ago, Emmy and I were convinced Eric was going to propose to her. Hell, he just about said that to me. But he didn't. And she hightailed it back to England right after. I would have tried to find her, but didn't have a clue. I only had her address and number while she was living State-side."

"Didn't you get suspicious when she just disappeared like that?"

"I would have been, except that Eric told me he had proposed and that she had turned him down."

Maggie raised an eyebrow in what could have been mistaken for curiosity. "So Eric lied. Why do you suppose?"

"I've been thinking about that." David washed down the last of his pasta with a swig of beer and wished again that he had garlic bread in the house. "And I don't have any kind of idea. Emmy told me today that they ended badly."

"I can imagine, if she thought he was going to propose and he didn't. Would she have accepted?"

"In a heartbeat." David cleared his throat. "She was crazy about him."

The question about Eric's non-existent proposal haunted him off and on over the next week. Why did Eric make up a story about being turned down? And why hadn't Emmy at least come to say good-bye before returning to England? More than that, what brought her back three years later?

He kept a lookout for her every time he went to lunch, and he went to lunch even in the rain so he wouldn't chance missing her, but she never showed. After a while, he could almost have believed he had imagined the entire encounter.

Except that Eric got weird.

They usually met twice a week or so for a beer after work. David always wondered why they had kept up those after-work drinks long after their first year out of college. They had been in the same circle of friends at school, but shortly after graduation most of the group had drifted away to other destinations, seeking better jobs or following love, marriage, and family. They probably met more out of habit than a desire to see each other socially. So here they were, still meeting at a corner tavern-slash-grill, usually on Mondays and Thursdays, not quite talking over old times, but somehow not discussing anything of any importance, either. Until Emmy reappeared.

At first, Eric pointedly ignored anything David said about her. After their first several meetings beyond Emmy's reappearance, though, he broached the subject himself. "You said she wanted me to know that she still loves me?" His voice had that strange, hollow quality that emerged when her name came up.

"Yup." David pulled the knot in his tie part-way down and unbuttoned his collar button.

"Why would she say that?"

"Because it's true?"

Eric took a gulp of his beer. "It can't be," he muttered, staring down at the table.

"Why didn't you ever propose to her?"

There was a long silence. "Are you still in love with her?" Eric finally asked. He was still looking down, this time at the label on his beer bottle, and David had to strain to hear him over the noise in the bar.

No hesitation on David's part. "Yes."

Eric shook his head. "Then you may not want to hear this."

"Just tell me."

"All right, then. You've been warned." Eric took a deep breath and released it with a sigh. "I didn't propose to Emmy because she's crazy."

"What?" David was stung. "What are you talking about? She's the sweetest, probably the most beautiful woman I've ever met. How can you say that?"

"Oh, she's all that you think she is. Beautiful without a doubt. And sweet? Sure thing. But there was always something wrong in her head. Some loose wire or something. But you'd never guess until you got to know her. She's certifiable." He favored David with a wintry grin. "Gonna hit me? For disrespecting the woman you love?"

"That could happen. Define certifiable."

"Aggression. Mood swings. I don't mean laughing one minute and crying the next, or even going from content to depressed. I mean extreme mood swings. Like laughing one minute and trying to claw

8

your eyes out the next. She was needy, clingy. And if I didn't meet her needs or cling back, she'd get angry. I mean *angry*."

"Like threatening to hold her breath?" David asked with a tinge of sarcasm. He didn't buy what Eric was selling, not about Emmy.

"I mean like I have scars from where she scratched me. I had bruises sometimes. She was flat-out scary. There was no way I'd ever propose to her. There's no way to be in love with a woman who's fifty percent demon and one hundred percent Lizzie Borden."

David had no response. He was torn between furious and unsettled. He had known Eric since high school; Eric might have been a jerk of the first order but the one thing he wasn't was dishonest. Especially if he could use truth as a weapon, which he might be doing right now for his own private enjoyment, just to push David off balance. But the bottom line would still be that Eric was telling the truth.

"You don't have to believe me," Eric said, and drained the last of his beer. "But it's true. Neither of us should ever see her again." He abruptly stood and left without saying good-bye.

But David did see Emmy again. Several days after that last beer with Eric, and they hadn't met for drinks again since, she turned up at the sidewalk café and sat down at the table as David was finishing his sandwich.

"Hello," he said, uncertain. "Where've you been?"

"Here and there. How's things?"

"Same old, same old." He smiled at her and gazed into those brown eyes. They were soft as he remembered, but did he see something else there, now? An edge, maybe? Some sort of shadow? Maybe Eric had gotten to him more than he realized. He shut his mind firmly against everything Eric had said, but he wasn't quite quick enough.

"What's wrong, David?"

"Not much," he said, voice light. "What could be wrong?"

She tilted her head and regarded him. "I know you better than that. What happened?"

"Eric and I went for drinks the other week." He hesitated. "He said some stuff about you."

Her eyes narrowed, then softened. "He told you, didn't he?"

"Told me what?"

"Did he tell you I was possessive, or jealous?"

"No, not that."

"Or that I was a madwoman? A clinging vine?" There was bitterness in her voice and that nettled him. "He told you I was crazy, didn't he?"

There was no denying it. "Yes."

She turned her head away for a moment, regaining her composure. When she looked up at him again, there were tears in her eyes. "David, can I ask you a favor?"

It was a question he had waited years to hear. "Name it."

"Do you think there's a way you could get Eric to meet with me? Just one last time? I'd like to make things right between us."

He remembered Eric's parting line. *Neither of us should ever see her again.* But there she sat, hands in her lap, gazing at him with wet, beseeching eyes.

"Bloody hell," he said without thinking.

She laughed in spite of her tears. "You sound like someone from home."

He smiled back. "I'll try," he said. "That's all I can say. But you know Eric. No one pushes him around, as I'm sure you know."

Her smile grew rueful. "Yeah, yeah, yeah, I know. But I'd appreciate it if you tried."

"I can do that."

"Tell him to meet me Friday around five-thirty, at the last place we saw each other. *You* know."

David remembered three years ago when he had carried a similar message from Eric to Emmy, a request that she be at a specific place late on a Friday afternoon. Eric had led him to believe that he was going to propose to her. Now it was three years later and he was being tapped to do it again, but in reverse. He sighed inwardly. "I'll tell him."

"And can I ask you one more thing?"

"What's that?"

"Could you be there, too?"

"Me?" He was surprised.

"I mean, kind of in secret. You know, so that Eric doesn't know you're there. I might need a good strong shoulder to cry on after it's all over. But if you're right there, he might not be as candid with me as he would if he thinks we're alone."

Sneaking around. The idea was just the slightest bit distasteful.

"Please?"

He sighed. "So I get to hide and listen to you two declare your love to each other?"

"Don't be stupid," she said. "Eric got over me long ago. I hear he's found someone else, eh?"

David winced. "Yes. They've only just started getting serious."

"Rumor has it he's planning to propose to her."

"So it does," he agreed, carefully neutral.

"I wish her all the best in the future," she whispered. "But I'd like to clear things up with him before we all move on, you know?" She took a deep breath. "Although I think I'll always love him."

"Okay. I'll tell him. Where do you expect me to hide?"

She made a face at him and it was adorable. He felt his heart twist. "You're clever enough to find a place. Just make sure you keep us in sight. And can hear us." She caught the way he was looking at her. "I want this on record, David. You're my record. If you already know what we've said, you won't need me to repeat it to you while I'm weeping all over your shoulder."

He conceded the point.

* * *

That night he dreamed about Emmy. It was late spring, the end of term, and she was standing on the small hill past the student union, backlit by the sun so that her hair took on a sheen of dark fire and her features were shadowed. He squinted against the brightness of the light and could see that she was smiling. She waved at him as he approached her, climbing up into the sun, climbing up to her, but before he reached her she vanished. When he jolted awake, stunned by her sudden disappearance, he found he had been crying in his sleep. He wiped his face with his hand and wished to his deepest depths that he had not agreed to be there when she finally confronted Eric. He wished he had never delivered any message, the one three years ago or the one this week.

* * *

"What's going on?" Maggie's voice was as brusque as she could make it: her voice pierced his cell phone like an arrow.

David did what he always did. He dodged. "What's going on?" he repeated, making his tone deliberately light and changing the inflection to casual conversation.

"Never mind. I'll be right over."

"Wait, Mags?"

She had already hung up. David thumbed the button on his phone with a sigh, not sure he wanted to deal with Hurricane Maggie in his present state of mind, but there was no point in leaving his apartment. She would simply hunt him down and she was good at that. Resigned, he foraged through his ice-crusted freezer for something dinner-like in appearance and was rewarded with a forgotten frozen pizza. That would work. It was just becoming fragrant when his doorbell rang.

He buzzed her in and went to the refrigerator to pull a beer and a diet soda. He hated when Maggie was dieting. It made her cranky.

The three sharp raps on his door underscored that observation.

"Come on in. Want some pizza?"

She sniffed. "The cheese is burning."

"I didn't put it in that long ago. That must be stuff that fell to the bottom of the oven."

"Or stuff left over from the last time you made pizza."

"That's unkind."

"That's you." She sat down at the table in front of the can of soda and looked at him. "Tell me what's going on," she demanded.

David twisted the cap off of his beer and took a swig. "Tell me why you ask."

She softened her voice to match his. "We haven't talked since last weekend. I know you said that Emmy was on your mind. And I know something happened when you spoke with Eric last week. So what's going on?"

"A mess," he admitted. "I saw Emmy again, almost right after I saw Eric. You'd think they timed it that way, or something. I mean…" He let his voice trail away. "I could have used more time," he finally said.

"For what?"

"When I had drinks with Eric, he said some stuff about her."

"Really? Like what?"

He hesitated before answering. "Like that she's crazy. Full-bore nuts." The look on Maggie's face did more than nudge him. "Eric says he never proposed to her because Emmy is crazy. Mood swings and aggression. And very needy."

"Wow. I didn't expect that." She was studying him. "And you don't believe him? You don't think she's like that?"

"I don't know what to think. Eric's a lot of things, but a liar isn't one of them. He's the kind of person who's more likely to beat you over the head with the painful truth just for kicks."

"Do you think he was doing that here? Knowing that you always had a thing for her?"

"I don't know." David thought back to the evening in the bar, remembered the sound of Eric's voice, the look on his face. "I don't think so."

Maggie let a few silent moments pass before hitting the crux of his dilemma. "And you also said you saw Emmy right after you talked to Eric?"

He looked away from her. "Yeah. She found me at lunch, like before."

"Why didn't you guys just swap phone numbers, or something?"'

"I don't know." His answer was honest. "We just never did."

"It doesn't matter. She finds you when she wants to, I guess."

"Yes."

"And she found you after Eric said all that stuff about her?"

13

"Yes."

"How'd that go?"

David frowned. "What does that mean?"

"Just that you're about the lousiest liar on God's earth. She must have known something was up as soon as she looked into your baby blues."

"They're green," he reminded her.

"Quit hedging. How'd it go?"

"She asked me about it. I mean, she figured out that Eric had told me she was crazy." He could picture her face in detail, down to the look in her eyes. Sadness? Bitterness? Disappointment? "She wasn't happy about it."

"Was she surprised?"

"Not really. I mean, she knows Eric as well as I do."

Maggie put her hand on his, something she never did. "David, do you believe him? Do you think she's crazy?"

He shrugged, unhappy. "Maybe. I don't know. Does it matter?"

"Does it? I mean, are you thinking about starting a relationship with this woman?"

There it was, spoken out loud. He imagined the words coming from Maggie's mouth in comic book balloons with bold black lettering for emphasis. "I don't know," he said again. What he meant was that he hadn't allowed himself to think about that. He knew Emmy was still in love with Eric; how could he possibly stand a chance with her?

"Is it Eric? Or is it her mental instability?"

Ouch. She should have been a war-time surgeon: all precise incisions without the bother of anesthetic. *"I don't know."* He put an edge into it. "Besides, what do you care? Are you jealous?" he added just to be annoying.

She rolled her eyes. "Well, make a decision soon," she said. "You're such a pain when you feel stuck. And I think your pizza's burning."

They talked of other things after that, but came around to the same subject shortly before Maggie left. "There's one more thing," David found himself volunteering. He had hesitated to mention Emmy's

14

requests but found that as Maggie was preparing to leave, he felt a sudden need to tell her. "Emmy asked me to set up a meeting for her with Eric, so that they can clear the air before she moves on from him."

"And did you?"

"Yeah. Eric didn't want to do it, but I got him to agree to tomorrow evening."

"That might help both of them."

"There's more."

"So?" she prodded him when he grew silent.

"Emmy wants me to be there, too, but somewhere that Eric won't see me. She thinks he might not be as open with her if he knows I'm there."

"Well, that's just weird on a couple of levels, isn't it?"

"You think so?" David's relief that Maggie agreed with him about Emmy's request was like a second wind to him. "Why?"

"Well, wanting you around in the first place is just strange. It's between the two of them, isn't it? And then wanting you to hide?"

"I thought so, too. But I said yes to her anyhow."

"Why? Are you their non-marriage counselor?"

"She told me she might need a shoulder to cry on afterward." He felt like an idiot saying it, but he was always frank with Maggie.

She thought it over. "Okay. Maybe not so weird. I guess I could see where she might want you around. You've got good shoulders." She smiled at him then and for just a second, David wondered why they hadn't been able to stay together.

* * *

Getting Eric to agree to the meeting was an act of Herculean endeavor. Just giving him the message taught David why the age-old tradition of not killing the messenger had become necessary. But in the end, Eric had said, "Okay, okay, I'll be there. But only because I know she won't show up. No way." He had glared at David as he spoke.

"You think I'm setting you up? Having a joke?" David demanded.

"I don't know what you're doing. I'll be there. But she won't."

Now David paced along a small bluff, occasionally glancing down at the water below. The area felt so isolated it was easy to forget that this little slice of country was still within the city limits. And although people knew about it, somehow it never got very crowded. In hot weather, there were too many trees harboring mosquitoes for anyone to stay around for long without serious insect repellant. David figured for all that trouble, most folks would probably just go to the real country. In winter, the snow-laden trees were beautiful, but the path to the view became a nightmare of slush, or worse, ice.

David rubbed his arms against the chill that came off the water now that the sun was just above the horizon, casting pink and orange fingers into the sky. He knew the area well—all the university students did— and had always been able to picture that dusk three years ago when Eric had proposed to Emmy, or supposedly had. David had always seen the two in silhouette against the rosy, darkening sky, Eric on his knee, Emmy with her hand to her mouth as she gazed down at, in David's imagination, the huge diamond-and-platinum engagement ring offered up to her with a mix of hope and joy. *Like a flipping greeting card commercial*, he thought cynically, but his imagination suggested no alternatives. Now that long-held picture had been smashed to pieces by both parties, but it wasn't leaving his mind easily. He still didn't know what to think. He certainly didn't know what to feel.

"Come on, you guys," he muttered, pacing back and forth over a small distance. "Just get this over with."

On cue, there was a scrambling sound at the base of the path. David snuck a quick look before retreating into the trees. Eric had arrived and was not happy with his lot in life. He pushed and struggled his way up the path, complaining to himself in an undertone the whole time. David nearly let out a nervous giggle. He wasn't often treated to the sight of a disgruntled Eric LaMark. There was still enough light for David to see streaks of drying mud on the lower legs of Eric's pants and the sight made his mouth twitch again with suppressed amusement. Weeks later Eric would still be pissing and moaning about his dry-cleaning bill.

Eric brushed himself off and glanced at the trees, the water, the sky, and then back down the path. "C'mon, Emmy!" he called out. "If you're really here, let's just do this!"

There was no response.

"Emmm –mmmy!" He called out.

Did David hear a mocking tone in that voice? He frowned as he listened.

"David says he's seen you a few times. Maybe he dreamed you, I don't know. But I don't think you're gonna show. Somehow I know this."

Not mocking, David thought. Eric had been drinking. Drinking and then driving. *What an idiot.*

"Now you know as well as I do, Emmy, there's no coming back for you. No. Coming. Back." He hurled the words out into the wind, his voice loud and somewhat slurred. David risked a peek and saw that Eric was standing in the wide-legged, slumped stance of the inebriated. "You can't come back. Not now. Not ever."

The import of Eric's words was beginning to sink into David's conscious thought and he felt unexpected goose bumps come up on the backs of his arms, the base of his scalp. He didn't want to follow his uneasy thought to its logical conclusion.

"Eric." Her voice came from everywhere, soft and unmistakable. "Eric, I'm here, lover."

David saw his friend jump. "You can't be." No more slurring in his words. Simple shock.

"Don't be ridiculous, darling." The British accent was no longer warm and inviting. There was only coldness, an undercurrent of dark promise. "I'm coming to you right now, aren't I?"

David slipped out from behind the tree, giving up all pretense of hiding, and saw Eric standing still, his posture one of frozen disbelief. "Emmy?" he whispered, not caring if Eric heard him or saw him next to the trees.

And then she came, but not from the path. As both men watched, one incredulous, one in horror, a pale hand appeared at the edge of the bluff, scrabbling and clutching for a handhold. At last it found purchase and the other skeletally pale arm appeared, clothed in a torn and muddy sleeve. In the last of the daylight, David could just discern the bright floral pattern now caked with muck. Awkwardly, she clambered up to even ground, pulling herself in disarticulated fashion. The smell of decay and water-rot wafted to him on the breeze and he choked silently on it.

The repulsiveness of the vision chilled David, paralyzed him in cold horror. The part of his brain that continued to function noted that several of her bones were broken. He could see that, he realized with a shock, because some of her skin and underlying tissue was missing in chunks. Her hair, long, snarled, and tangled with twigs, rotting leaves, and strands of limp weeds, hung down past her shoulders. "You made me wait so long, Eric. That was amazingly rude of you." Her voice was raspy now as it issued from the torn and mangled throat. "It took me so long to get back to you..." She shuffled closer and raised one half-shattered arm to touch him.

Eric flinched and backed up two steps, and David backed away with him, trying to melt farther back into the trees. He could see that Eric was poised to run. If he broke the spell, if he could force his feet to move, Eric would flee down that path and David would be close behind him. He readied himself, one hand against the solid bole of the tree beside him.

"Don't you dare," she said in high-pitched, tearful tones, filled with anguish and yet unmistakably dead. "Don't you dare back away from me. You who put me into that water. You who should have been with me there, if you were truly going to leave me."

"Emmy, it was an accident... You fell. I couldn't catch you—"

"You pushed me away!"

"You were crazy," Eric's reply was little more than a whisper as she came closer and closer to him. "Scratching, hitting..."

"You hurt me, Eric. You hurt me so badly." Emmy's voice was also quieter, but no less hard. "And after I fell, what did you do?"

"I...I—"

"What did you do?" she persisted. She was face to face with him now, and David winced against the horror that the face he once loved and cherished had become. She was a mangled nightmare, an eyeless, lipless, twisted visage and the rosy pink of the sun's last rays somehow made everything worse.

"I ran," Eric whispered.

"You ran," she said contemptuously. "Didn't bother to check on me—"

"I could see you were beyond help. Your neck—"

"And the lies? Eric, the lies about me going home?"

"The truth was worse."

"How?" Her wail, keen and sepulchral, brought a crawling sensation to the back of David's neck.

"Should I have told everyone I never meant to propose to you? Because you were crazy? That you fell to your death because you were a mental mess? Emmy, every day I waited to hear that your body had come back, floated up, whatever. Every day. And it never happened. I would have come forward. I swear it. But I waited."

"Instead of going to the police and having them search at the time?"

Eric grew still. "I was afraid," he said. "I was just afraid."

"I'll show you fear," she promised, a hiss from her lipless mouth.

Then Eric did something unexpected. He dropped to his knees in front of her and gazed up at that terrible, ruined face.

For just that short moment, David saw the silhouette he had always imagined, backlit in the splendor of sunset, Emmy gazing down at Eric's upturned face. Except—what was wrong with this picture? The suitor was within an inch of a heart attack and the bride was splendidly dead with shattered bones, crowned with rotting weeds and leaves. The little voice at the back of David's mind whispered the details deep within and he bit back a panicked, hysterical sob of laughter.

"I'm sorry, Emily," Eric said. "I'm so sorry."

"I accept that apology," she said after a long pause. And then, "I love you and we were meant to be together. So I've come back for you. Come to get you before you make the mistake of choosing another woman."

"Emmy—"

"Shhh."

19

David watched, frozen, as Emmy put her shattered arms around Eric's neck, cried out when Eric didn't struggle, didn't even resist, as she pulled him toward her and down. Eric turned David's way just once and their eyes met for the smallest fraction of a second, but David would never forget that look: the resignation, the sadness, the doom... He watched, frozen, as Eric and Emmy merged and then... were gone—down into the earth? Melted away? He watched, frozen, long after there was nothing left to see. Then some part of him thought to fumble the small flashlight from his pocket, fingers clumsy and wooden. With caution, he approached the spot where the two had vanished and shone his light upon the ground. Nothing, not even footprints. No, wait. He bent and retrieved a strip of muddy fabric, the floral print of it dull beneath its coating of age and grime. He stared at it for a while and then, as if his brain finally admitted the horror he had just seen, he found himself tearing down the hill, ignoring roots and branches, dumb instinct guiding his every step as he fled to the sanctuary of his car.

* * *

Pounding. Loud, incessant pounding. David rolled over in his bed and groaned. What time was it anyway? He opened one eye and peered at his clock with suspicion. Saturday. After nine. He presumed that was nine AM. The pounding continued.

He knew it was Maggie. He could tell by the way the door was shaking in its frame. "Hold on," he mumbled, still trying to wake up. He couldn't remember how to think. He felt as if something had been holding him underwater, underground. He felt like he hadn't been breathing for hours.

"David? David, are you up?" Her voice was reaching screech level. The neighbors would love that.

"What? What the hell, Mags?"

She pushed her way in as soon as he cracked the door open a fraction. "I wanted to make sure you were okay. I wanted to check on you."

"Wait, slow down. I'm okay. Why wouldn't I be? What's the problem?"

"You didn't hear? You didn't see the news?"

"See what?"

"Eric LaMark. Your friend, right? The young hot shot on his way to the top of the financial world? He was found dead in his bed this morning."

For a second the world went completely dark and David was back on that bluff at sunset, watching as Emmy took Eric into her fleshless arms. "Wait. Wait," he said, trying to make sense of it. Had he just been dreaming? Had everything been a dream all along? "Eric was found dead in his bed?"

"Yes."

"But that's impossible. I just saw him last night." He looked at her. "I told you he was supposed to meet Emmy. And he did. I saw him. I saw *them*."

"But that's what I'm trying to tell you, David. They found him dead this morning, but they think Eric's been dead longer than just last night. They think maybe yesterday morning, or even the night before that. There's no way you could have seen him." She looked at him, concern in her hazel eyes. "There wasn't a mark on his body. They won't know what it was until the autopsy."

David stumbled to his sofa and sat down hard. On the coffee table before him he saw a scrap of muddy floral fabric, and choked back the urge to scream aloud. He had been at the bluff. They had *all* been at the bluff. He could have believed it was a dream but for that horrid strip of her blouse. There was a faint scent of stagnant water and death coming from it. He closed his eyes and wondered if he could ever find a way to forget.

"Maybe Eric had a heart thing," Maggie offered.

"Maybe." David stared at the coffee table, mouth bitter from the lie he had just uttered. *Maybe*? No way. He knew what had killed Eric, and no autopsy was going to find that. He would accept Maggie's suggestion in an attempt to stay sane. A heart thing. Good. Sure. But he would always know differently.

Eric had a heart thing all right, the kind where someone else stopped it for him. *I love you and we were meant to be together,* Emmy had declared, twining her rotted arms around her lover's neck and pulling him down to oblivion, pulling him down to join her. And she had wanted it on record. He put his hands over his face, resigned to the nightmare he now carried.

Yeah, yeah, yeah.

SMOOTH CRIMINAL

by

Andrea Jones

As I run, I hear only my breath—trembling, gasping, panting. I rush into blackness.

When I come back, I hear my own voice shouting.

"Annie, are you OK? Are you OK, Annie?"

I pound on her door. I don't care who hears me this time. "Annie!"

Past panic, I'm frantic. My heart bashes my ribs. My fists sting from beating on her door. Will she open? Is she able?

Does she know it's me?

I cringe when I hear the sirens yowling. The sound shoots up my spine to hit my brain, like those cheap, cheating carnival games with the bludgeons and bells. But— finally— the cops are here. Even in *this* neighborhood, I expected them to show sooner.

In the dusty dark of the hallway, the orange of sunset seeps under her door. The girl never shuts her blinds. I twist the knob, making sure it's locked. If my heart beats any harder, I know it'll explode. Everything I've seen and heard, everything I've *not* seen, shrieks in my skull, swelling and swelling, a crescendo of chaos.

There's a riff of staccato as the screen door's ripped from its hinges. The cops come stomping into the building, all jingling and boots. The noises amplify the pain in my head.

"Up here! It's Annie. I can't get her to open up!" As two white officers in black flak jackets converge on the door, I slip to the side. I don't press my hands to the dirty wall, and I don't go too far. I need to be the first to see the scene.

One of the officers towers over me. The corridor constricts. "You're the one?"

I stop dead.

"The one who called it in?" He has a voice like a bullhorn. He punches every syllable, like white cops do.

I nod. I swallow. His eyes look me up and down, sizing me "down." I'm puny next to him. I control the urge to smooth my hair.

"Clear the area."

I stand my ground. I'm a little tougher than I look, but my eyes tear up.

He jerks his jaw toward the wall, and I turn to face it while he pats down my jeans, one-handed. On his other hand, his finger's on the trigger. I don't keep my back to him any longer than I have to.

The noise level rises as Annie's shabby batch of neighbors collect to gabble in the hallway.

"...some guy in a ski mask..."

"Those gang-bangers, runnin' in this 'hood. You oughtta lock 'em up!"

After a hard stare, the cops ignore the residents. All authority, they hunker down and aim their weapons at her door. The shorter one raises his boot. "Police!" The door gives way with a squeal of old wood, an echo of what's in my head. Nobody moves as it swings to slam against the wall.

"Sweet Jesus." It's Miz Tabitha, the old lady next door, adding a soft note to the discord in my brain. "An' on a Sunday, too." She's missing her walking stick, so she totters in front of me on her swollen ankles, clutching my elbow to peer in at Annie's kitchen. Like me, she got a grip that's tighter than you expect. I have to see the apartment my own self, so I shake her off.

The room looks just as bad as I imagined it. A chilly wind smacks me in the face, and I know that the back window, the one in Annie's bedroom, is broken. Minutes before, I heard the glass shatter. My nerves shattered with it.

"Ma'am!" bawls the Bullhorn. "Police officers! We're coming in."

I am right on their big fat heels. I don't trust these pigs not to spoil the scene.

We jerk to a stop and stare around. Annie's kitchen table is overturned. It's flipped right over, smashed a hole in the yellow-painted plaster. It's undressed, the tablecloth heaped on the floor. I see the sugar bowl in shards on the linoleum, her china tea pot— the one from her gramma, all pink and white and innocent— is lying in a pool of its own innards. The two chairs sit gawking, like it's all too much for their spindly minds to grasp.

But where is Annie?

"Annie!" I holler, "Are you OK?" My voice bounces off the kitchen tile, then dies on the rug leading to her bedroom.

The cops' eyes dart around, looking for the perp. I guess by now it's obvious even to them that some thug attacked her. I knew it all along. A with-it woman like Annie doesn't just start screaming. And a neat freak doesn't throw furniture 'round. Takes a slob like me to mess up a woman's kitchen. I feel sorry, now, 'bout the few times ever I lost patience with her.

More cops bound up, flipping notebooks and herding the neighbors toward the lawn. "Let's move it along, people. Names, please." I turn my back on the naked table, and shut the door for quiet. I touch the lock, but I don't twist it. My head still rings with screams. I want reassurance. I want to hear it in Annie's voice— if she can talk.

The cops don't stomp now. They creep. At the bathroom door, one turns sharply. It smells like Bon Ami in there, and mildew. He snaps on the switch. The bulb flickers to life, illuminating the rust stains in the sink. Annie's make-up waits on the edge, lined up and ready. She only ever spends money on her looks. The cop noses his gun in the shower, crinkling the curtain, then he turns toward the bedroom again. As soon as they enter, I stumble in behind them. I picture it before I see it.

Bloodstains, on the carpet. Little drops, dark, and wetter ones that get bigger.

Annie isn't where I expect, on the rumpled-up bed. She lies on her side, one hand on a dresser handle, the other clutching her face. From the nappy trail on the carpet, it looks like she crawled there. It's cold, and I see goose bumps on her arm, each one standing out like the skin of a basketball.

I see the blood. Welts, all over her, but I don't see the wound. Her fine, lady's legs poke out beneath her blue silk robe. I blink and look again. The robe isn't blue any more. In some spots, it's purple. It matches the side of Annie's face.

"Annie!" I run to her and fall to my knees. They slide a bit on the blood.

"Step back, sir. This is a crime scene."

"Don't you think I know that?" I grab onto Annie. Her flesh is cold, but alive. "Where's that ambulance?"

The Bullhorn makes a half attempt to pull me away, then shakes his head. This kind of neighborhood, who gives a rat's ass about procedure? He snatches a radio from his belt. While he makes noises into it, letting its static charge the room, I rub her arms to warm her. It's hard to miss the welts, and I wonder, does she feel the hurt? I kiss the damage on her face. No make-up's going to fix that.

Holding her head to my chest, I find the source of the blood. A sticky red mess on her scalp identifies it. Now her blood's all over me. It's under my nails. My prints are everywhere. My brain still pounds in my skull.

"OK, son," the shorter cop says. "Move aside now." He's down on one knee, his holster creaks, he smells like coffee. He feels for Annie's pulse, pulls her lid to open one of her eyes. It rolls to look at him, a gorgeous gold-flecked brown, then turns toward me. I wait.

Will she know it's me?

He lets her eye close.

The cop lays her back down. He gets up with a grunt, and searches around for the weapon. With blotches like Annie got, I know it's a cane. He wades toward the window through junk that spilled from the bed stand, kicking a pile of paperbacks aside. Glass snaps under his boot, and he stops. He stretches his neck, squinting out the broken pane at the parking lot, half a story below. He rests his fists on his hips. "Goddamn hoodlums." When he turns around, his billy club bangs against the bureau. The soft wood dimples. It matches the mark of another blow. One I heard earlier.

I'm back on my knees, howling along with my brain, "Doggone it, baby, wake up!" The room's getting darker. Shadows in the corners. Shadows, looking bad, on her face.

"Dog*gone* it, Annie!"

She whimpers. Her moan only rolls in my head, like a marble in a spray-paint can, scrambling with all the other sounds.

I sniffle, try not to cry.

Mascara bleeds down her cheek. She turns her head. Her eyes open, then they widen.

She knows me.

"Annie— are you OK?" I wipe my nose on my sleeve. "Won't you tell us that you're OK?"

"I don't know..." It's a whisper. It doesn't hurt my head.

"Who came in here, to your apartment?"

"I don't know..." Such a faint, soft voice. The pain in my cranium shrinks.

"And the bloodstains, on the carpet? Who came here?"

"I don't know..."

"Who? *Who?*" I want to shake her.

"I...know."

A scream explodes in my head. I grab at my skull, and the agony escapes through my throat. "Ow-ww!"

The Bullhorn butts in, "Ma'am, it's over now. We'll get you to a doctor."

Annie stares at him, then turns her gaze upward, toward me. Her slick, lipsticked mouth opens to speak.

"Annie," I shake my aching head. "Don't—"

Her bloody hand finds mine. It's slippery, but I squeeze it, tight, like I'll never let her go. I see her wince, but then, like a miracle, the girl tries to smile at me.

The shrieks are fading from my brain. They are morphing now…into laughter.

I'm grinning back at her. *O-K!* My heartbeat calms.

She didn't know me.

She doesn't know. Me.

It was me.

I'm giddy, like a criminal let outta lockup.

Below the broken window, the ambulance burns rubber as it plunges into the parking lot. Throbs of red whirl around the room. The siren blares in crescendo, then cuts off, like a victim. Like Annie. It dies, in a last, short whine.

The sun goes, too. Only that mechanical crimson blazes now, off the ambulance. If Annie ever shut her blinds, now would be the time.

The Bullhorn shuffles up. His puffy pink hand pats my shoulder. "Sorry, son. We gotta move 'er."

I sniff, but I can hear my own thoughts again. Taking care to use my un-bloody hand, I smooth my hair. I'm a little tougher than I look.

"Doggone."

I breathe, in relief.

Dog-gone!

I'm OK, Annie.

Annie…

I'm OK.

SATISFACTION

by

David McAfee

March 31

His hands shook as he ran them under the steaming hot water. The fear was gone, replaced by amazement. Not at what he had done, as might be expected. He was amazed it had taken him so long to do it. He should have done this years ago. Years! He had expected to feel many things after his first time: guilt, fear, even shame, but not euphoria. That was unexpected.

But euphoric was the only word that would fit. His heart had yet to slow to a normal rate, and the pain in his head was gone, finally. Had he found the cure for his migraines? It sure seemed like it. Not a day too soon, either.

The Rolling Stones played in the background as he scrubbed the blood from his fingers. There sure was a lot of it, much more than he'd expected. The woman—he had not read her ID yet, so he didn't know her name—had bled out fast. Too fast, actually. She was already cool to the touch, and was it his imagination or had rigormortis already begun to set in?

What the hell did he know? He wasn't a doctor. She was dead, that was good enough. Well, almost. It would have been better if she'd lasted a little longer. He blamed it on first time nerves. He would do better next time.

From his CD player, Mick Jagger complained about satisfaction. Until a short while ago, he could relate. But not anymore. Now he had found what he needed.

That there would be a next time was certain. This couldn't be it. It just couldn't. For the first time in years the constant, painful pressure in his temples was gone. He stood in the bright light of the bathroom without pain, without anxiety. He finally felt human again. He couldn't remember the last time he'd felt so whole and undamaged.

No, this could not be the only time.

But he would have to wait a while. Once the police found her body, the investigation would begin. Those bastards would start looking for him. They would find nothing, of course, but it would still be prudent to wait a bit and give the trail a chance to get cold. No sense giving them two cases to investigate at the same time. If he waited long enough, they might not even connect the next one to this one.

Hands clean, he walked over to the table where she lay, her body stiff and cooling in the early Spring air, and sat on a stool next to the shower door. He'd set his workspace up in the oversized shower to make clean up easier, and now he was glad he did. The blood had slowed, but there was still a steady *drip, drip, drip* from the table to the floor. The blood pooled a bit around the drain before vanishing through the grate into the sewer. The coppery smell of it filled the air, mixing with the scent of her perfume and taking his mind back to that moment. The expression on her face when his knife broke her skin for the first time…her eyes had opened so wide he could almost have driven his car into them. They were still open, staring vacantly at the wall behind him. The blue had just begun to turn glassy. Her mouth was still open, which reminded him of the way she had gasped for breath near the end, like a fish dying on the shore, her lipstick forming a bright red O in the middle of her face.

He found himself getting aroused, which was odd considering he had gone through the entire death without so much as a twitch from his nether region. But now, in the afterglow, he was getting excited. Very excited.

"Why not?" he asked aloud as he reached for his zipper. After all, it wasn't like he had to worry about her seeing him.

When he finished, he found himself staring at the gaping wound in her chest. The red stains around the pink flesh were like a magnet for his eyes, and he wanted to remember this image for the rest of his life. For a moment, he was tempted to take out his phone and snap a picture, but then he remembered that he'd left his phone at the house. His phone had GPS, and while he didn't know if the police could use that against him, he hadn't wanted to chance it.

The song had started over several times, and now Mick was singing about men and cigarettes. It reminded him that he hadn't had a smoke since he picked up the woman, and suddenly he needed one badly. He zipped up his pants, then walked over to the table and grabbed a cigarette. What kind of cigarettes did Mick smoke, anyway? Not that it mattered. He brought a Marlboro to his lips and lit it with a match. Lighters were for pansies.

He inhaled deeply and watched as the smoke swirled in the air between him and the woman. Even the dripping had slowed by now. The steady *pat pat pat* of blood on the floor was gone. His heart had finally slowed to normal. Even the twitching in his hands and fingers had stopped. He finished the cigarette and tossed it into the small pool of red under the table. It landed with a low hiss as the burning cherry touched the coagulating blood.

Mick's voice continued to fill the small bathroom.

She wants you to come back next week. Huh, Mick? He thought. Screw that. To hell with the woman and her 'next week' crap.

"You just don't know, Mick," he said aloud. "You just don't, man."

Maybe if Mick had experienced the kind of thrill that he'd discovered tonight, he would be less worried about cigarettes and woman who told him to come back next week. Maybe this song would never have been written at all.

Maybe Mick would have some satisfaction. Finally.

Screw Mick.

He stood up, walked over to the CD player, and switched it off.

He grabbed his hacksaw from the table. Time to start cleaning up. This part was crucial to his future success. He couldn't just dump the body somewhere. The cops would find it soon enough and would start looking around. He'd be extra careful, and he would scrub the hell out of everything, as well as burn the woman's clothes and identification. But still, it never hurt to take extra precautions.

He walked over to the body, set the blade of the saw on her wrist, and got to work. His plan was simple. Fifteen pieces: wrists, feet, shins, forearms, thighs, arms, head, and two pieces for the torso. He'd save them in his deep freeze, taking out one piece every week and driving it a hundred miles away to dump it in the woods. The police would never find all of them, if they ever found any at all. The face and hands would require more attention, of course. He'd burn them along with the clothes, then dump the bones out in the woods somewhere. There would be no identifying the remains even if they were discovered.

In short, he'd thought of everything. He was confident that, using this method, he would be able to operate in safety for a very long time.

The radio was off, but inside his head, Mick was still whining about not getting any satisfaction. *Stupid ear worm!*

The hell with Mick. Keith, too. Hell with them all.

Satisfaction was easy to find, as long as you were willing to take it.

April 30th

It was supposed to take fifteen weeks to dispose of the last body, but it had only taken four. The first week, he took her skull out into the woods and dropped it off, then he settled in to wait for the next dump day. But the waiting was hard. Much harder than it should have been. Then the pressure started to build inside his head again, making things much more urgent. He knew he needed to be careful. Rushing things would be a great way to get caught. But still, the pain in his head would not let him be.

The second week, he'd gone out three times, taking the charred remains of her hands and one foot out to three separate locations, all of them over fifty miles from his city. He realized that it didn't really matter how much time passed between drops, just as long as he made sure they were spaced very far apart so no one could connect the pieces to each other, so to speak.

He laughed every time he thought of that pun.

The local news programs had yet to mention her, which struck him as a bit odd. Perhaps they considered her a runaway? Who knew? In any case, it didn't hurt his feelings to know that the police weren't looking for him. Yet.

The third week, he'd taken the other foot, both shins, and both thighs. He'd gone out five times that week, and his gas tank was feeling the pinch. But the pressure in his head kept building. He had thought he would have more time before it became painful, but by the beginning of the fourth week, his head felt like it was moments away from splitting open and spilling his gray matter onto the sidewalk.

By Wednesday of the fourth week, he had dumped every single piece. He'd spent hours and hours in his car in those few days, making three drops a night for two nights straight to get rid of the last six pieces. True to his plan, he didn't keep a single souvenir.

That's how people get caught, he told himself.

Now here he was, barely four weeks out from his first kill, stalking new prey. Mick and the gang were in the CD player again. Same song. Right now Mick was singing about the radio and useless information. *He sure seems to complain a lot for a guy worth millions.*

Useless information, indeed. They weren't even talking about the girl on the radio. The local news was full of juicier gossip about the mayor's alleged affair with his secretary. Having met the mayor on numerous occasions, he did not doubt the rumors. He could spot a fellow predator from a mile away, and the mayor was always on the hunt for young, nubile women to screw. To each his fetish. After all, he wasn't in much of a position to judge.

There! There she was. Like the last few nights, she closed the door to the diner and crossed the parking lot to her car. She always parked in the same spot, which was usually the farthest one from the diner's front door. He assumed this was because the diner's owner did not want the employees to take up the good parking spaces. Not that it mattered. Her space was on the far side of the lot and there were no windows on that side of the diner. In addition, the lighting was poor, which would make sneaking up on her relatively easy.

He watched as she got into her car and drove away, keeping his eyes on her taillights until they disappeared around the bend. Her right taillight was out, which would make her easy to follow. All he had to do was start the car and go. Fast. Right now, before she got too far away for him to catch up without drawing attention to himself.

The pressure in his head mounted, and he fought back the urge to peel out of the parking lot and follow her.

No, he told himself. *Who knows where she's going or when she will stop? No, this needs to happen on my terms, not hers.*

A bright flash of pain sliced through his head, and he almost cried out. He put his palms on his temples, pushing them inward in an attempt to keep his skull from splitting open. God, his head *hurt!* He needed this. He needed *her.* Otherwise, where would he be?

Mick's voice hit the chorus again. He almost punched his radio.

"Tomorrow," he breathed. Tomorrow night. The pain in his head eased as he confirmed it to himself. Tomorrow night, he would take her.

"That all right with you, Mick?" he asked the CD player. The song ended as soon as he finished his question.

"I guess that settles it…"

May 3rd

"Tomorrow, my ass," he grumbled as he rinsed his hands. The pink-tinted water splashed into the sink, then swirled away down the drain.

"Two days. Two damn days!"

The girl hadn't shown up for work on May 1st, then again on May 2nd. The pain in his head had been so bad that he almost hadn't gone in on the 3rd, but he simply couldn't imagine starting all the way over from zero. He'd been rewarded for his perseverance when she had gone in to work. As he stood there at the sink washing her blood and skin from his hands, he chastised himself for being shortsighted and missing the obvious. He should have foreseen that she might have some days off. He hadn't watched her long enough to get a full sense of her schedule. That was not a mistake he would make again.

He finished washing his hands and turned to face her. He'd wanted to slow this one down and savor it. The first woman had died too quickly, he realized. That was probably the reason the pounding in his head had returned so soon after. As such, he had planned to slowly bleed the waitress out, savoring her death like a fine glass of wine. But by the time he'd wrestled her out of her clothes and strapped her to the table, his adrenaline had been pumping through his body like a jackhammer. His pounding head felt like a log under a splitting maul, and before he could stop himself, he rammed his hunting knife through her chest.

Then he did it again, and again, and again. He didn't bother to count the number of times he'd stabbed her, but to judge by the amount of blood all over his clothes and the shower wall, it must have been a lot. Looking at the mess of his sanctuary made the heat rise in his neck, and he slapped himself across the face.

That wasn't the plan. He needed to get control of himself before the next time, or he'd probably mess everything up.

Losing control is how you get caught, he reminded himself.

"I gotta be more careful," he whispered.

Mick was on the radio again. How long could one guy complain about not getting any satisfaction? Forty years or more, apparently.

"Go to hell, Mick," he growled.

At least the pain in his head was gone. He stared at her still body, at the bloody, gaping wounds in her chest, and was not surprised at all to find himself hard as a rock again. He unzipped his pants and let his hands go to work. When he finished, the pain in his head was completely gone.

Peace, at last.

He'd screwed up last time and dumped the body parts too fast, but he would not do that again. No way.

As he fetched the hacksaw, he promised himself that next time, he would be patient. Next time, it would take a good, long while for the woman to die. He switched off the CD player just as Mick got to the chorus.

"Satisfy that," he said as he walked back to the body.

May 14th

One week. One lousy, stinking week. Then the pressure in his brain was back and Mick and the Stones started singing their damn song again. This was probably Mick's fault, the bastard. Who the hell can sing on and on and on about not getting what they want? Maybe he should just toss the CD out the window...

No, he couldn't do that. The song was part of the ritual now. Still, Mick's voice was as annoying as a canker sore. How had the Stones gotten so huge with that whiny jerk at the helm?

He had fully intended to follow through on his original plan to dispose of the body over a period of fifteen weeks. But when he drove out to the neighboring county that first night, he'd accidentally brought the skull and both feet instead of just the skull by itself, as was the plan. He wasn't sure how he'd missed something so crucial, but figured he might as well toss the other pieces out since he already had them with him. At least he'd driven another twenty miles between pieces. It wasn't the fifty mile radius he'd been wanting, but it should still be plenty.

The next night he'd gone out ahead of schedule and dumped a few more pieces. And the night after that he dumped the rest of them. He couldn't help but be a little irritated at his own lack of patience, but he figured as long as he kept up his habit of driving around to dump them, the timeline wouldn't matter. Besides, the reports on TV hadn't said anything about foul play yet, although one news station had apparently shown the pictures of both women side by side to compare them, along with a number to call if anyone should happen to see them somewhere.

That's when he realized he'd made a mistake in his selection. Both women were young, attractive brunettes. Thankfully, one had blue eyes and the other had hazel, so they probably weren't quite sure about a pattern. Not yet. He'd have to keep it that way.

He sat in his car and watched as Number Three left the jewelry store and walked to her little blue Mini Cooper. Her hair was much lighter in color than the first two. That should throw the police off a little. The cops in this tiny little town were dumb as dog turds, anyway. It was unlikely they'd make a connection, especially since no bodies had been recovered.

And they won't be, he thought. He was far too careful for that.

She was almost to her car. His head pounded. He was surprised she couldn't hear the sound of his headache from where she stood. It felt like a blaring, bright orange beacon in his mind. A red-hot poker in his brain.

He really should wait.

Mick's voice poured from the speakers, filling the inside of his car with his whining.

Shut up, Mick!

Get reckless and you'll get caught.

I don't care what you can't get, Mick. Shut up!

Not tonight.

Fine! I'll show you satisfaction, asshole!

A hard stab of pain. Right behind his eyes. Enough to make him whimper.

He opened his car door and got out. Tonight was as good a night as any.

May 15, Early Morning

Damn it!

Holy friggin' crap, that hurts!

He scrubbed his hands under the sink, the water so hot it almost burned. Clouds of steam rose into the air, fogging up the mirror and making it difficult to breathe. He reached up and touched the scratches on his face. They were deep, and they stung like hell. Probably leave a scar, too. He wasn't sure how he was going to explain them in the morning when he went to work.

That bitch!

She'd fought him like the devil. How the heck was he supposed to know she knew karate? Or was it Tai Kwon Do? Hell, he couldn't tell the difference.

You would have known that if you'd bothered to do any recon first.

"Shut up," he said aloud. He'd spent no time learning about this one before going after her. Another mistake. And one he wouldn't repeat. And this time he would wait the fifteen weeks, by God. No more screw ups!

Screwing up is how you get caught.

From his CD player, Mick sang about white shirts and guys on TV.

He looked down at his shirt, which was white when the night began, but now looked like a Jackson Pollack painting. Splatters of blood covered it. Most of it was hers, but some was his. He'd have to make sure he removed any trace of DNA from her fingernails. Although, burning them should take care of that, shouldn't it?

He walked over to the hacksaw and got to work. It didn't occur to him until after he was done that the sight of her body hadn't given him an erection this time.

Mick wasn't the only one who couldn't get any satisfaction, it seemed.

"Screw you, Mick," he grumbled.

May 20th

He could barely see her past the wall of pain. He wouldn't be able to wait. Tonight. It had to be tonight. Right now.

He tossed the trash bag with the blonde's feet and forearms in the back. He'd have to wait and dump them later. He'd driven fifty seven miles from home with the intent of dumping the pieces in the woods of the next county, but the pressure was already back, making it hard to concentrate on driving. Then he'd seen her, walking out of a small gas station/tourist shop. He'd pulled in and parked on the north side of the station, near where she was fishing her keys out of her purse. She was distracted.

Mick was singing about Satisfaction again.

He got out of the car.

May 21st, Early Morning

That one had been easy. Too easy. No whirling kicks or flailing fingernails this time. She'd wilted almost as soon as he grabbed her. She hadn't even screamed when he tossed her in the back of his car with the pieces of the blonde. Shock, maybe? Fear? Either way, she'd presented no challenge at all. She'd even sat, staring at him, when he pulled the pieces of the blonde woman out of the bag and tossed them out the window on the way home. Mick was back, singing about the girl again.

"Some chick told you to come back next week. Yeah, Mick, I know."

He finished scrubbing his hands and picked up his hacksaw.

The pressure was gone, but he could feel it waiting. Building just behind his eyes.

Already.

Not a good sign.

May 25th

Steamy water. Scrubbing hands. The Stones playing in the background, and another body cooling on the table. He hadn't even gotten rid of the last one yet. The pieces sat in his freezer, along with the last two parts of the blonde before her. The pain had come back that same day. Why was it coming back so fast, now? Why wasn't this working?

His first kill had kept the pressure away for several weeks. Now he couldn't even get a few hours of peace?

Maybe he needed a better kill.

You're losing it, he told himself. *This isn't the plan. This is how you get caught.*

"Shut the hell up!"

Something new, maybe? Something different?

Mick again. Still complaining.

He could relate. Satisfaction was hard to come by, it seemed. What would it take?

He got to work on the newest body, then stopped halfway through as a fresh spasm of pain split his skull.

The hacksaw fell to the floor as he put his hands on his head, trying to hold the two halves of his skull together.

This wasn't enough anymore.

He needed something better.

But what?

May 28th

The body lay still on the table, and he scrubbed the blood away from his fingers. The reflection in the mirror stared back at him with bruised eyes and a busted lip. He smiled, he couldn't help it.

That had certainly been different.

The man on his table had fought him, as he had known he would. He was strong. Very strong. In the end, however, he hadn't been strong enough. Somehow, that made this kill better. The fact that he'd physically overpowered a strong specimen made him feel that much more alive. A true Alpha male. He'd masturbated over the body almost as soon as the heart stopped. He hadn't been able to help himself.

Christ, he was getting excited again just thinking about it!

Mick was on the radio asking if the man smoked the same cigarettes as him.

"No idea, Mick," he said.

A man this time. That ought to throw the police off.

News reports still hadn't picked up on the murders much, though there were a number of reports regarding the missing women, no one had yet used the word "homicide." He felt a little jilted by that, like they'd robbed him of his chance to be feared. Still, he supposed it was good news for him, as it meant they still hadn't realized what they were dealing with.

He'd been looking for another woman that night, but there weren't any out and about. At least, none that would suit his purposes. The pressure in his head increased to mind-bending levels. Then he'd seen the man walking alone, and knew what he had to do.

It had never occurred to him to kill men. But since he wasn't having sex with any of his victims, then why the hell not? And after it was all said and done, he felt that the man was his best kill yet, so maybe there was something to this new line of reasoning.

He grabbed his hacksaw and got to work.

Sixteen pieces this time. One extra.

Not a bad way to go about it, eh Mick?

He smiled. His headache was gone.

May 30th

The last piece of the blonde was gone. Tossed out the window. Not quite thirty miles away, but he had a lot of catching up to do in the disposal department. His freezer was full. If he was going to get rid of all the pieces, he'd need to step up his efforts, which meant more trips. He'd have to maximize them by taking more pieces out at a time.

He needed to get rid of them all before he killed again. He just didn't have the space in his freezer for any more bodies. But his head pounded, making it difficult to drive.

Mick wasn't helping matters much, singing his stupid song again.

Find your own satisfaction, Mick, he thought, *and leave me to mine!*

When he drove past the store and saw the man in the jogging suit, his headache flared. The pain was so intense he had to pull over to the side of the road to keep from running into anything.

41

Mick reached the chorus.

He knew he couldn't wait.

May 31st

He scrubbed his hands clean under the steaming water. He felt like punching himself in the face. What the hell was he going to do with this body? His freezer was stuffed. He couldn't squeeze so much as a finger in there.

What was he going to do?

He'd have to dump the whole thing, he supposed. He'd have to be careful, though. He'd drive it out over a hundred miles to dispose of it. It meant he was in for a long night, but it couldn't be helped. He'd been too careless, and a long night was a small price to pay to cover that up.

Being careless is how you get caught.

He dragged the body out to his car, swearing and cursing at his own lack of patience. When the pressure in his head started to build up, he slammed his head into the car door.

"Not now!" he said.

The jolt brought fresh pain to his forehead, but at least it cleared away the pressure. For now, anyway. It always seemed to come back. Faster and faster these days. Ever since he began hunting, it seemed to get worse instead of better. That was not what was supposed to happen. He got into his car and turned the key. Almost immediately, the Stones came on the radio.

You still can't get any, Mick?

Something warm and wet trickled down the side of his face. He looked in the rearview mirror and was surprised to see a fat stream of blood rolling down his cheek. He'd cut open his skin. Badly. No wonder the pressure was gone.

He'd have to remember that trick.

June 1st

He punched himself in the face. Hard. The blood of his latest conquest smeared his nose and cheek, but he didn't stop. He hit himself again, then a third time. Still nothing. Finally, he rammed his head into the sink. The bright flash of pain seemed to clear his head, and when he looked at his reflection and saw the fresh cut in his forehead, the pressure eased.

He wiped the blood with his hand, smearing it with the blood of the woman on the table.

Another woman. This one had been the least satisfying kill yet. The pain in his head hadn't let up at all. Not even a little. As soon as she died, he'd come to the sink to wash his hands. But the pain made it difficult. At least he'd found a solution. Albeit a painful one.

He paused to listen to Mick's voice in the background. *No satisfaction, indeed.* Mick was right. It wasn't working. Nothing was working. He looked over at the body and felt nothing. No triumph, no elation. The blood on her chest didn't excite him at all. What was wrong? Why wasn't this working?

Maybe he needed another?

The pressure began to build again. It wasn't painful, not yet, but he knew it would not take long. In a few hours he would be an incoherent mess again. But how to stop it?

He couldn't find another victim so soon, could he?

No. Besides, even if he did, he wouldn't have any place to put the body. As it was, he was going to have to dump the woman whole, like the man before her. That was extremely risky, and certainly not part of the plan.

Though, to be fair, his plan was toast by this point, anyway.

The news reports still hadn't said much about the missing people. As yet, no body parts had been found, so at least he was doing that much right.

But if he was going to keep this up, he'd have to stop screwing up.

That's how you're gonna get caught, he thought.

He needed to be more careful.

June 2nd

The woman's body from the night before lay in the corner on the floor, while the new body (a man this time) sat cooling on the table. He hadn't had time to dispose of anything before the next wave of pressure and pain had hit.

His face was battered, and his head bled from numerous cuts. He'd smashed his face into a mirror in an attempt to ease the pressure, but it had only provided a temporary relief. In the end, he'd been forced to seek out new prey.

Mick's voice rang through the room. Satisfaction again.

"Screw you, Mick!" he screamed. "Screw you!"

He looked at his face in the mirror and barely recognized himself. The blood smeared over his cheeks hid his features pretty well. His eyes were bloodshot, and his nose tilted at an odd angle. He must have broken it. That would explain all the blood.

Still, the pressure would not go away.

What would it take?

He had a fresh victim on the table, and he'd beaten the crap out of himself, but nothing seemed to work. His head still felt like it would split open from the inside. He couldn't keep going on like this. Sooner or later he would get caught, or killed. That is, if his head didn't crack open on its own. What was left? What could help?

He looked over at his latest kill, the knife still protruding from his chest, and after a moment he had his answer.

The ultimate kill.

The more he thought about it, the more it made sense. What better way to cement your status as Alpha than by killing the Alpha?

He reached the table and grabbed the knife's handle. It was slick with blood, but he yanked it out with no trouble. He then shoved the body onto the floor. It landed with a sickening thump, sending tiny sprays of blood from the numerous cuts.

He climbed on the table, his head surprisingly clear.

The pressure behind his eyes was gone, he noted. Hell, he was even getting excited again. He thumped his member through the fly of his jeans, wincing at the slight pain but marveling at the hardness in his pants. That's when he realized he was on the right track. Finally. He almost reached into his pants, but he stopped himself.

"Not this time," he said. "This time is special."

This is right. This is what I was supposed to do all along, he thought.

He held the knife up over his chest, took a deep breath, and rammed it home. The pain was delicious!

"Yes!" he screamed. "You hear that, Mick?"

He pulled the knife out, then rammed it home again. Blood spurted from his chest, arcing across the room. He'd missed his heart, but that didn't matter. He'd scored a hit on a major artery. It would not be long now. He pulled the knife out again, but this time it was more work than it should have been. He raised the knife up.

Had it gotten heavier?

He plunged it down again.

This time, when he tried to pull the knife from his chest, he found he couldn't get it free. It was too heavy. He held on to the handle as the room grew darker.

From the CD player, Mick was singing, but the words sounded different. Had they changed?

Finally got some satisfaction...

Was that how the song went? Or had Mick altered it just for him?

"Know what, Mick?" he asked. "You're all right." He coughed. Blood bubbled on his lips. His fingers tightened on the knife handle, and then there was nothing.

Jun 15th

The smell hit him first. He covered his nose and motioned for his partner to do the same.

"Yep," he said. "Something is dead in here, all right."

They'd received a call about a strange smell coming from the attic apartment above the general store downtown. When they arrived, they found the door to the apartment locked, but the smell flowed from underneath it. Death. Decay. Something inside was rotting away in the early summer heat. He'd knocked for several minutes with no response from inside, so they'd gotten the store owner to bring up the spare key.

Now the door was open, and the stench of death was strong enough to gag them both.

They walked into the room, exchanging confused glances.

Everywhere they looked there were body parts. Hands, feet, legs, forearms, even a few heads. They looked plastic.

He picked one up and examined it. The ragged edges were colored red.

"Looks like red magic marker," he said. His partner nodded.

The smell seemed to be coming from the bathroom. He set the plastic hand down and crossed the room, his hand on the butt of his pistol. When he got to the door, he peeked in. His breath caught in his throat, and he took a step back.

"Well?" his partner asked. "What is it, Mike?"

Mike shook his head, then motioned for his partner to take a look. "You're going to have to see for yourself, Cole."

Cole walked forward and looked in the room, then promptly stepped back, gagging and retching all over the floor. Mike could relate, he was having a hard time keeping his lunch down, as well.

A body lay on a table, which sat in the shower stall. All around the corpse were more red streaks. They looked to be from the same type of red marker. Underneath the table, the entire floor of the shower was colored red. The body's hands were wrapped around a toy survival knife, which had also been colored with red. Around the knife, the flesh of the dead man's chest was red, as well.

"Holy crap!" Cole said. "Is that Will?"

"I think so."

"Looks like he decided not to let the cancer get him."

"Looks that way," Mike said. Will had been diagnosed with a malignant brain tumor back in March. The doctors had only given him a few months to live. He hadn't been seen much around town since then. A few people swore they saw him driving all over creation, but no one had actually talked to him for weeks.

There was a broken CD player on the shelf next to the table. The door was broken off and the CD inside looked cracked. From this angle, he saw the Rolling Stones CD case on the floor. The thing wasn't plugged in, though. Not that it would have mattered.

"What do you make of all this?" his partner asked. He held up a plastic hand and waved his hand in a wide arc. Mike looked around at the various plastic body parts strewn around the apartment, then he looked back to the body on the table. There were three long, red stripes on Will's cheek, as well as a few on his forehead. Around his eye, it looked like he'd switched from red markers to a dull purple. Mike couldn't begin to fathom why, unless Will had wanted to look like he had a black eye. A very cartoony one.

He shook his head.

"Well," he said. "I guess now we know who's been stealing the mannequins from downstairs."

SWAMP WITCH

by

Donnie Light

Young Virgil and Vernon ignored the rumors and warnings. After two hours of trudging through black muck and picking their way through brambles and catbriers, the twins found themselves deep in the Black Bayou. It was a dark and forbidden place of legend and lore, where fable and truth blended into a single reality.

In the bayou, curious green reptiles slithered and clung. Snakes hung thick from the Cypress trees, like heavy ropes on a barn hook. Alligators suspended themselves in the murky water with only their eyes above the surface, keeping watch for easy prey. The nocturnal chorus produced by crickets, peepers and bullfrogs was endless here, because even the days were dark in the Black Bayou.

When one stepped into the bayou, a thousand eyes watched your every move. Smaller creatures slunk away from approaching footsteps. The bigger and more dangerous ones remained camouflaged, nearly invisible, but ever so close.

Virgil and Vernon knew to stay away from the path to old Hattie's shack, but one day curiosity overcame them.

Vernon and Vergil were as close as two bothers could be. No secrets could be kept one from the other. They shared everything, including their thoughts and dreams.

As younger boys, stories of the swamp witch Hattie often scared them into sleeplessness, prompting them to pull the sheets over their heads and perhaps light a candle to chase away the shadows. But since they turned twelve, those old stories didn't scare them anymore. They wanted to find out for themselves if old Hattie the swamp witch was a real person or a being of myth and legend.

"It's kinda creepy in here, Vern," Virgil said as he pulled his bare foot from the sucking mud. Their shoes remained at home, reserved for school and Sunday morning church and not for mucking around in the bayou. Their daddy always talked about how the great depression left little money for buying things like new shoes, and how he hoped President Roosevelt could turn things around.

"Don't be a scaredy-cat," Vernon said. "Ain't nothin' back here but more creepy-crawlies." Vernon was far more adventurous than his identical twin. His daddy said he took that after the paternal side of the family. Virgil was far more cautious by nature, and his daddy said he took that after his momma's side.

Vernon pulled a wriggling black leech from his ankle and tossed it deeper into the swampwater. A trickle of blood seeped from the bite. "I don't believe ol' Hattie lives back here anyway. Pa told us those stories to scare us and make us mind."

It was true that many grownups in the nearby town of Yellville used tales of old Hattie to persuade youngsters into a proper behavioral pattern. *If you don't mind me, old Hattie might come and carry you off,* flustered parents told rambunctious children. One story claimed old Hattie turned a man into a large snake that now guarded the way to her shack. Another tale said that old Hattie took lost or wandering folk and chopped them up to feed her pet alligators. She never got caught because what went into the Black Bayou and crossed paths with old Hattie—never came out again. Legend told that Hattie cast spells and worked dark magic. Some said she could see in the dark and walk on water amongst other interesting feats. Any unidentified sound coming from the swamp was often attributed to Hattie—or one of Hattie's victims. When some regretful thing happened in town, blame often fell on the swamp witch. The stories about Hattie seemed endless.

The people in Yellville lived mostly off the bounty of the swamp, but had enough dry land to plant gardens and graze a few cows and goats. They were a trustful sort who never locked their doors at night—unless somebody took to telling stories of old Hattie. On those nights, locksets clicked and wooden bolts were thrown before the lights went out, because nobody wanted Hattie getting in.

"I think we ought to turn around," Virgil said. He swatted at the mosquitoes that swarmed about his head.

"Tommy Coultrain said you had to pass a giant Cypress tree, bigger than any other in the swamp. When you come to it, you'd be almost there."

Virgil slapped another mosquito. "And how's Tommy Coultrain know that?"

"His cousin told him," Vernon replied.

The pair sloshed further ahead, wading in ankle-deep water. Virgil didn't like the dead-fish smell of the bayou, or the mosquitoes that sucked his blood from above the water, while leeches sucked his blood from below it. The dampness mixed with the heat to create an oppressive, insulting atmosphere.

Virgil grabbed Vernon's arm and pointed. "Look at that tree!" he said in a muted shout.

Vernon looked in the direction where Virgil pointed and saw the biggest Cypress he had ever seen. It would have taken a dozen men with joined hands to circle the trunk of that giant tree. It ascended so high that the top was lost in the canopy of the swamp. The cypress knees were taller than most men and rose like jagged teeth from the shallow black water.

The boys looked at each other, suppressing their fear. They spoke in whispers.

"That's gotta be it," Vernon said. "I ain't never seen a tree that big before."

"I think we ought to turn back," Virgil said. "It's gettin' darker." While it was the middle of the afternoon, this deep into the swamp it seemed like twilight. The vegetation overhead was thick, and Spanish moss drooped in masses like gobs of coarse hair.

"Let's get on past the tree," Vernon urged. "We might never find it again."

"Let's don't and just *say* we did," Virgil replied. "We'll tell ol' Tommy we found it."

Vernon looked at his twin and grinned. "You're scared."

"Naw," Virgil said, shaking his head. "I just think we ought to get back." He looked at the surrounding swamp. "Look how dark it's gettin'," he reminded his brother.

Vernon moved away, forcing Virgil to follow or be left alone. They made it to the giant Cypress tree when Vernon stopped and pulled a small jackknife out of his pocket.

"What are you doin'?" Virgil asked in a hushed but anxious tone.

"Carvin' my initials in this tree."

"What for?"

"To prove I was here, o' course."

While Vernon carved on the tree, Virgil kept watch for anything that moved. He looked past the huge tree into the gloom of the Blackwater Swamp. He noticed what appeared to be fog hanging over the water, but caught the scent of smoke. What ran through Virgil's mind was the fact that somebody was burning something this far out in the bayou. He then spotted a thin trail that twisted its way deeper into the swamp. It was nothing more than a muddy rut that cut through the cordgrass and seepweed as it wound around the edge of the murky water. As his eyes followed the path he saw the tops of some weeds move. His eyes stopped on that place as he wondered what unseen thing was moving at ground level. The boy stared as a slithering form emerged from the vegetation—dark in color, its skin glistening with wetness.

He tapped Vernon's shoulder but couldn't utter a single word. He pointed with a shaking finger to the path a few yards beyond the big tree.

Vernon saw it too. The creature pulled its entire length onto the path and looped upon itself. Each coil of the great snake seemed as thick as a man's thigh. It sat in an enormous heap; as if someone had dumped a pile of old tires on the path. It turned its serpentine head toward the cowering boys who were frozen in place with their jaws hanging open.

The snake appeared to stare at them with yellow eyes. Its tongue flicked in and out as if it were altogether another creature—an ugly forked parasite reaching out to taste the humid air.

As if the giant reptile wasn't enough, the boys looked beyond the snake and watched an old woman emerge from the tall weeds. She wore a dark, raggedy-looking dress that drug on the ground. The bottom of the skirt was wet and muddy. Small leaves and debris clung to it like ticks clinging to a host. Her long gray hair hung down over her face in thick strands which covered one eye. The other eye, dark like a deep pit, was staring at the boys. She raised an arm and pointed a crooked finger in their direction. Then she made the strangest cackling sound blended with a few unrecognizable words in a thick Creole accent. The boys only heard one word clearly.

"*Git!*"

And they both got. They turned away, tripping over each other to gain distance from the old hag. Their pounding hearts thrummed in their ears. They were barely aware of the racket they made as they crashed through sawgrass and duckweed. Each scrambled over Cypress knees which seemed malevolently intent on slowing them down. The boys leaped over rotted logs, slipped on swampy slime and crawled through muck and brambles. They ignored stubbed toes and fine cuts as they fled.

After what seemed far longer than it was, Vernon chanced a glimpse over his shoulder to see if the swamp witch was following them. He half-expected to see her gliding through the air, that crooked finger pointed at him, that dark, wet dress flapping behind her.

But she was not there.

Virgil never stopped to look back, and Vernon didn't catch up with him until they got to the dirt road that led back to town. They both flopped down on the road and rolled onto their backs, chests heaving as they pulled in long breaths. Their feet were bleeding. The sawgrass had made fine cuts all over their hands, forearms and shins. They were soaked to the bone from running through muck and shallow water.

After catching enough breath to speak, Virgil said, "I ain't never goin' back in there."

"Me neither," said Vernon. "Not in a million years do I wanna see anything like old Hattie again."

"You figure that was old Hattie?"

"You kiddin'?" Vernon asked. "Who else could it be?"

"You saw the size of that snake. I'll bet it used to be a man—like in the stories."

"Ain't no way I'll let old Hattie turn me into somethin' awful like that. I'm never going back to the Black Bayou."

Vernon and Virgil walked back to town, swearing never to tell anybody that they ran across old Hattie for fear they may be locked away for being stupid, or because old Hattie might hex them with her swamp-magic voodoo.

* * *

Yellville was the kind of town where people worked hard, helped one another in a time of need, and celebrated about any occasion with a crawfish boil and fish fry in the town square. A dance typically followed any community gathering. The sound of fiddles, banjos and guitars floated over the square like a musical mist. The old folks tested their dancing legs while bashful boys hooked elbows with giggling girls at the urging of friends.

Although Vernon and Virgil swore they would never tell about their encounter with old Hattie, the fear wore down and the memories of what *had* happened became mixed with what they *thought* happened and they told their buddies. The story was told differently the first few times. In one version, Hattie had no eyes—just deep holes where eyes should have been. In another rendition, lightning flew from Hattie's fingertips, narrowly missing Vernon, but catching a tree on fire.

And of course, those friends who heard the stories were sworn to silence, and each other person they told was sworn in the same way, and soon the town was buzzing with talk about Hattie.

Virgil grew ever more curious about Hattie the swamp witch, which prompted him to visit old lady Greenwood. Everyone in town called her Granny Greenwood, and she was known to serve up home-baked cookies to anyone who might stop and visit for a spell.

Virgil stepped up to the screen door and knocked.

A heavyset woman waddled toward the door, looking over her reading glasses at the boy. She clutched a skein of yarn and a pair of knitting needles in one hand.

"I ain't buying nothing," she said. She looked at Virgil through the screen.

"Not selling anything, Granny," Virgil replied. "Just wanted to ask you about the old days," he said, knowing she had a fondness for telling stories about the town's history.

She waved Virgil in as she hobbled toward her rocking chair. A black cat scurried into the darkness of a back room.

"You takin' an interest in Yellville history?" Granny asked. She motioned for Virgil to have a seat on the threadbare sofa.

"Well, ma'am," Virgil said, "I truly wanted to know something about old Hattie."

"Oh, Lord," Granny said as she picked up a hand fan and began waving it before her plump face. "Everybody's talkin' about Hattie again." She eyed Virgil with a suspicious look. "Which twin are you? I never see one of you without the other."

"Virgil, ma'am," Virgil replied. "And I'm curious about what is fact and what is fiction in regards to old Hattie."

"Fact and fiction," Granny repeated. "I know a few of the facts," she said. "I knew Hattie back in the day." The hand fan sped up. "I knew her momma better."

Virgil nodded, encouraging Granny to go on with what she knew.

"Hattie's momma fell in love with a Choctaw Indian," Granny said. "She would sneak off into the swamp to meet with this Indian fella. They had to keep it all secret, you see, because Hattie's momma was white, and this fella was an Indian. His tribe was hidin' in the swamp, because the government was roundin' up all the Indians and sendin' them out west." Granny paused a moment to think. "Oklahoma, I believe," she said.

"Hattie's mamma was named Nell, and her and her Indian beau kept meeting in secret whenever they could. Then one day, Nell's papa noticed how his daughter was bulging a bit in the middle." Granny looked at Virgil, uncertain on how to continue this part of the story.

"She was *with child*," Granny said.

Virgil nodded in understanding.

"The folk in Yellville ain't got nothin' against the Choctaw," Granny said. "Unless your daughter is carryin' a half-breed baby inside her. Nell's papa was furious when he found out about her Indian lover and kicked Nell out of his house. She went to live with the Indian in a little shack at the back of the Black Bayou.

"A few months later, Nell died giving birth to Hattie. Nell's daddy felt horrible. They had the funeral here in Yellville. On that day, Nell's father buried his only daughter and met his little granddaughter, Hattie."

Virgil was slowly shaking his head.

"Hattie grew up with her Indian daddy in the bayou," Granny said. "She came to town once in a while, but never stayed long. She would stop and see her grandparents, but it was always an uncomfortable visit for all involved. At some point, she stopped coming to town altogether."

It seemed to Virgil as if Granny's story was nearing the end. "So how did she turn into a witch?" he asked.

"Well, that's where fact begins to blend with fiction, and I reckon nobody but Hattie knows for sure." Granny began to rock while continuing to fan herself. "Some folk say the Choctaw tribe never took her in because she was half white. But rumor has it that a Choctaw Medicine Man taught Hattie the healing arts."

Virgil was nodding, as if the story made sense to him. Then a frown crossed his face. "But that don't make Hattie a witch," Virgil said.

Granny acknowledged Virgil's statement with a nod. "But there came a time when Hattie's daddy went off toward New Orleans," Granny said. "And folks say that he came back to the bayou with a dark-skinned woman from a place called Haiti. I never saw this woman," Granny said, "but others did, and they say she knew black magic and Voodoo. Folks were afraid of that dark woman," Granny said.

Virgil sat silent, enrapt by Granny's story.

Granny stopped rocking and leaned toward Virgil on the couch. "I don't know if this is fact or fiction, but the story goes that the Voodoo lady lived with Hattie and her daddy. And of course that would explain how Hattie got to know black magic and became the swamp witch."

Granny got up and went to her kitchen. She returned with a small plate of cookies and offered one to Virgil.

"Some who knew Hattie back then say that she wanted to know her family in Yellville, so she stayed close. But she never really fit in and was never accepted by the townsfolk.

"What about the Choctaw tribe?" Virgil asked.

"There are still a few Choctaw up north of here," she said. "But Hattie stayed out in the only place she felt at home—the Black Bayou—halfway between the Choctaw tribe and Yellville."

Both Granny and Virgil sat in silence for a moment as Virgil ate his cookie. Then Granny spoke again. "I guess that's been Hattie's life all these years; livin' halfway between the Choctaw and Yellville, and never bein' fully accepted in either place."

* * *

The stories about Hattie swirled around Yellville for a few days before it took to raining. The sky darkened and a light breeze carried the smell of brackish water from the nearby coast. A dark sky turned into a black sky as the rain fell in large, fat drops on the tin roofs of the houses and shacks in town. At that point, talk of the weather overtook talk of Hattie.

The older townsfolk knew that a big storm was churning out in the gulf and prepared for a heavy rain. Some secured tarps over leaky roofs while others did outdoor chores ahead of the storm. Firewood for cooking was stocked in kitchens to keep it dry.

The big drops turned to a steady rain. The wind grew stronger and drove the rain at steep angles. It pounded the windows and doors, finding its way through the smallest cracks in the houses. People walked on wet rugs as they watched puddles grow on their linoleum floors. They kept the kitchen stoves stoked and hot to chase away the permeating dampness.

Outside, things that were not fastened down blew around, banging into other things which set them all in motion across the town from west to east.

And it continued to rain.

"The road's gone under," Bobby Monroe said to his wife. There was one road into town, and during hard rains the rising water covered it.

This was not unusual for the town of Yellville. Living in the swamp meant dealing with water. There was no such thing as high ground in the swamp—there was simply *higher ground*—which might only be a few feet higher than the normal water level in the bayou. When the water rose, the low spots in the dirt road into town went under. There were only a handful of people in town who owned cars anyway, along with a couple of trucks folks used for hauling things. But during high water times, there was no car or truck going to leave Yellville.

But the boats floated just fine despite the high water. The folk in Yellville didn't fret over a flood. It happened often enough that the folks learned to wait it out.

An old man sat under the covered porch in front of the general store in Yellville. He looked out at the steady rain and saw one of his friends approaching on the boardwalk.

"Mornin' Harold," the sitting man said when his friend got under the porch.

Harold shook the water off his raincoat and pulled off his hat. "Do you think it'll ever stop raining?" he asked.

The old man on the bench looked at the soaked town. "Always has," he replied.

And after four days of steady rain, it finally stopped. The sky remained gray, but life in Yellville went on. People picked up the clutter from the storm, patched broken windows, and dried out their belongings.

Birds flew and squawked again, fish found that their world had grown larger, and the people and critters of the swamp settled for a new normal.

* * *

Doctor Jeremiah Jackson awoke one morning well after the storm. When he put his feet to the floor, he realized that he felt odd. His face felt flushed as he stroked the gray whiskers on his chin. His lanky frame groaned as he tried to stand up. He sat on the edge of the bed and placed his hands to the sides of his feverish head. His hands were clammy and moist. He lay back again, thinking that this awful sickness would pass.

He could see the gray skies outside his window. The clouds churned on a high-altitude breeze that Doc Jackson wished would come though his open window and relieve the stifling heat.

Just as Doc Jackson drifted into a restless sleep, someone banged on his front door. The sudden sound startled Doc into wakefulness, but he felt even worse than he had before. He remained on his bed, though he urgently wanted to get up.

"Doc! Hey, Doc!"

Someone shouted at his open window. The shouting seemed compelled to rouse the good doctor at all costs. It was a familiar voice, but in Yellville, most every voice was familiar.

"It's Wilma, Doc. My little girl is sick somethin' awful!"

Doc Jackson tried to answer Wilma, but his voice was so weak that it was drowned out by the song of a distant mockingbird.

A few minutes later Doc's front door issued a familiar squeak as it swung open.

"Doc?"

Wilma Upchurch stood in the doorway to Doc Jackson's front room, listening for any sound. She called the doctor's first name.

"Jeremiah?"

Doc could not answer, but summoned his strength to reach over and knock a copy of *The Good Earth* by Pearl S. Buck from his nightstand to the floor.

Wilma heard the thump of the falling book. "Doc? Are you all right?" She walked to the stairs and listened for a reply. "Are you up there?"

Wilma often helped Doc with cleaning and dishes and sometimes cooked the elderly neighbor a good meal. He had become a father-figure to Wilma, and often told her stories of his life beyond Yellville. Doc was one of the few people in town who had traveled to the world beyond the swamp. He had been to cities like New York, Boston and St. Louis. He had even gone overseas when he served in the military. People enjoyed his tales of far-off places, and always gravitated toward him when he was around. Every small town has a hero, and for Yellville, their hero was Doc Jackson.

Wilma climbed the creaky stairs and peeked into Doc's bedroom. The old man struggled to raise his head. She looked into his eyes and saw fright. She saw the sickness in his eyes as well, and didn't have to ask him how he was feeling.

"Doc, little Emily's burnin' up inside," she said. "And by the looks of it, you ain't doing any better than she is."

There was obvious desperation in Wilma's voice. The old man struggled to rise, and when Wilma helped him do so, dizziness overtook him. His head pounded with a headache, he felt nauseated and could not stand.

"Swamp fever," he croaked. "High water and mosquitoes..."

Wilma hitched a breath when Doc mentioned Swamp Fever. There had not been a bout of the fever in many years, but Wilma knew the stories—the awful stories of Swamp Fever plagues taking hold of the bayou. It took a certain set of circumstances to trigger an outbreak, and Wilma figured those conditions must have been met.

"What can we do, Doc?" Wilma asked. She took him by the hand and gasped when she realized how hot it was.

Doc Jackson rolled his eyes and wheezed out another breath. He looked at his friend and with a struggling voice, he simply said, "pray."

* * *

Later that same night a fog drifted in from the Black Bayou and old Doc Jackson succumbed to the fever. Two neighbor ladies sat with him until he passed because Doc had no family left in Yellville. He took his last breath thirty minutes before midnight. The women said a silent prayer in thanks of Doc's service to the community. They said a second prayer that the plague would pass quickly and take few.

Little Emily survived until the following day, her youthful immune system allowing her to fight off the infection for a few hours longer. Her parents were heartbroken at the loss of their youngest and watched their other two children with a wary eye, checking for fever every few minutes. By the time news of the deaths had passed around town, several others fell sick with the same fever.

Virgil awoke to the sound of his mother speaking softly. She sat on the edge of Vernon's bed with her hand held over his twin's forehead. She noticed Virgil stirring.

"Your brother is hot with fever," she said.

The worry on her face said everything Virgil was afraid of. "Is it the swamp fever?" Virgil asked in a hushed tone.

She turned her face away from Virgil and her shoulders shook. Her lack of an answer was answer enough.

Virgil climbed out of his bed and pulled on his trousers. He spoke to his mother as he worked his arms into shirt sleeves. "I'll be back, Momma," he said in a rush.

His mother barely noticed the door close as Virgil left the house.

Virgil was connected to his brother in a way that only twins would understand. His brother was like an extension of himself, and he could not bear the idea of life without Vernon.

Virgil hurried through the swamp on the same path that he and Vernon had taken only a few days ago. It was the route that led to the back of the Black Bayou. The same path that he swore he would never take again for fear of crossing paths with Hattie the swamp witch.

But now it was Hattie that he sought. Virgil's fear of Hattie was nothing compared to his fear of losing his only brother. If anyone could save his brother, Virgil figured it was Hattie.

He found the great Cypress tree and saw his brother's name carved in the bark. He looked ahead to the path, but the water was higher than it had been, and things looked different. He trudged and waded and made his way deeper into the bayou than he had ever been before. The canopy of the trees was so thick over his head that is seemed like darkness had fallen only an hour after sunrise.

Virgil looked around and spotted a small shack in the gloom ahead of him. He pulled up and stared at the small shack. Its roof was covered in moss, and the wood was so dark and damp that it appeared black. The front door was partially open. Only darkness lay beyond it.

"Miss Hattie!" Virgil called. He took a few steps toward the shack. "Miss Hattie!"

Virgil saw the front door of the shack slowly close.

"Miss Hattie?" There was no response.

A channel of deeper water lay between Virgil and the shack. He looked for a way across and spotted the eyes and nostrils of a large alligator in the black water. He saw no other way to cross.

"Miss Hattie, the people in Yellville are sick and dying from the swamp fever," Virgil shouted. The big alligator submerged at the sound of Virgil's voice. He heard a soft shuffling sound from inside the shack.

"Don't mean to trouble you, Ma'am," he said. "But good folks are dyin', and I was hoping you'd be able to—"

A loud, angry cackle came from the shack, cutting Virgil off. The boy stood his ground while every muscle in his body tensed.

"Miss Hattie," he called. "Truth is, my brother is sick with the fever. He's my twin, and I love him more than anything." Virgil's voice gave way to a sob. "I need your help, Miss Hattie, and I'd be eternally grateful if there was anything you could do."

A softer, smoother cackle came from the dark shack. The door opened just a bit.

Virgil sat with his head in his hands and cried. "I can't live without Vernon," he wailed. "If he was to die... well, you might just as well turn me into a snake."

Virgil heard a sound from the shack. A giggle? He sat for a long while before he decided he'd said his piece. No sounds came from the shack, so with his head hung low, Virgil began the trek back to Yellville with his mind on his brother and best friend.

* * *

Three days after Doc Jackson died there were several fresh graves next to the Baptist Church. The townsfolk held mass funerals to bury their dead while others still suffered on their deathbeds. After the funerals, most of the somber community gathered around the churchyard. The only ones missing were those who sat at bedsides caring for the sick.

"Ain't never seen anything like it," a man said as he stroked his chin. "Been livin' here all my life and there ain't never been a plague like this."

"It ain't natural," another man said. "Like the ol' Devil takin' a shot at Yellville."

Others nodded, and another spoke up. "My guess is old Hattie brought this on us. You know them twins claim to have seen her a few days ago. Right after that, we get a storm and a flood, and then... well, this." He waved toward the graveyard, and then slapped a mosquito that was feasting on his neck.

The men looked at each other. "And the 'skeeters," one offered, "I ain't never seen them so thick."

During a moment of silence as the men stood around, one of them had a hateful idea.

"I think we ought to go fetch old Hattie and put an end to this."

"How you mean to put an end to it?" another asked.

"We tote her back to town and show her the end of a rope," one boasted.

"Hang old Hattie?" one criticized. "If you ever found her, hangin' would be too good for her."

Heads nodded and eyes glanced around the group trying to determine if anyone was serious about finding old Hattie and hanging her.

Just about then, an eerie sound came from the swamps behind the graveyard. It was a sound so haunted and sad that some of the men shuddered. It could have been described as a wail, or perhaps a howl, but it sounded like something that was injured and dangerous.

The men looked at each other again, but this time with doubt in their weary eyes. One decided to lighten the mood and took another by the arm.

"You gonna let a little swamp cackle spook you?"

Some of the men put their hands in their pockets and others dug into the mud with the toe of their boots. Everyone who lived in Yellville for any length of time had heard what the locals call a swamp cackle. Most attributed the sounds to Hattie, but others knew that there were plenty of things in the swamp that made mighty strange sounds. Nobody knew what it was, and nobody wanted to go find out... especially after the shadows grew long and the night creatures began to move. A swamp cackle could send shivers up the spine of a confident man.

"I say we fetch a rope, and when morning comes, we head out to the bayou, find old Hattie and put an end to this once and for all," the same man said. "I'm tired of livin' under her spell..."

Another swamp cackle echoed off the trees and the dark water and carried to the small group of men who could not help but move closer to the church. One of the men saw his wife emerge from the open doors.

"There's my wife," he said as he moved toward her. "Better git on home."

Others searched for their wives and kids and within minutes the group of men had disbanded, all thoughts of a hanging quelled, but thoughts of the swamp witch heavy on their minds.

* * *

Few folks in Yellville slept well the night after the first round of funerals. Many were still suffering from the fever themselves. Those who weren't sick sat and watched over others who were.

The widow Evelyn James lived alone in a two-story house next to the town square. Like many folks in the autumn of life, Evelyn often found it difficult to sleep. She spent many nights looking out her bedroom window, watching stray dogs and cats and noticing when a light came on at a neighbor's house. Her insomnia had worsened in the months since her husband of forty-three years had gone to be with the Lord. She missed cooking and caring for him. Since his death, Evelyn ate simple meals and tried to keep busy cleaning the house that nobody messed up.

But on the day of the first funerals she had missed her afternoon nap, so when she retired for the night she was more sleepy than usual. She managed to fall into a slumber while listening to the lullaby of the frogs, crickets and owls in the bayou.

Something awakened her in the small hours of the morning. It was such a gentle awakening that she lay there confused for a few minutes wondering why she was awake but still so sleepy. She listened, certain she had heard something unusual, but puzzled by what it might have been.

The clock on her dresser ticked in a routine rhythm. Thinking that a forgotten dream likely woke her, she adjusted herself and her light covers and closed her eyes again.

Then a sound triggered a faint memory of what had awakened her.

She heard someone whispering. It was too faint to make out the words, but definitely a whisper from somewhere just beyond her room. The voice was unique, raspy and high-pitched. Evelyn noted the delicate clink of metal and a watery sloshing sound.

She was about to get up and look out her window when another strange sound broke the silence.

Laughter.

That same unusual, unfamiliar voice chuckled ominously. It was a hideous, deceitful laugh that sounded like a hyena circling a wounded animal. The laugh turned to a chant, a soft and melodic chant with the cadence of a poem being read in a hush.

Then there came another soft, metallic clink, followed by more chanting.

She could no longer resist a peek out her window. She swallowed her fear and crept to the windowsill. She stood to one side, peeking toward the square. She saw a firelight flickering on the wall of a storage building, but could not see the source. Embers lifted upward, dancing toward the sky. A shadow crossed the same wall. Some hideous, crouching form moved about the small fire, casting a dark, distorted shape upon it.

Evelyn rushed back to her bed. She broke out in a cold sweat under her cotton sheet. She dared to wipe the sweat from her brow, but was careful to be as silent as the dead. Something was out in the town square—and Evelyn felt content in her ignorance of what it might be.

The whispering continued, broken from time to time with that ghastly muted laughter.

Dark, dreadful images filled Evelyn's head until she wished she could have been snoozing instead of wondering what lay beyond her small house whose walls suddenly seemed insubstantial.

She closed her eyes and pulled the sheet over her gray hair, pulling it tight despite the heat in her core and the cold sweat on her skin.

Sometime toward dawn, the strange sounds ceased, but Evelyn prayed for sunlight to fall upon her windowpanes. But daybreak brought a dismal gray sky, as if night was hesitant to let go.

When the sound of voices—normal voices—drifted through her window, Evelyn looked outside. There were several people gathered at the town square, talking as much with their hands as their voices.

Evelyn knew everything that went on in Yellville, and there were no scheduled gatherings in the town square that morning. She rushed herself into her house-dress, pulled on a head-scarf, and set out to see what was happening, ever mindful of the strange sounds she had heard in the night.

As she approached the gathering of people, she realized they were all looking into a kettle that hung from a steel tripod over a small bed of hot coals. The community used iron kettles for crawfish boils and other celebrations that involved cooking. Beside the kettle she saw a crude sign—a sheet of parchment with a stick poked through it at the top and the bottom and shoved into the soft ground. A single word was written upon it:

CURE

The word had been scrawled onto the paper with some coarse writing instrument, perhaps a sharpened twig dipped into some dark, inky liquid.

Evelyn peeked inside the kettle and saw a bubbling green brew, thick and noxious. Flecks of various colors surfaced then rolled back under to be replaced by other colorful bits of things that might have been herbs.

Evelyn saw the confusion on the faces gathered round. "It's from old Hattie," she said. "I heard somethin' out here last night, making all sorts of strange sounds."

Virgil joined the gathering crowd. "Did you see her?" he asked.

Evelyn shook her head. "But it was Hattie, I swear."

All eyes were upon Evelyn now as she described the sounds and the chanting and how scared she had been.

Evelyn looked into the pot. "I ain't touchin' that stuff," she said. "Probably turn you into a goat or somethin' if you drink it."

Heads nodded all around her just as Pastor Turner approached. The short and rotund preacher peeked into the kettle. He had listened to what Evelyn was saying and tossed forth an opinion. "It's the work of the Devil," he said as if he knew with certainty. "The Devil and his minions are trying to deceive us."

That must have sounded right to the majority of folks gathered around. A few whispered *amen* and others said *sweet Jesus, save us* under their breath. Pastor Turner lifted his ever-present Bible and led the group in prayer, asking forgiveness for sins and salvation from the swamp fever and the Devil.

Virgil kept his eyes open during the prayer so he could watch the bubbling green liquid in the kettle. It was a mesmerizing sight and he could not pull his eyes from it. But he wondered if Hattie had actually made a cure, or if this might be a trick because he had dared to ask for her help. The kettle could be full of poison for all Virgil knew.

It was then that Big Bill Jennings walked into the growing crowd. Big Bill was called Big Bill not because he was a large man, but because he had a son who everyone called Little Bill. But Big Bill *was* a big man in Yellville. He was the closest thing to a mayor the town ever had.

Big Bill was level-headed and generally made good decisions on the town's behalf. He was Yellville's go-to man when emergencies arose. When Big Bill had something to say, the people of Yellville listened.

Big Bill stepped up to the kettle and was brought up to speed on the ideas surrounding its appearance in the town square.

After considering all arguments, Big Bill took off his hat and spoke.

"Little Bill has taken the fever," he said. "His momma is watchin' over him, but the boy's burning up. He's talkin' crazy... don't even seem to know who I am." He hung his head at the sadness of his own story.

Faces drooped at the news of Little Bill. The boy was fourteen years old and always on the right side of things. He helped people out when he could and was admired by all in town.

Big Bill spoke up again. "The road is underwater, and those who are sick would never make it out of the swamp by boat. Doc Jackson is gone, and I'm afraid there isn't much more we can do." He paused for a minute, seemingly looking at his boots. Then he raised his head again. "If there is any chance this brew is really a cure, then I'm all for trying it." He looked into people's eyes, seeing the sadness and fear reflected back to him. "I don't see as we have anything to lose."

Big Bill took the ladle that hung from the side of the kettle and dipped it into the churning green concoction.

The preacher warned him again that it was the work of Satan.

Evelyn told him that there wasn't anything good that came from old Hattie and the Black Bayou. "Swamp witch magic will do you in!" she admonished.

But Big Bill cautiously sipped the cooling mixture with all eyes upon him. Not a breath was exhaled until Big Bill slugged down the ladleful and was still standing. He belched, excused himself, and then licked his lips. "Ain't that bad," he said. "It smells worse than it tastes."

He dipped the ladle again, letting the overflow drip back into the kettle. He then took the full ladle and walked toward his house which was a block away.

Half the crowd followed him. The others stayed back and talked about what a foolish thing he had just done. Someone offered that he might now be under old Hattie's spell and should not be trusted. Many agreed.

Within a few minutes, Little Bill's mother spoon-fed her child the green substance with some folks looking in from the parlor and others peeking in the windows of Big Bill's house.

An hour went by with no change in Little Bill, but his mother said he seemed to be cooling down. The crowd started to dwindle, many having sick of their own to care for and chores that had to be done. But a few stayed around and watched, curious about what effect the brew might have on the ailing boy. Virgil watched, ready for a sign that he could use the brew to save his twin.

Another hour passed and Little Bill told his momma he was thirsty. She gave him a cool drink and felt his forehead. The next hour he was sitting up in bed, waving at the folks outside his window. News spread and the crowd gathered again, and all witnessed the miracle of Little Bill's apparent recovery. Then the gathering moved to the mysterious kettle in the town square.

Not a soul in the town of Yellville could bear the thought of another funeral. Almost everyone knew someone who had a fever and feared it would continue to spread. Many folk were on their deathbeds when the word of a cure got out, and the whole town took part in ladling out cups of the liquid and giving it to the afflicted, then drinking it themselves for good measure. Virgil ran home to fetch a cup, filled it, then ran the cup back to his mother. She had heard the news as well and she helped Vernon take his dose. She sent Virgil back for a precautionary dose for himself. By sunset, every person in Yellville had partaken, but for two: Evelyn James and Pastor Turner.

* * *

The next morning, the sun was shining in Yellville. It was the first time since the storm that the skies were blue and bright. The folks of Yellville stood talking to neighbors, inquiring about loved ones whose fevers had broken and were just about feeling right again. The waters had begun to recede, reduced to a few deep puddles in the lowest spots. It seemed hope had returned to Yellville.

Pastor Turner fell sick the night before. His wife poured the cure-brew into his mouth when he seemed too near death to struggle against her. He awoke that morning claiming an angel had come to him in the night and cured him with a single touch. Nobody ever told him the truth.

Evelyn James never took the fever, but the sights and sounds of the dark shape in the town square fueled her nightmares for many months.

While sadness permeated the town, the remaining people reveled in the sunshine and went out about the work that needed to be done to bring Yellville back to order. The same group of men who talked about finding old Hattie and hanging her just the night before, were now talking about what a wonderful thing old Hattie had done by bringing a cure to the stricken town.

"You know, a bunch more would have died had old Hattie not left that cure."

All agreed that it seemed Hattie had saved the community from becoming a ghost town.

"Kinda makes one wonder what other things old Hattie can do," said another of the men.

"With Doc Jackson dead and buried, we need someone who knows how to heal folks," said someone else. "It ain't gonna be easy to find another doctor willing to come to Yellville."

"Old Hattie might not be so scary after all," someone offered. "Maybe we can go and fetch her, and bring her back to town."

"Yeah," one man agreed. "That swamp witch magic might do some good around here."

The men stroked their beards, twisted their mustaches, and wrung their hands while they thought about this new idea.

"We could offer her a house here in town where life will be much easier than livin' out in the Black Bayou."

"The old DuChamp place is empty," one fellow stated. "We could fix it up a bit, and let her stay there."

Another moment of silence ensued as they worked out plans in their heads and dreamed about what old Hattie might do for the folk in Yellville.

"I wonder if she can make crops grow bigger?"

"Or make some kind of spell so we can catch more fish."

"If she can turn a man into a snake, she can prob'ly do most anything."

"If nothin' else, we need to at least thank old Hattie for savin' the town."

With their minds made up, ten men gathered themselves up and headed out to the back of the Black Bayou. They followed the paths through brambles and mud, waded through the hydrilla and muck following the path the twins had described a few days earlier. They found the big Cypress tree, and upon close inspection, saw where Vernon had carved his initials in the bark. They nodded to one another and looked beyond for a path to old Hattie's shack.

"The water's still a little high," one of them explained. "The path might still be underwater."

"Or the floodwater done washed the path away," another suggested.

"It's gotta be back this way," one man said as he led them on.

So nine men followed one who didn't know where he was going, but knew where he hadn't yet been. They marched deeper into the swamp where the trees and vines grew bigger, and the light faded to gray. The muck was thicker and tried to suck the boots off the men's feet as they struggled to make progress. The man who was in the lead tried to pick a path that offered the least resistance, which resulted in the group wading aimlessly in the Black Bayou.

There was no sign of Hattie's shack when darkness fell on the group.

"Where the hell you goin', Tom?" one man asked with disgust. "We passed by this spot more than an hour ago."

Others sympathized, realizing they had been going in circles.

"Can't see a damn thing out here," one shouted. "We need to get out of this swamp!"

"Then you lead the way," a humiliated Tom offered.

Then true darkness fell upon the swamp. They had never intended to be in the bayou this long, but they were tired and lost.

They all calmed down enough to know that they needed light to see by, so two men climbed trees to gather some dry Spanish moss which hung in clumps. Others fished in pockets for wax envelopes of dry matches. In a short time they had managed to make a few torches.

After lighting the first one, they realized how many glowing eyes were watching them. In every direction they saw pairs of eyes reflecting the glow of the flame. Some were green, some were yellow and others were red. Most were small, but some were large enough to garner concern from the men.

"I ain't gonna sleep in this swamp tonight," one of the men stated.

"I heard that," another chimed in.

"Then somebody better figure out the way back," someone else demanded.

The men made a pretty good racket as they slopped through the muck and shallow water. Many of them swore and wondered whose idea this was anyway. Then someone spoke up with some urgency.

"Hush!" a man shouted. Everyone stood in place, quiet as they could be. The only noise was drips of water falling from their clothes into the swamp.

Off to one side came a splashing sound. Something big was churning up the bayou. It sounded as if something was running through shallow water, each footfall making a splash.

Then came the most god-awful swamp cackle any of the men had ever witnessed—and it was close. Another man lit a torch.

More splashing followed a hideous howling sound.

It was closer.

The men all took off in the opposite direction, almost climbing over one another to take the lead. They tripped over roots and cypress knees, got tangled in the thick vegetation, but kept moving away from the God-awful howls.

Another swamp cackle from their left caused them to turn to their right and continue their flight as best they could. The torches were extinguished one by one as men fell into the water or lost their grip in the panic. The men caused so much commotion that roosting birds flew into the darkness and smaller swamp critters scurried away from the chaos.

Now the crazy cackling sound came from their right, and the men instinctively turned left to put distance between themselves and the unseen monster that seemed to be stalking them.

The men continued to flee from the horrific sounds with their hearts thumping like pistons. They were all exhausted. But fear is a mighty motivator, and they kept moving despite being spent. Some ended up urging others along, either dragging them by their arms or pushing them from behind.

The man in the lead took another step but realized that the step was much easier than the previous one. He stomped his foot and to his amazement, discovered he was standing on dry ground. The others soon caught up and were thankful to be out of the clinging mud of the Black Bayou.

The men stood on the land and pulled in deep breaths. A couple fell to the ground, bone-weary and wet. The others listened, only hearing the peepers and bullfrogs and crickets. One made another torch and set it ablaze. They all felt more secure in the presence of light.

The man holding the torch looked around. "Hey, I know this place," he said. "I bring the kids fishing down here. The road is over yonder," he pointed into the darkness.

"Thank God Almighty!" one man shouted.

Everyone gave thanks to Their Maker as they took inventory of themselves. They all had mud slung across their faces, their clothes were soaked, and one man found he was missing one of his boots. They all looked at each other and laughed as if they had not been afraid at all while lost in the swamp.

Another torch was lit while the men picked leaches off their arms and pulled hydrilla from their pockets. One of the men spotted something at the edge of the light. He tapped the man holding a torch and pointed.

The two of them called the others. They all gathered around, looking at a stump with a parchment note held to it with a rusty nail. There was a message scrawled in the same crude writing as the note on the kettle found in the town square. This one read:

DON'T COME LOOKIN' AGAIN

The men all looked at each other in amazement. How had she known they would end up here?

While they looked at the note and scratched their heads and wiped their brows, the most dreadful, ghastly swamp cackle yet let loose from the darkness beyond the torch's reach. A mournful howl, followed by a screeching wail filled the men's ears, striking panic once again into their minds.

They all scrambled up a muddy levee, pulling and pushing each other to be the first one to the relative safety of the road back to town.

* * *

Virgil sat with his recovering twin on the front porch of his house when the men walked past mumbling about the swamp witch. He had not told Vernon about finding Hattie's shack, but no secrets could be kept from one another. But now was not the time to tell of that adventure into the swamp. Virgil just scooted over and wrapped an arm around his brother and best friend, glad to know that he was going to be okay. He looked out toward the swamp.

An old woman watched from the darkness as the men dragged themselves into town. Now that she was sure they made it, she turned back to the depths of the Black Bayou, the place she called home.

A short but loud cackle rose from the darkness and the men hurried for their homes.

Rococo

by

Connor Millard

"It has been almost one year exactly since Rachel was assimilated into the main group, but it is only during the last few days that she has seemed close to settling on a keyword," Bob said, his computer quietly recording every word. He looked away from his scope to make a few minor marks in his notebook. "This is, of course, unusual. With most subjects—"

"Null-Seven," Phil said.

Bob stopped the recording. "What?"

"Subject null-seven." Phil turned in his chair to face him. "You called her Rachel again. She's not Rachel anymore."

Bob moved his head back from the scope but did not look away. He stared out at the decaying cityscape, all filthy concrete and window frames full of glittering glass teeth. He could see the tiny, blurry shapes of the kids in distance, milling about the ruined intersection that served as their camp.

"Bob, you assured us that you were okay. That you could be objective. That's the only reason you were allowed to stay on the project. Having an observer with a personal connection to one of the subjects is about as non-kosher as it gets already. If you—"

"I'm fine," Bob said, looking at Phil. "Just a slip of the tongue. I'm fine. I can still do this work. Really, I'm fine, Phil."

Phil looked him in the eyes for a few long moments. His face softened. "Okay," he said. "Just...keep a better eye on what you're saying, alright?" Satisfied, he returned to his own work.

But it wasn't just his mouth. It was his heart threatening to fall from his chest into his stomach whenever he saw her through the scope, laughing or acting like a normal seventeen-year-old. It was his eyes burning and threatening to tear up when he heard her voice over the field microphones, speaking gibberish, but her voice nonetheless. It was his whole body, multiple times during any given day observing the kids, telling him to run out to their crude encampment and hold Rachel again, as tight as he had ever held her, and hope that somehow he could just squeeze it out of her, every strange word or phrase, everything that wasn't her, and that she would be his daughter again.

It took a lot to not let any of it show, and it was a blessing that he made as few slip ups as he did. Whether Phil didn't see any of these things or pretended not to wasn't of much consequence to Bob. All that really mattered to Bob was that he hadn't said anything to anyone else, allowing him to spend time as close to her as he could, now.

* * *

He felt a tug on his shirt.

"Daddy?" Rachel said, looking up at him. He pulled her up onto his lap.

"Yes, bun?"

"Who are The Kids?"

Bob took a moment before answering. "What do you mean?"

"You and Momma were talkin' about them yesterday. And the day before that. And before that. And Saturday, and the day before that...."

"Well...." He took another moment to think. "You know what I do for my job, right?"

"Scientist!" She smiled her goofy, incomplete, toddler's smile.

"Right. And you remember what that means?"

She scrunched up her face. "You...figure stuff out. And tell people."

"Yes. So, the kids." He took a breath and let it out in a half-sigh. "The kids are sick, in a way that we haven't seen before. I'm trying to figure it out, so we can help them."

"Are they, uh...can they make other people sick?"

"Contagious? No. Not that we can see, at least. We don't know how they get sick. Why?"

"I don't wanna get sick."

Bob put his arm around her. "You don't have to worry about that, honey. Ever. I promise."

She didn't say anything.

"Okay?"

"Okay." She hopped off his lap. When she was gone he looked back to his computer screen, but didn't start typing. Eventually his gaze drifted off to nowhere in particular as he sat there, thinking. Trying to decide if he had made a promise or a lie.

* * *

"I think she might be close to a keyword."

Bob put down his forkful of potato. "Really?"

"Yeah, listen to this." Phil set an audio player on the table and pushed play. There were a few voices. Rachel's, of course, and Bob recognized a few of the other kids. Balter, Excavate, Rake, and either Yin or Yang, he couldn't quite tell. He felt a twinge of guilt, as he usually did, that he never knew, and still did not know, their real names.

"Sun-green balter trees shine preamble baltering butter sun-wise to waiting," Balter said.

"Steel excavated streams and pork barrel anomalous oxygen for excavation, sans dread," said Excavate.

"Balter balter of prudence off to nigh."

There were a handful of 'hm's and 'mm's.

"Raking predetermined manse onto rake bellowed tarps it guarded," said Rake.

"Of groaning rococo made quell by once quelled breaking above the broken abstract rococo rococo," said Rachel.

Yin or Yang said something after that, but Bob wasn't really listening at that point. "So rococo is the front-runner then?"

Phil nodded. "Break and quell are up there, too. It'll probably be a few days before she settles on something, but I just wanted to let you know. I...thought you might want to try and pick up some extra rotations for the next few days. To...y'know. See it as it's happening." He gave Bob an intent look.

Bob weakly smiled. "Thanks," he said. "I *would* like to be there for it. I'll see if Crane and Hill are willing to swap."

Phil nodded awkwardly and started off towards the lunch counter.

"Phil?"

He turned back.

"I—thanks. Really. Thank you."

Phil smiled with one corner of his mouth and made a vague gesture. Something half-way between 'it was nothing' and 'you give me too much credit'.

Bob watched him walking away for a moment, then went back to his lunch. He smiled in earnest.

* * *

"Dad?"

"Yeah, Rach?" he said though a mouthful of breakfast.

"What was it like? Before, I mean. When...how do you always put it? 'When things made sense'?"

He took a long drink from his glass of water, considering, and swallowed. "Well," he said. "The city was whole, for one. And peaceful. Relatively, anyway. Now that it's a ruined husk I realize how much I took things like it for granted, but—"

"That doesn't really help. I barely know the city *now*, remember? Not everyone gets to see it so often."

"Right right. Sorry." He smiled. "Taking things for granted again. Hmm." He trailed off and didn't speak for a while. He put the tip of his thumb under his chin, absentmindedly, the way he always did when he was thinking.

"Dad?"

"What? Oh, sorry. Yeah. Before. Before. Well, for one thing, there were so many more people. Especially in the big cities. You could walk for hours and hours and never see the same person twice. And in five minutes you could find out what was happening two towns over, or half the world away. It was brighter, too. The days were longer, most of the time anyway, and there wasn't so much fog.

"The biggest thing, though. I'm sure you've heard stories that float in from other places. When we get a strong signal on the radio, or someone wanders in from miles away. Stories of strange things. Of dangerous things. Spectacular things, too, but mostly dangerous things. Mist that swallows up whole towns and leaves nothing behind but forest. People that can say what's going to happen tomorrow, or the day after, or even further, and be mostly right. Wolves taller than men. Men that talk to wolves.

"Before—not before you were born, but before you were old enough to remember—people talked about similar things. Smaller things, but otherwise the same. But we knew that, for the most part at least, these things weren't true. Or had an explanation that we could understand."

"And now?"

"Now we never know what the hell is real. The world used to be a lot more...boring, I guess. Boring, but in a good way. A bit safer. More comprehensible."

"Mmm," Rachel said. "So." She paused. "The Kids. There wasn't anything like them, before?"

A few people sitting at the same long cafeteria table softly cleared their throats and slid a little further down.

"No," Bob said. He brought another spoonful of cereal halfway up to his mouth. "Well…." He stared into space for the barest of moments. "No." The spoon went into his mouth.

"Aw, come on!" Rachel said. "Tell me!"

"They aren't anything you need to concern yourself with."

"Considering that I could be joining them one day whether I concern—"

"Don't!" He put his spoon down with a sharp clatter. "Don't—just don't."

Neither of them said anything for a while.

"Look," she said. "I know—I know you're scared. You and mom. And everyone else with kids."

Bob said nothing.

"But don't I deserve to understand what might happen to me one day?"

He sighed and pinched the bridge of his nose. He pushed his bowl of cereal away.

"If it manifests, it begins to do so around sixteen," Bob said, keeping his voice low. "Give or take."

"So," she said, her voice low. "Next year." She pressed her lips tightly together.

He put a hand on her shoulder. "It's the hardest year. But you'll be fine."

She tried to smile. "Keep going."

A few people at the other end of the table left. Some others started giving Bob sideways glances.

"The subject shows an abnormally improved vocabulary. They won't notice anything, and those around them won't either, for a time. It starts off small, a few uncommon words here and there. Then more and more until they start sounding like a dictionary. It's usually not until the last few weeks that it becomes obvious. And I've always considered that a small blessing. A short time to contemplate.

"Their use of the words starts to become strange. Odd or idiosyncratic usage, things like that. We can normally make sense of what they're saying, albeit with difficulty, almost up to the end. At that point it devolves into nonsense, even more nonsense than what the kids in the city spout. The end stage is usually accompanied by some seizing, but not always. Occasionally they just pass out."

She was quiet, staring at her father and hardly blinking. Perhaps a little pale.

"After that, they're gone." His voice cracked at 'gone,' and he stopped. He licked his lips and swallowed, then continued.

"We're not sure how much of themselves they remember. They don't engage with us while they're here. At the beginning, we tried to restrain them, keep them from leaving. But they fought. Wrested themselves from strong hands, struggled violently against every restraint we could find, and attacked anyone trying to keep them from going where they somehow knew they needed to go. Yelling their mish-mash of speech through all of it, voices warped with remarkable rage.

"So we let them go, then, as we do now. Partly because it's futile to spend so much time and effort keeping them here without unintentionally injuring them, partly because of how…difficult it was to see them like that. They find their way to the others. We don't know how, but they make it there, and safely. And they're calm when they get there. The picture of calm. Eerie, sometimes. We bring food to them every few weeks, to help them along, and they're all smiles and indifference. No foaming anger or flailing punches.

"Cognitively, they function. On some kind of level, at least. They talk to each other. We don't know if they're actually articulating anything to one another, but by every appearance they seem to communicate. They manage to coordinate themselves somehow, because they survive together. They gather food, they prepare shelter, and nothing gets neglected.

"They occupy themselves in their down time as well. They chat, far more than could possibly be necessary just to figure out who's going to do what and when. It's impossible to tell what they're talking *about*, of course, but sometimes from the tone, or the inflection, or the affect, you can get a feeling for the conversation. Very engaged, whatever it is they're saying." He trailed off.

Still pale and enrapt, Rachel asked, "Tell me about the sculptures."

He smiled. "Yes, of course you've heard of that. There isn't much to tell, really. More often than not, they have some kind of structure in progress. Scrap metal, wood, salvaged furniture, plastics, whatever they can get their hands on that isn't necessary for survival, they put into it. Strange, misshapen things that don't look to be attempting to capture the likeness of anything. Abstract. Building for the sake of building, or some attempt at art, or something else, we don't know. Still, they're definitely…interesting to look at." A few images flashed in his mind of the twisted shapes, full of sharp points or edges that almost seemed to attempt at some recognizable form, but ultimately dissolved into nothing. He shook them away.

"Once they've finished a structure, they destroy it," he continued. "Tear it down or, more frequently, burn it. And they all gather around it and watch it go…." He trailed off again, putting the tip of his thumb up under his chin.

She waited, but he didn't start again. "What else?" she said.

He didn't answer.

"Dad?"

"What? Oh. That's it, really. We don't know very much, to be honest. When a new case becomes apparent, we'll study the patient for as long as we can. Do some brain scans, if possible. We've gathered a lot of data, but whatever this is, it doesn't seem to play by the rules. The way the rules were before, anyway. As we understood them. Maybe there were never any rules to begin with."

She didn't press him for any more, and they picked at the rest of their breakfast in silence. The sideways glances from fellow breakfast-goers stopped after a bit, but every so often someone would shift uncomfortably in their seats.

"They really don't look like anything?" she asked after a while. "The things they build, I mean."

"No." He put his spoon down, his appetite evaporated. "Sometimes we see things in them. The way you see shapes in the clouds. Or anywhere. Just the human brain trying to make sense of random input."

* * *

Voices crackled out of the speakers.

"Rococo splash rococo gnash down preternatural glossy sieve of rococo. Patter spots the pattern lump rococo to the lingering apple of dye down rococo."

"Excavate grounds preaching towering rinds toward excavated slumber. Wear brake streak with moss flute to the excavation."

"Yin."

"Balter and fry?"

"Rococo rococo rococo down drive petal shute rococo leaf dreads rococo pine."

"Numinous rumblings from parted swords in numinous."

"Rococo rococo."

"Anapest of prodigious hearth to wasted anapest smiles on top of winter."

"Rococo drives rococo plinth for rococo blizzards doomed toward forward hives."

"Hmm."

"Mm."

Bob and Phil sat at their posts, still and listening. Bob with thumb under chin, Phil with hands folded in lap.

"It's obvious she's found her keyword," Phil said. The speakers still spewed the kids' mangled English.

"Yes."

"But the frequency is strangely high."

"Mmm-hmm."

"Which we've seen before. Just not *this* high, as far as I can remember. And definitely not persisting for this long. And on a few occasions, the other kids have said 'rococo' back, almost like they're responding. Or catching on to something she's saying."

"Right."

"Bob? Are you listening?"

Bob blinked and looked at Phil. "Hmm?"

"What do you think it means?"

He started to tap his chin. "It might not mean anything. Just because it's new doesn't mean it's significant."

"What if it's not? The number of cases has gone down drastically. The protocols have worked, or something else has. Maybe our children's minds have just gotten stronger, somehow. I don't know. But whatever going on, what if It's...." Phil hesitated.

"What?"

"...Mutating. Changing itself. Trying to overcome immunity."

"You make it sound like it knows it's being resisted."

"Is that really so crazy?"

"...No."

"Exactly. I—"

"Rococo," came Rachel's voice over the speaker.

* * *

"What do you think?"

"It's...a whale?"

Rachel grimaced. "Of course it's a whale!" She waved a hand at the small sculpture she had placed on Bob's desk. "What do you think about it? Is it good? Is it bad?"

"It's...it looks a little menacing, actually. Is that what you were going for?"

She sighed. "Sort of. But less menacing, more...imposing. Monolithic. Working in small scale makes that all but impossible, though. And I *know* we can't really spare a whole lot for non-essential stuff. It's still frustrating though."

He was quiet for a few seconds as he scrutinized the sculpture. "Why a whale, though?"

She shrugged. "It's supposed to be, like, Leviathan. I was skimming through some of the books in the library. Something about a huge, unstoppable, powerful *thing* just kind of resonated with me, I guess. A big mysterious thing that can't be comprehended. The idea stuck in my head. It felt relevant, I think. To the world today. You know, with everything going on." She looked away.

Bob smiled. He tousled her hair. "Well," he said, "you're well on your way to tapping into the zeitgeist, if nothing else. That's valuable to an artist."

She tried to fix her hair with little success. "Not if it's the last zeit to ever have a geist."

He took a breath to say something, but stopped. He chewed his bottom lip. "Maybe. Or maybe it's more important now than ever to leave something behind besides ruined wonders and broken tools."

"Why? Anything we leave will be long gone by the time anything else comes this way. Aliens or otherwise. We are the only things that give what we do any meaning."

"Have you been reading Nietzsche again?"

"*Dad.*"

"Fine, fine. Alright, look. It's going to take more than a few ghouls and ghosts to finally do us in. You've been reading what history texts we have here, right? Plagues, meteors, global warming, nuclear weapons, and one super-volcano. We almost didn't make it, did you know that? No one's really sure of the exact number, but the ancient human population once dipped down to somewhere under ten-thousand. Some radical estimates of a mere thousand. And before the Collapse, we were over nine billion strong. We're survivors."

"That's only true until it isn't."

"That's why you need to be positive. Tenacious. Ready to bite and scratch to earn the future of the species. We will do what it takes to persist, even if that means having to radically change. We should always be hopeful we can continue on along the path we started, the way we are now, but if we can't, if we continue to be beaten back…. Well, then the ones who survive the culling will get to decide what the species becomes. Even if that means we have to become monsters to survive monsters."

"Now who's been reading darkly realist philosophy?"

"Evolution doesn't have any preferences, Rachel. What becomes useful to survival, survives."

* * *

"*Bob.* Bob! Bob come on you need to hear this."

Bob was woken from sleep by furious, violent shaking. He mumbled a handful of curses, nearly falling out of his chair. Satisfied, Phil went back to his own chair, pulled up as close to the speakers as it had ever been.

"What," Bob said, after righting himself on his own chair.

"Just listen."

"Rococo," Rachel's voice said.

"Balter?" said, of course, Balter.

"Numinous post!"

"Rococo."

Bob frowned and his brow furrowed. "Sounds like—"

Phil shushed him. Bob continued to listen.

"Balter post!" said the speakers.

"*Rococo*," Rachel said, her voice slow and deliberate.

"Excavate!"

"Rococo," burbled over the speakers, again. But it wasn't Rachel.

Bob sat up straighter in his chair.

"Mmm, Rococo," said Rachel.

"Rococo," said Balter.

"Excavate?"

"Numinous?"

"*Rococo*," Rachel and Balter said together, in an almost rhythmic fashion. If Bob's attention wasn't entirely focused, his mind might have drifted to the thought of a pair of singers harmonizing.

"Rococo!" said Excavate.

"Hmm! Rococo!" said Numinous.

By now Bob had pulled his chair up and was staring at the speakers with the same look on his face as Phil had had from the start. "But. What? How. Why."

"Yeah," said Phil. "This has been going on for maybe…half an hour? Granted, it's slow. But she seems to convert a small group, starting with one, then that sort of cascades, and then she moves on to the next. I would have shaken you sooner, but at first I wasn't sure it was really happening. I thought maybe sleep deprivation had finally started to catch up to me."

"It's recording, right?"

"Of course."

"Rococo!" came from the speakers, from a multitude of voices. Bob couldn't discern how many or which of the kids it came from.

"Should we do something?" Bob asked.

"Like what?"

"I don't know. Call in? Take it back to the others?"

Phil scratched his temple. "I don't know what good it could do," he said. "We'd probably do more good just observing a while longer. See if it persists."

"Persists?"

"They seem to stick to rococo once she…'convinces them' I guess? But it's barely been an hour. There's nothing to say it couldn't die away. Fade out. Let's just watch for now. First hand, out the windows here. See what happens."

"Yeah," Bob said. "See what happens."

* * *

Bob knocked on the door frame. "Rachel?"

"Acknowledge patriarch."

He walked into the infirmary. Rachel was the only occupant, so she got the bed closest to the door. The doctor and nurses were out; they had the room to themselves.

"I came to…I just wanted to…soon." He rubbed his eyes. "It will…probably be soon."

"Prophecy has been vindicated." She sat on the infirmary bed, hands folded in her lap. Still but for the faintest of shivering.

He pulled a chair up to her bed. "I'm staying here." He took one of her hands in his. "Nothing is dragging me away."

She squeezed his hand. "Condemned exile unsettled at gates."

He wasn't surprised to find her eyes were dry. He had suspected she had done her crying in the days before, in her room. Where he couldn't see.

"I—" His voice cracked. He cleared his throat. "I'm sorry."

"The people do not understand Galileo."

"This shouldn't be happening. I should be able to fix this. Nearly a decade of observation, of theories, of work—I should know how it works. Know how to stop the gears, make it go backwards. But I don't. I only just barely have some concept of what it is, and it's not enough."

He leaned forward on the bed, head hanging. "Every day I'd come back to you and your mother, watching you grow up, wondering 'Will she need me to save her? Will I be ready if the time comes?' And then we lost—lost your mother—"

She squeezed his hand again. A few solitary wet spots had appeared on the sheets below his face.

"Ragnarok," she said.

Bob smiled, just a little bit. They sat in comfortable silence.

* * *

Bob and Phil stared blankly out the window at the kids. The intersection was sparsely populated now; the kids had begun to move further into the city.

"How old is William, again?" Bob asked.

"Three."

It was a few minutes before either of them said anything else. The kids outside were busy working on their latest sculpture. It was the most solid—and simple—of their efforts to date: a four-sided, tapering column that ended in a point. It looked remarkably like one of the obelisks of ancient Egypt, and Bob wasn't so sure it was a coincidence.

"That's the youngest so far, right?"

Phil slowly blinked. "Yeah."

Silence, again.

"How—how many is that, now?"

Phil scratched his temple. "Under the threshold age? Or, what *was* the threshold age. I don't know. A dozen, maybe? Two? More? Less?"

"All starting with rococo. Hardly any build up, and scarcely any seizures at the conclusion. It's like It fully colonized a single word. Worked out the kinks."

Phil grunted. The kids abandoned their obelisk, most likely to find more material.

"Do you think," Bob said. "Do you think it was always headed toward this? Or did something change?"

"All I know is that things started feeling weird once your daughter showed up at the kids' intersection."

"You got something you want to say to me, Phil?"

Phil closed his eyes and pinched the bridge of his nose. "No," he said. "No, I'm sorry, I'm just…tired. Scared. Empty."

"So am I."

They watched the deathly still cityscape for a while longer.

"It's a shame they won't let anyone try to place some more cameras, deeper in," Phil said. "Just imagine what's going on in there. It's where most of them are sleeping, living, building, now."

"Be glad we're even still here at the observation post. Julia wanted us to close it down two days ago. Crane and Hill still haven't shown up. Not even a signal from their transponders. I would be surprised if anyone was willing to go out to put out more cameras now. The kids had been so *docile* up till now, but those last radio transmissions from Crane and Hill are still haunting my dreams."

"Pfft. Hill. I bet Hill did something to piss them off. Always poking what shouldn't be poked. If someone else went, discreetly, I bet we could get at least one cam—"

"Phil. You've been on about seeing their new camp for days. What help do you think it would be? A decade of research hasn't yielded anything, and we're even fewer now, besides."

"It would give us something to occupy our time, for one thing. And besides—isn't it human nature, wanting to see the eye of the storm that's about to swallow you?"

* * *

"I have a theory," Phil said.

Bob was lying on the couch in his quarters, staring at the ceiling. He said nothing.

"Okay, I'll just continue. Rachel, she—she progressed rather fast, didn't she?"

"Mm," Bob said.

"I know she was working on her vocabulary, right? Always rolling some new word around in her mouth. And, you told her a lot about the kids, right? Probably had more concrete details than most of the other children or teens here."

Bob mumbled something.

"So, a thought occurred to me: what if it works on some kind of souped-up memetics? The idea of the kids—the gibberish, all of it— spreads through communication. When it finds a mind with fertile ground—a brain full of a variety of words—it grows."

Bob sat up. "That—that's something. We could...we could slow it down. Couldn't we?"

"That was my thought. Stop talking about the kids outside of those of us studying them, stop it from spreading."

"Could it be that simple?"

"Well, we'd have to cut back on advanced English for anyone under the threshold age."

Bob paused. "Those are vital years," he said. "What would it do to their overall mental acuity? Could they make up for lost time after they've cleared the danger?"

"Does it really matter? If there's a chance of it working, it must be done."

Bob took a deep breath. Let it out. "Yeah. You're right."

* * *

The bulkhead was unlocked and ready to open. Bob stood before it dressed for his hike: down jacket, boots, backpack with supplies, including a field camera.

Phil had his hand on the release lever. "I feel like I should try to talk you out of it," he said. "But mostly I'm trying to figure out why I don't want to go with you."

Bob adjusted the shoulder straps of his backpack. "There's still work to be done here. Even if we're the last watch for this place."

"Yeah." Phil drummed his fingers on the lever. "They haven't all gone," he added quickly. "Maybe some of the children will...stay. There's still Paul, Edie, Quincy, Michael...Dirk and Melinda's daughter...um...." He looked off to the side, thinking. "That can't...that can't be all of them, can it?"

Bob just looked at him with a half-smile devoid of all mirth.

They stood in silence, not sure what else to say.

"Do you think it'll ever take *us*?" Phil asked. "You know. The 'old' people."

Bob looked up the ceiling, tapping his thigh. "No," he said, finally. "There's always a husk that's left over. Inedible."

Phil nodded. He pulled the lever, and the bulkhead groaned open on its old hinges.

Bob took a single step over the threshold. "I'll do my best to get the camera up," he said. "Before I try to find her."

"It's appreciated, Bob." He smiled. "You're giving me an all access pass to the strange new world. Try to make it back. So you can help me tend to the old one while its light sputters out." He waved, as did Bob.

Bob turned away and the door shuddered shut behind him. He heard the locks thud and grind as they engaged.

He walked until sunset, then set up a simple camp; nothing more than a fire and his bedroll. Looking up at the stars, he felt a strange peace. There were any number of things out there, old and new, that could prematurely end his trip while he lay there in the dark, alone. But still, he felt more content than he had in months.

He reached the edge of the city just before midday. There was no rush, so he took his time, enjoying the hike. It felt like an age since he had been here last.

As he got closer to the familiar ruined intersection, he started to see small sculptures. Placed in empty window frames, on mail boxes, perched on long-defunct fire hydrants, seemingly no more thought put into placement than where they could sit without falling over.

And something new: graffiti. Simple, like the kids' earlier sculptures, but still something. Mostly hand-prints and wiggly shapes. A few scribbles and possible attempts at representation here and there. Bob took some time to appreciate them.

He started to hear them when he got to the intersection.

RococorococorococorocococoRococo! Rhythmic, and harmonized. One voice. Sometimes it would seem to come from ahead, sometimes behind, sometimes the right or left. Mostly it seemed to float around the buildings, to circle around Bob like some kind of aural predator.

Rococorococorococorococo!

He headed out from the intersection in the direction they had guessed the new camp was. As he went he began to see larger sculptures lining the streets, most the kind of abstract nonsense that become so familiar. But a few of them, a few, started to show legitimate form. Something spider-like with a body and spindly legs. Something like a disembodied arm: a main trunk ending in a slab, with a number of finger-like appendages branching off. Something with four legs. A smattering of humanoid shapes.

Rococorococorococo!

He used the sculptures as a guide, following wherever they got bigger or more complex. Left, right, right, left. He noticed he was headed in the direction of the downtown plaza and veered off the path of trash figures to find his own way there. There was a building on the plaza that was still sound as high as the third floor.

Rococ020corococoro!

As stealthily as he could, he found his way to the back of the building and up to the third floor. He walked over to a smashed out window and he saw it.

In the center of the plaza there had been a statue of a man riding an elephant. A silly looking thing, but it didn't matter now because even if it was still there it was no longer visible. In its place was a massive...*mouth*. Rising from the floor of the plaza, sheet metal, plywood, roof tiles, floor tiles, street signs, aluminum foil, anything flat that could be nailed or wrapped around it made up its skin. Jagged window panes and polished triangles of metal were its teeth. It might have had eyes, but he couldn't see them from his vantage point.

"Leviathan," he whispered. He shook himself out of his trance and set up the camera, making sure to find a proper place for the antenna and solar panel. He made his way back down and walked out onto the plaza.

Rococo!

They seemed not to notice him at first. The song still continued, although not all the kids at the plaza were participating. Even at the center of everything it still seemed to come from all around him, deep from within the recesses of the city. He moved closer to the center, near the Mouth, hoping to draw attention.

A boy materialized in front of him. "Ro," he said. "Roco co rocoro coro."

"Rococo," said a girl a few steps away.

The boy pushed Bob. "Ro!"

The girl and another boy pushed him again, and this time he lost his balance, hitting the ground rather hard. "Rachel!" he said. "I'm looking for Rachel."

More kids had gathered, but didn't make any indication of understanding him. They started to kick him, aiming for his stomach, his head, his groin, anything soft. He tried to protect his head, but it proved almost useless.

Suddenly they stopped. Bob looked up, pain in his sides and skull. It was Rachel.

"Ro ro ro co," she said.

He pulled himself up onto his knees and pulled her into an embrace. He squeezed long and tight. Pulling back to look her in the face, he thought he saw a flicker of her old self in her eyes. Whatever it was, it was gone in an instant.

"I don't know if you can understand me," he said. "And I know there's no chance of you suddenly being able to communicate." He wiped some blood from his mouth. "But I needed to see you, see you face. Once more." He spat out a tooth. "And I thought I might—"

She pushed him back onto the ground.

"—might as well ask, and see what happens. What does it mean? At least give me that. Why that word?"

She leaned down. Close, close to his face. She put her mouth right to his ear and whispered.

"Rococo."

THE DEVIL WENT DOWN
TO GEORGIA, AGAIN

by

Ann Fields

In a half-formed state, the Devil partially reclined, partially hovered upon Its golden throne, and with one simple command, a command thought not spoken, conjured a screen made of smoke. Immediately, the screen began flickering with images, showing snippets of billions of lives as it searched for one specific life, a boy. While patiently waiting for the screen to settle on that one life, the Devil disparaged those who used crystal balls, prayer, tarot cards, divining rods, amulets, meditation, chants and such to tap into knowledge. It didn't need any of that, just a smoke screen, *if* It felt like it, and thoughts, *if* It felt like it. But then again, It *was* the Devil, a being greater in strength, wisdom and knowledge than the lower life forms who relied on those other tools; a being with enormous power. *But not enormous enough*, the Devil thought with contained anger as It peered at the screen on which appeared the boy, Johnny, a grown man now. The Devil stared at Johnny thinking, *such a common name for a boy with exceptional talent*. A talent so big that had It won their bet all those many years ago, It could have used the boy's gift to match the power and might of God. No more fallen angel status but a God to God.

Deeper into the screen of the material world It stared and well, well, well, what do you know? The Devil's smile, slicker than oil, spread across Its half-formed face. Its anger wiped clean. It knew that look on Johnny's face. It recognized that posture, that aura. The boy, Johnny wasn't happy. In fact, it looked like Johnny would never be happy again. Pleased, very pleased, the Devil banished the screen and with Its smile growing more calculating than devious thought, *Finally, all these years tracking that boy and now, it's time.*

Wasting not one moment, the Devil transformed wholly into a see-through gray energy. It sifted through the heavy, red atmosphere, shimmied through cracks in Earth's solid layers, slid past its fiery core, upward through giant-sized boulders, streams of water and steam, tangled roots, malleable clay, and finely minted dirt to filter through a split in Mother Earth. The wisp of energy shaped Itself immediately into a form that humankind approved of. The Devil hated to do it; hated shedding Its natural form to accommodate lower beings, but this mission was too important not to.

With the transformation into a tall, good-looking, well-preserved human man completed, the Devil scanned the area. Nothing had changed in this rural part of Georgia. Strips of wild grass still bordered cultivated rows of sprouting vegetables; rugged wood fences still marked boundaries that didn't even matter out here. And that ole hickory stump. It, no, he frowned in remembrance as he approached that stump. It still sat stubbornly in the middle of a generous intersection from which sprung roads leading everywhere but here. He kicked at it, still solid and wide enough to hold three oversized grown men. He sat upon that ole stump and with nothing but thoughts, formed a fiddle made of gold. The Devil held the instrument in his hands. Inspected it, admired it, deemed it excellent bait. Then out of the air, he plucked a bow and without even rosining it or tuning up, he played a song so magnificent, so sweetly endearing that the birds hushed their singing to listen. As the final note died, the Devil thought about playing another song but no, this was no pleasure trip. He had business here; a soul to win.

The Devil stood and with one hand stuffed in a pocket and the other carelessly holding the fiddle by its neck, he took off down the lightly traveled road, heading to the other place he knew well. He was early but he could wait. For an opportunity such as this, he had nothing but patience.

* * *

The black luxury tour bus, with cursive gold lettering on each side proudly proclaiming "Johnny, *the* Fiddler," swerved into the oncoming lane of traffic. If any cars had been in that lane or the other for that matter, the drivers of those cars would have assumed quite correctly that this was an unplanned move, an impulse action that could end with deadly results. It did not thanks to the driving skills and calm demeanor of the doughy man behind the wheel. With one hand, he pushed the angry man off him and away from the wheel. Then with both hands again on the wheel, he steered the hulking bus back into the proper lane, then onto the soft shoulder, then onto the grassy patch of land that separated state from private property. All the while ignoring the two men arguing in the aisle behind him.

The bus driver brought the bus to a smooth stop, idled the motor, applied the emergency brakes then pulled the lever to open the doors. Only then did he slump over the wheel and expel a long, thanksgiving breath.

The doors had not completely swished open before a lanky, dark man slip-sloshed his way down the three steep stairs. Anger, disappointment, frustration, and desperation mixed in him to keep him moving, out the bus, over the recently mowed grass to the rugged wood fence. There he paced, failure oozing out of him unseen except by those who had the gift of spiritual sight.

"All I'm saying is you didn't hafta…"

"GOD DAMN, CHUCK!" The angry man spun around hard, his dark face darker with fury. "That bitch don't know shit. And you don't either for booking me on her show." Johnny, *the* Fiddler, resumed his hard pacing, supremely pissed at even having to have this conversation with Charles "Chuck" Goddard, his business manager/childhood friend/music promoter/cousin/music producer. Muttering viciously, more anger escaped through words. "Comparing me to Thomas King. Got her damn nerves. King ain't shit. Can't play worth a damn!"

"Johnny, you losin' it. You on edge, man. How 'bout we take a little time off?" Chuck moved a little closer, hand outstretched as if trying to measure Johnny's anger through the air between them. "Head to Florida, to the beach. Watch the girls walk by. Gain a little perspective."

"You take some time off." Johnny turned sharply to face Chuck again, dark eyes glaring. "As a matter of fact, take off permanently." Suddenly, it clicked. Hearing those words out loud, feeling the truth of them in his soul, Johnny instantly knew why he didn't have the recognition, the fame, the success that Thomas King, a lesser musician, had. It was Chuck. All Chuck's fault. "You're fired. FIRED!"

"Mannnnn…"

"Did you hear me?" Johnny stomped to his longtime friend. Long fingers, perfect for playing the fiddle, shot out, poking Chuck in his chest. "I done wasted enough time with you. You holdin' me back. You the reason I ain't nobody. I'm done with you, man." Johnny gave Chuck one last poke. His eyes, his posture dared Chuck to push back, to fight. But in the logical part of his mind Johnny knew Chuck wouldn't. Chuck was a talking man, a thinking man. He wasn't the type to get physical. Oh, he could out talk, out think, out figure any man, but to get down with it? Naw…*that* was Johnny's thing. A holdover no doubt from his childhood where "a beating a day" had been his father's motto.

The two men stood there in the bright sunshine, eye to eye, chest to chest. Each one waiting, hoping for the one thing the other would never do: Push back. Quit anger.

One beat. Two beats. Three beats. Nothing. Then Johnny saw the shift in Chuck's eyes, the capitulation, the "I give."

"Okay, man," Chuck said in a low voice that cracked. He nodded his head, looked down at the ground, looked at the trees beyond the fence, looked anywhere but at Johnny. His face reflected what Johnny had seen in his eyes—resignation. "Okay, man," he said again, this time with less hurt in his voice. "You're right." Chuck swallowed hard, straightened his backbone, and finally met Johnny's eyes. "It's time to part ways. I've taken you as far as I can." He held out his hand for his cousin to shake.

Johnny didn't reach for it. He stared down at it, stalled by the magnitude of the moment. For twenty years, it had been him and Chuck. Johnny and Chuck in Memphis at the Blue Note. Johnny and Chuck in Los Angeles at JR's Blues Tunes. Johnny and Chuck at the Imperial Room in New York City. Johnny and Chuck in Paris at LaFontaine. At the Caribbean Jazz Fest, the Montreal Blues and Jazz Festival, the Oak Cliff Revue in Texas. All over the world and country they had traveled, forsaking all others for the love of entertaining music lovers with the gift of Johnny's fiddle playing. One hand shake would end it all. Well, not all. Johnny would continue to rosin his bow. Johnny would continue to delight audiences. His name would continue to blink in neon red, blue, orange and white outside of clubs and performance halls. He would continue to headline concerts and festivals all over the world.

Johnny smiled, envisioning the new levels he would reach without his cousin holding him down. He would hire a new manager; one with influence and deep, broad connections in the industry. Heck, he might even call Curtis Barnes, Thomas King's manager and let him know he was available. Hell, if Barnes could get King TV music specials, gigs playing for kings and statesmen, *Billboard* features and crossover record deals, Johnny couldn't even imagine what he could do for him, the better fiddler. No, the best fiddler on the planet.

Johnny thrust his hand into Chuck's and pumped it enthusiastically. "It was a good run," he said sincerely to his cousin. He could afford to quit his anger now that he saw the future clearly, saw his name and image embedded among the stars.

"Yeah," Chuck replied softly, "it was."

They shook one more time then their hands fell apart. Silently, reflectively, the men turned as one and headed for the bus.

* * *

They arrived in Atlanta a little after ten that evening, bringing with them the dust and dirt from interstate highways, farm to market roads, city streets, country lanes, and freeways so congested it seemed like opening day at the track. During the fourteen week tour, Johnny and his talented band had played in big cities, small towns, suburbs, ghettos, and places not even on maps. They had whizzed by historical markers, impressive monuments, indescribable works of nature, and Johnny's favorite—a stump. A big ole hickory stump. One that sat in the middle of nowhere from which roads leading east to west and north to south extended. When they'd passed that stump, vivid memories from twenty years before had overtaken Johnny. In his mind, he saw his 18 year old self…

…a tall, skinny boy, the ink barely dry on his high school diploma when he grabbed his fiddle case in one hand and in the other, a small cardboard box which contained his birth certificate, about two thousand dollars in cash, and a stingy assortment of clothes and toiletries. Pushing the screen door open with his shoulder, he burst out of his father's tense house, skipped down the porch steps, and without a backward glance or word of good-bye, set out on foot for Atlanta, leaving behind what promised to be a small life in Mississippi. He hitched the occasional ride, but walked a good portion of the state and the next state and finally reached the Georgia line. A few miles into what would become his new home state, he came upon a hickory stump. It seemed a good place to rest with the sweet, wild grasses bending carelessly to the wind; rows of nearly ripe vegetables adding color to the greens and browns of summer; and plenty of birdsong to please the ear. Inspired by the birds' melodies, Johnny took a seat on that ole stump and pulled his fiddle from its case. After rosining the bow, he joined the birds in song. He didn't know how long he'd played before he came back to himself, and there in front of him, a stranger stood. Blinking up at the man, Johnny wondered why he couldn't get the sun out of his eyes until finally he had the sense to lower his gaze and there at the man's chest was the reason why he'd been unable to focus—a bright, shiny fiddle that outblazed the sun.

Shading his eyes, Johnny reached out to it, mesmerized. Touched it; it felt hot. Snatched his hand back then finally looked up into the man's face.

The stranger smiled friendly-like at Johnny and without a word of greeting sat down on the stump. The stranger's smile turned deadly when he faced Johnny and said, "A bet. You win, you get my fiddle of gold. I win, I get your soul."

No consideration was needed on Johnny's part. He knew before the stranger had finished issuing the challenge that he would take the bet *and* win. He'd spent 13 years under his father's instruction and even though his music teacher father had told him every day those 13 years that he was average and would never make a name for himself in music, Johnny knew better. Something deep, deep-down in his soul told him he would be a great musician. Johnny held tightly to that belief and knew this challenge by a fellow musician was merely a test of his belief, just as his father's destructive words and handling had been a test. With that conviction and a teenager's invincible, egotistical spirit, Johnny eagerly said, "I'll take that bet," then smiled slyly and finished with, "Take care with my fiddle."

The challenger played first, thrilling the air with such a happy, energetic tune that the air enthusiastically carried it to all the nearby creatures, great and small. Soon, the challenger ended his song and while the final notes lingered in the air, Johnny began clapping and whistling, sincerely impressed with the stranger's talent. He even patted him on the back and said, "Not bad ole boy but..." He picked up his fiddle and tucked it under his chin. "...let me show you how it's really done." Before Johnny had played a lick, those great and small creatures popped out of their holes, burrows and caves to better hear. Even the angels in heaven stopped frolicking to get a better listen. And God, master of all, peeked below to see just who in blazes played like that.

Far too soon, Johnny brought his masterful, heart-and-soul playing to an end and when his final note sounded, the other musician hung his head and handed over the golden fiddle. The stranger vanished in a poof, but Johnny neither knew nor cared. He cradled that fiddle and smiled down at it like it was a newborn babe.

Johnny considered that day the start of his musical career and now, twenty years into the future, look where that starting point had taken him. Around the world and most recently around the country and now back home to Atlanta. Johnny looked past his reflection in the bus window, thinking more about that day at the stump. No doubt because it held even greater significance than being a start. It also represented proof. Proof that he *did* have the guts to leave his father's house and words behind and go after the success his schoolteacher father had been too afraid to even attempt. Proof that he *did* have the talent and skill to make a name for himself as a professional musician. And finally, tangible proof of his convictions: a fiddle of gold. Johnny smiled at himself in the window and said, "That had been one happy day."

And other happy days had followed. Days in Atlanta filled with making the rounds of clubs; of hanging out at studios; of practicing and composing; of creating head shots, demo tapes and other marketing materials; of moving from one residence to another with each successive home becoming less and less desirable. Then one day the happy days ended. The timing coincided with the last of the money he'd been saving since he was eight years old. For even at that age he knew his father's house would not be his home. Neither would he claim a homestead in the small town where he'd been born and raised, and where his mother's remains rested.

To re-initiate the happy days had required a sacrifice: sell the fiddle of gold for money. Money to keep club dates; to pay for studio time and back-up musicians; to promote his talent; and to move Chuck to Atlanta and buy them a corner house out of which they had lived and worked. Then, the sacrificial money had been needed for a tour bus; to buy a studio; to distribute his records; to meet payroll for his band and a small staff of five and to purchase the office building next to the studio for the staff. Later still, the fiddle money had been used to buy separate houses in different parts of town for he and Chuck; to pay for the latest digital recording equipment; for even more marketing, promotions and wider distribution. The sacrifice had been worth it. The money had sustained him during what could have been years of famine and drought; what other musicians and artists called "a time of paying dues." And while there remained sacrificial fiddle money in one of his bank accounts, Johnny was grateful that his earnings had kicked in years before to surpass even that.

With his mind now focused on money and success, Johnny didn't notice that the bus had taken its final turn and soon they would be arriving at Fiddler Music. He slouched in his seat, long legs splayed, ignorant of the stirrings of his band members as they counted down the minutes to home. Tuned inward, he simply frowned at the fact that money had never been the issue with his music career. If his success in the music business *had* been money based, he could have bought endorsements, lifetime achievement awards, Grammys. He could have bought the people who selected the musicians to write scores for Broadway and Hollywood, to perform at the Kennedy Center and other "by special invitation only" venues. But it wasn't about money. Hell, it wasn't even about talent, although it should be. It was about connections and the influence and power to transcend his chosen genre, and that's where Chuck had failed.

"But it's all good now," Johnny affirmed to his mirror self. He couldn't stop the smile that re-surfaced and took over his entire face. Now that the dead weight of his cousin had been lifted, even the sky was no limit. Dreams of his name and image growing larger than life crowded out reality and he missed the bus's entry into the back parking lot.

* * *

Well before the bus driver applied the brakes, the men, and one lone woman, a young drummer with unbelievable talent, were on their feet, retrieving duffle bags, instrument cases and sacks of souvenirs for loved ones. Even before the driver switched off the motor and opened the doors, the musicians were lined up, anxious to escape this rolling home and retreat to their real homes. As soon as the doors opened, they stepped off, one by one, moving slowly, weary from playing fifty-six gigs and logging thousands of travel miles.

It only took fifteen minutes for the musicians to disperse, the bus driver too who raced by Johnny and Chuck, waving and tossing out, "I'll be back tomorrow to clean her up real good. Inside and out." Johnny returned the wave, Chuck nodded, both watched as his red rear lights faded into black. That left the two of them, Johnny and Chuck, standing at Chuck's car, under one of the parking lot lights.

Chuck had always led the business discussions and Johnny saw no reason to change that now. So he waited patiently, his fiddle case in hand, as Chuck stowed his travel bags and laptop case in the trunk of his Cadillac. Finished, Chuck slammed the trunk closed and when he turned to face him, Johnny stiffened inside and out. He didn't want to hear any begging or pleading for his job back but as he searched his cousin's face, Johnny saw no sign that Chuck planned to do so. In fact, there was nothing there. No regret, no hurt, no emotion whatsoever. That was good because his mind was set; his future, too. Johnny relaxed.

"How 'bout six tomorrow night?" Chuck suggested, looking his cousin strong in the eyes. "We can meet here. Finalize the separation."

"Fine by me." Even though Johnny had not planned to be moving about by that time tomorrow, he could afford to be accommodating now that an unfettered future awaited him.

"I'll ask Roger to come too. Address any legal matters."

"Sure." Johnny agreed, but couldn't imagine what matters that might be since he had full rights to all his creative works. And there was only one owner of Fiddler Music—him. Chuck was an employee just like one of the band members or the office staff. But then again, that wasn't the right description either. Chuck had been the *first* employee. Chuck had had his back from the start, taking on every responsibility so Johnny could remain focused on the creative side of things. And never once in twenty years had Chuck shown himself to be anything but loyal to him and Fiddler Music; a very uncommon experience in the music business. At that reminder, Johnny flirted with guilt and regret but only for a moment. For then those big dreams pushed their way back to the forefront and the justification began.

He'd done right by Chuck. His business manager was financially set. Even with a monthly child support payment that rivaled that of some professional athletes, Chuck still lived a good life with a house in an exclusive neighborhood, luxury cars, college money for all six of his children, and investments as solid as Gibraltar. And professionally, Chuck, the music producer/promoter was set. He had a solid reputation in their genre and once the record labels heard he was available, they'd come courting. Even if they didn't or if Chuck turned them down—the more likely scenario—Chuck had a skill for picking talent. The outstanding band that backed up Johnny had been scouted by Chuck who practically lived in clubs and studios doing just that—sniffing out talent. Any or all of his future picks would likely be stars, guaranteeing Chuck professional longevity. Lastly, on a personal note, the man was set. He was smothered in love. His current live-in had given Chuck two beautiful, smart daughters. The previous two had given him a boy and a girl each. Chuck drowned all of his kids in love and attention, and they in turn treated him better than a king. Chuck would be fine. He had a life most men would wager the Devil for.

"It's been real, cuz."

Chuck's deep voice brought Johnny back to the now. He glanced down and saw Chuck's hand posed for a shake. This time, Johnny did not waste any time grasping his manager's hand. He squeezed it tightly once and let go. "Sho' you right."

They chuckled at the inside joke, a reference to the incomparable Barry White, and then in a low tone that trembled slightly around the words Johnny said, "Kiss the girls for me."

Chuck nodded and they both turned, in different directions.

* * *

Johnny didn't drive home immediately. He needed time to key down. It was always like that after a tour or a major recording session or a creative stretch where the notes jumping around in his head were transferred to paper in beautiful arrangements. Transition time is what Chuck called it, that period of time needed to come down off the high of being a performer to again become an everyday man, to again engage in life's rote experiences such as taking out the trash, retrieving the mail, and buying groceries. Over the years, Johnny had learned that his transition back into an everyday man never happened suddenly, but gradually over the span of hours, days, sometimes weeks. But eventually, he'd get there and for now, driving alone, on the dark, nearly deserted streets of Atlanta would start the process.

This Johnny did for quite some time until a big yawn shook him. Soon after, his eyelids started to droop. *Time for home,* he told himself, noting that bits of gray had started sneaking in around the edges of a black sky. A look at the clock on his dash confirmed that dawn would take control of the sky soon and by that time he hoped to be stretched out in his bed.

Anticipating home, Johnny thought about its secluded quietness. No, his neighborhood wasn't like Chuck's gated community with 24/7 security, but it was one where you had to arrive by map because of the crazy bends in the main road and the splintered side streets. Not only did its creative layout lend itself to privacy, but also its low turnover in home ownership. About ninety per cent of his neighbors had built this neighborhood, raised their families there and now lived as retirees in paid-for, well-kept homes. Not him though. He'd been one of the lucky ten percent to find this piece of heaven and stake his claim. He loved the peace, the maturity of the neighborhood, but mostly he appreciated the invisible lines of respect. He knew his neighbors and they knew him but they kept the knowing to a surface level. No personal stories. No shared secrets. No regular visits or invitations. Just innocuous conversations on polite topics while passing each other on the street or in the grocery store. Just the way Johnny liked it.

Even though their relationships were superficial, that didn't keep Johnny from watching out for his neighbors which he did now. As he rolled toward the Patrick's house, he frowned as he spotted a dark colored SUV on the street in front of their house. Knowing the couple, husband and wife, did not tolerate unaccounted for vehicles anywhere in the neighborhood, Johnny wondered at this until he noticed the luggage carrier on the roof of the SUV and the out-of-state license plates. Then he remembered the summer guests they had been eagerly expecting. *Good for them*, he thought, driving slowly past the house and SUV. A few feet on, the road took its first bend which his Lincoln took smoothly. A couple of houses past the bend, down on the right, Johnny saw another development, and a burst of humorless laughter shot out of him. "Poor Mac." Johnny referred to Mac Murphee, the only neighbor he had gone deeper than surface level with because they both loved music and often swapped albums. Poor Mac had finally lost, or surrendered, to Mrs. Murphee because a huge, brightly colored "For Sale" sign now hung on his speed boat. With a sad shake of his head, Johnny drove past the reminder of why he'd never acquired a Mrs.

The road curved again and began a gentle rise but Johnny had driven this street so many times, he maneuvered automatically, freeing his mind to contemplate the give-and-takes, the back-and-forths required in any relationship. Not just romantic ones, but business too. Hell, he and Chuck... Johnny stopped there. There was no more he and Chuck, just he and whoever was going to assist him in reaching the next level. More success, more achievements. Johnny smiled as he hooked an easy right into his cul-de-sac, which was literally *his cul-de-sac* because although it was a circular street with room for five houses, his was the only house in the circle; the other lots having been labeled as "too expensive to develop" because the previously gentle rise had graduated to a ridiculously steep incline. He however had lucked out because his house, a tan and blue split level, sat solidly, stubbornly on top of the incline, which it seems had been snipped off for just that purpose.

As he always did when approaching his house after having been gone awhile, Johnny inspected her, as much as he could in the mixed grays and blacks of the morning sky. From roof to basement, corner to corner, he searched for signs of wear, damage, invasion or loss. Just as he was about to declare all well, he saw movement up top, on the porch. He wasn't one hundred percent sure because the glow of the porch light didn't extend to the point where the porch and steps met, but certain he saw something, Johnny stomped on the accelerator and screeched the final few yards into his driveway. He slammed to a stop, a dangerous inch from his garage door, and yanked the gearstick into park. Pushing out of his car, he left the engine smoothly ticking and the car door hanging open to take the stairs three at a time up the crooked, tri-level stairway that led to his porch and front door. Even when blocked by the over-abundant landscape, his eyes never left the spot where he'd seen movement. He hit the final turn of the stairway, stopped dead on a dime and stared. A long, lean man sat on the top step of his porch. The man smiled at him, as if welcoming Johnny to the neighborhood for the first time. This, more than the invasion of his privacy, ignited Johnny's anger. He advanced a step, fists balled, his face contorted, eyes livid. "I'ma be nice and give you three seconds to get the hell off my porch."

"Johnny, Johnny…" the Devil interrupted smoothly. He shook his head as if deeply disappointed. "…so much violence." He reached to the side and pulled an instrument case forward, situated it across his bony knees.

"One," Johnny said, taking another step up.

The stranger opened the case.

"Two." Johnny took a second step up, almost putting him on eye level with the trespasser.

The stranger turned the case toward Johnny, tilted it so the musician could see the contents full on.

Instinctively, Johnny looked. His mind went blank; his fists uncurled. In the midst of black crushed velvet lay a golden fiddle. He glanced at the man then back to the fiddle where his gaze locked. A moment or two passed before his mind started functioning again then he managed, "My fiddle." He bent forward a bit to be sure. "My golden fiddle."

"*Your* fiddle, Johnny-boy?" the Devil asked slyly then shoved the case and its valuable contents off his knees to the side. The case slid a few inches on the slick concrete then stalled near the iron railing. Johnny's eyes followed its short journey and the Devil watched

Johnny. Then, the Devil glanced at the discarded prize and asked, "The fiddle you sold for…?" He spread his hands, shrugged his shoulders. Of course he knew the answer but intentionally left the question hanging to give Johnny a chance to think about his past decision and what it had and hadn't gotten him. After all, the Devil never wanted it said that he hadn't been fair.

"Nonea yo' damn business is what I sold it for," Johnny answered indignantly. His face again assumed frightening aspects, not unlike his father's right before serving up a beating. "Where'd you get it?"

The Devil shook his head again, let his head hang for a second before raising it and smiling all gator-like again. "Is that the question you should be asking, Johnny?"

"You gonna quit saying my name like you know me and answer my damn question. Or, I'ma beat yo' ass."

The Devil's eyes flickered for a moment, then turned solid black—a deep, soulless black. He slowly rose to a height equal to Johnny's, which was no slouch of a height. That height plus standing on the top step put Johnny's head eye level to his chest, forcing Johnny to look up to him. His voice was frigid when he declared, "Still got that giant ego, don't you, boy? That blinding pride?"

Johnny never met a challenge he couldn't rise to, never met a fight he didn't like and in this moment, he felt more than capable of handling both. He stepped up, still on unequal footing with the stranger but that didn't matter to Johnny. He could take him. His father had taught him well. He took another step. Two more steps would make them equal but Johnny didn't plan to let it get that far. He met the stranger's stare dead on and balled his hands into fists. Just then, something in the stranger's eyes prompted a memory; one tucked layers deep, which began struggling to the surface of Johnny's mind. That confused Johnny, making him think he ought to quit his anger and give the memory time to come into being. But Johnny wasn't weak enough to let the unknown trip him up. He held fast to his anger and decided he'd given the stranger enough warning. Figuring a left punch to the kidney ought to be enough to let the stranger know he was through playing, Johnny tensed his body, preparing to swing…

But the Devil in a deadpan voice said, "What you should be asking is what songs you should play on the number one rated morning talk show. You should be asking where's the list of questions the reporter with *Billboard* is going to ask you. And of course…" The Devil leaned forward, his black eyes boring through Johnny, "…you *should* ask what's my price for giving you your dreams."

Johnny stared, wide-eyed at the man with a host of questions weighing him down: *Who is he? Have I met him before? How does he know my dreams? Did Chuck contact him? Where did he get my fiddle?*

"Exclusive gigs," the Devil continued over the racket going on in Johnny's head, "Crossover record deals. Cameo appearances in film and TV. A-list status." He paused now to smile, a smile so big that Johnny saw in the midst of a crowd of perfect white teeth, one gold tooth. It sparkled as brightly as the golden fiddle lying near the stranger's feet.

That spark of gold caused Johnny to shift his gaze to the golden fiddle. It laid there, raising even more questions and confusion just by its presence and forcing Johnny to look back up at the man. He studied the stranger's face, taking time now to see if he recognized him as family, friend or foe. He didn't, but somehow that study prompted that memory. A memory that was still trying to surface, wanting to tell him something but was yet too far out of reach to be clear or helpful. The only memory Johnny could lay hold to was the one from earlier. That day at the stump where he'd won that fiddle of gold, where he'd gotten his start and his proof. But this man wasn't the man he'd won the fiddle from. He had never seen that man again even though he'd looked for him in all the many circuits and venues he'd played. What had happened to that man? Johnny had often wondered. He'd been one hell of a fiddler. Just not as good as Johnny.

As he always did when confused, fed up, tired or feeling like he was being played, Johnny resorted to type; his type—anger. Johnny tensed his body, furled his fists, warned one final time, "I don't know…"

"Name's Abraham," the Devil interrupted. He stepped down off his roost, putting him closer to Johnny. He held out a hand. "I'm your new manager."

Johnny ignored the man's hand. "I got a manager."

"Hmmm…" the Devil shoved his hand into his pants pocket and began moving, down the steps, shouldering past Johnny. Not touching him, not looking at him.

Johnny turned with him, keeping the man in sight.

When he reached the turn between the first and second level of stairs, the Devil stopped. He looked back at Johnny and speared him with a deadly stare. "Today you're going to get a call, booking you for a top rated show. Tomorrow, you're going to get a call from a high-ranking official to a king, booking you for his anniversary ceremony. The third day a caller will request your presence at a meeting with a high profile musician who'll want to collaborate with you. After that, I'll be back." The Devil smiled one more time, then turned, saying with a chuckle, "Johnny *the* Fiddler." Shaking his head, he sauntered down the stairs, hands in pockets, whistling a tune that Johnny knew well. It was one of his own songs, a creation from his soul.

* * *

Even when he'd lived in his father's house, Johnny had slept hard and heavy, and certainly so in his own house where peace filled every room. It was therefore by the grace of God that he happened to be up, but still more than half asleep, in the bathroom, when the phone rang. Johnny was no slave to electronic devices, phones included, so he finished his business at his leisure, stumbled back to bed, and was two ZZs from being comatose-sleep when the phone rang again. "Damn!" Johnny reached out and snatched up the receiver. "Yeah?" he grumbled, too tired still to work up a nastier tone than that.

"You probably just got to bed, huh?" Chuck asked with humor in his voice.

"Damn, right! What you want?" Johnny asked in false anger. He peeked through one eye and, registering the time on the clock, cussed in his head. He'd been sleep about three hours. He wasn't ready for conversation, business or otherwise.

"Some TV producer from New York called the office," Chuck replied, all play out of his tone. It was all about business now. "They insisted on speaking to your booking agent. I took the call figuring you should tell the office staff first before the rest of the world hears we ain't a team no more."

A shortage of sleep made his thinking slow so it took Johnny some time before he patched everything together, and when he did... Oh, shit! He *had* fired Chuck yesterday and that Abraham dude said he'd get a call today. The importance of Chuck's words caused Johnny to tumble out of bed. He snatched up the cordless unit then plowed to the kitchen, listening as he made his way.

"They want you in New York tomorrow morning as the featured musical guest. Two numbers plus some B-roll. I'll have the travel information and all the other details for you within the hour. The band members ain't gonna be happy. They tired as hell but I authorized a bonus. I figured that'd get their asses out of bed. And I figured you wouldn't mind since this is your big break."

Johnny heard every word out of Chuck's mouth, but thundering over Chuck's deep bass voice was the question in his head. He felt he knew the answer, but he had to hear it from Chuck. Chuck wouldn't lie to him. "Did you arrange this?"

"Wish I hada," Chuck replied with some longing in his voice. He paused before continuing, "I called Daron to let him know you'd be rollin' through and I didn't care if he was cuttin' Jesus' long-ass hippie hair, he needed to move that man to the side and trim you up."

"Thanks, man," Johnny said in sincerity, but mechanically too. His mind was on Abraham and his prophecy. A call today from a primetime show. A high profile gig to follow *and* a cross-genre project. If it really went down like that, Johnny knew he'd found his man. He smiled big thinking about all the goodness headed his way until that part of him he'd inherited from his father rose up and turned that smile the wrong way. His father would be skeptical, unbelieving and Johnny was too. Not about his talent or that he deserved success but about the man,

Abraham. Yeah, the man had delivered on one promise thus far but twenty years he'd been in the business and he'd never heard of an Abraham. But then again, Chuck had handled the business end; Johnny, the creative. There were artists Johnny knew that Chuck didn't and people Chuck knew that Johnny didn't. That was how it worked with them and that being the case, Chuck might know. Of course, given their present situation, it wouldn't be right to ask him, but hell, his and Chuck's roots went deep. Chuck would want to give him this as a parting gift so Johnny asked, "You know a man named Abraham? …in the business?"

Chuck didn't waste words. His silence meant he was processing, going through that database mind of his in search of an Abraham. Johnny remained silent too, fiddling with the coffee maker while filtering again through his own memories for an Abraham. Finally, Johnny heard, "Naw, but I can do some checkin'. What's the other name?"

"Only got Abraham."

Chuck grunted in reply and in the background Johnny heard some papers being pushed around. If he knew Chuck, which he did, he was looking for a pen to write the name. Why, when his cousin had a mind like a vault, Johnny didn't know. But it had always been Chuck's way and no doubt would continue to be.

Another empty second or two passed and then Chuck said, "Debbie's on her way to the cleaners to pick up your suits. She'll bring 'em to the office and I'll be there soon."

"Fine," Johnny said, and since all had been said that needed to be said, the men hung up.

* * *

On the Sunday following his whirlwind week, Johnny had not intended to open his front door to the Devil but when he opened the door to usher his female company out, there the man stood. The surprised look on Johnny's face didn't last long. He hurriedly kissed the woman good-bye, patted her on her backside as she slid by him then stood aside to let his visitor in.

"I see you like 'em big-boned," the Devil commented as he and Johnny watched the woman switch away.

"I like 'em anyway I can get 'em," Johnny said with an appreciative smile. Crooking his head toward the kitchen he offered, "Coffee?"

"'s long as you got sugar. I got a terrible sweet tooth."

Johnny led the man through the living and dining room but stopped in a nook that separated the dining room from the kitchen. There was nothing in that nook except a glass display case, five feet wide and six feet tall, and in that case rested the most precious tangible memories of Johnny's career—a copy of each of his CDs, fliers from some of his shows, before and after photos of the Fiddler Music building, some fan letters, news clippings, photos of he and Chuck in various venues, and more. The most recent addition was the golden fiddle that Abraham had left on Johnny's porch. He pointed to the fiddle and said, "You left her the other night."

A snake-oil-salesman smile curved Abraham's lips. "Consider it a signing bonus once we finalize the deal."

Johnny started to smile at that but it happened again. That nagging memory. The one that had tapped at Johnny's consciousness the morning he and Abraham had met. Several times now over the past few days, it had played peek-a-boo with Johnny, making him pause at whatever he'd been doing at the time and then grow frustrated when he hadn't been able to latch on to it. Before he let it get to the frustration point this time, Johnny moved on into the kitchen, forcing a change of thought and action.

"Cream?" he asked Abraham as he worked around the remains of breakfast to re-fill his mug.

"Of course."

He partially filled Abraham's mug then scooted it across the counter to him. While his visitor spooned in the additives, Johnny jumped right to business.

"Chuck said you got a solid reputation. A whole stable of musicians, singers and actors. Most of 'em successful, many at the top of the pile." Johnny felt excitement bubble to life in his belly at this second telling of fact. He'd had the same reaction when Chuck had told him initially. But he couldn't let his excitement show. He had to maintain a neutral façade to avoid losing any advantage at the negotiations table. Although, Johnny thought, no real negotiations were needed. He was ready to ink a deal now given the man's resumé and the golden fiddle as an incentive.

"I can put you there too, Johnny." The Devil glowed with assurance, his salesman smile still intact. "You got the talent. You got the desire. All you need is the connections, which I got."

Johnny humpfed. "You proved that, didn't you?" Johnny leaned over his coffee mug, arms stretched wide, hands flat on the counter, thinking about the last four days. They'd been the busiest four days of his life. There'd been the flight to New York City, all the pre and post activity for the show, then a flight back home. Before he'd recovered from that Chuck had fielded a call from an ambassador. Seems the king of his country was a Johnny *the* Fiddler fan and couldn't envision his anniversary celebration without his favorite musician. Out of the call had come a booking and a ream of paperwork, including security clearances for Johnny and his band members—all of which Chuck had generously handled. Finally, there'd been another hurried flight to New York City late Thursday night to meet with one of the biggest music producers in pop music. They'd spent Friday, the entire day together, kicking around some ideas, playing around in the studio. They'd gotten so caught up in the possibilities, Johnny had almost missed his red eye flight back to Atlanta. He'd walked into his house after four o'clock Saturday morning, exhausted and planning to sleep til Monday but before he made it to bed, the phone started ringing. Normally he would have ignored it except these were not normal days. He answered and who was on his line wanting a meeting? Curtis Barnes, Thomas King's manager. Even though he and Chuck had put off the meeting to finalize their separation, even though he had not announced to his band members or staff that Chuck would be leaving Fiddler Music, it seemed Curtis already knew. Johnny thought that odd until he figured Chuck must have done him another solid by calling Curtis and giving him the lowdown. Needing time to speak with Chuck first, Johnny had put Curtis off until Monday with a promise to call then.

"It's just starting for you, Johnny." The Devil's siren-song voice reached Johnny, distracting him from his thoughts. "I got even bigger plans for you."

Johnny liked the sound of that—his big dreams linked to Abraham's big plans and big connections—and it looked even better in his head—oversized marquees with his name in bold, tuxedoed men and slinky-dressed women clapping enthusiastically for him, his name and songs at the top of sales charts. Yeah, that combination sounded and looked mighty fine. This time, Johnny didn't even try to hide the fact that he was hooked. His smile was as big as the sun.

"Fame. Recognition. The world will be yours, Johnny. And the only thing you have to give in return…" The Devil's eyes changed to a deep, abiding black and the pretense of being friendly and persuasive dropped, especially that smile. "…is your soul."

Still caught up in the dream, still smiling big, Johnny nearly missed the Devil's offer. With a lift of his brow and a shift of his smile, he repeated, "My soul?" Just to be sure he'd heard right.

"It's nothing in exchange for living all of your dreams and…" Its words were as cold and hooded as Its eyes. "…for finally silencing your father's words."

The rest of Johnny's smile disappeared. The good feelings too as the Devil's final few words cycled in his head. *Silencing your father's words. Silencing your father's words.* The promise of fame was nice. As were the offers of manifested dreams and owning the world, but that which appealed to Johnny above all the others was *silencing your father's words.* With his soul in Abraham's care, he could finally overcome the hurtful words that had thrived in him, driven him during his career. With Abraham in charge of his soul, he could finally return to his father's house and make him recant every dream-killing word, make him admit his son *had* made a name for himself, that Johnny was the best, always had been. The opportunity to break his father and expose him for the lying, dream-stealing, soulless, angry bastard he was won Johnny. It would be worth the sacrifice of his soul. In fact, if he had two souls to give he would gladly sign over both.

The Devil looked at the vengeful smile on Johnny's face. It noticed the wicked twinkle in the boy's eyes and knew It had him. It was time to deal. In a low, dark voice It issued the final vow. "I give you your heart's wishes. You give me your soul." The Devil raised Its hand, ready to shake.

Johnny lifted his right hand, looked down at it, looked at Abraham's hand. Imagined the two joined as one and stalled. But why? he wondered. Abraham offered him everything he'd ever wanted in exchange for his soul which was nothing, an invisible substance that couldn't even be... Johnny's mind stopped. That haunting, nagging memory had returned and finally exposed itself fully. And turned out it wasn't the memory after all for the memory was that day at the stump. Rather, it was the point the memory was trying to impress upon him. That being, what had happened to the musician from whom he'd won the golden fiddle? That musician had vanished into nothingness, and as great as he'd been, he should have enjoyed some level of success. Which led him straight to his father and the unfulfilled life he led in Mississippi. The chance—no matter how small—of being his father, of living life as his father did, of dissolving into nothingness like the other musician frightened Johnny to his core. In fact, it was his greatest fear. He hated to take on his father's trait of questioning a gift instead of simply saying thank you, but he had to be sure. Because there was always a flip side to consider, right? There was always a chance of plans failing, of dreams laid fallow, of people lying, and before he made this pact, he had to be certain that chance was removed.

Johnny dropped his hand back down to the counter and looked Abraham in the eyes. "What kind of guarantee?" His tone clearly held no give, no compromise.

The Devil's skin tone deepened two shades. Its black eyes sparked briefly and Its long fingers clenched and unclenched—all of these signs that the Devil was angry. Johnny, of course, had no idea, and for Its part, the Devil contained Its anger. There was no hint of it in Its voice when It said, "I proved myself, Johnny. I gave you my word and followed through. Now it's your turn to do the same."

Johnny had never liked repeating himself but in this life-and-death matter, he'd give it one more go before he gave into impatience, which always led to anger. "What guarantee you gonna give me that I won't shoot up like a rocket and fizzle out like a firecracker? Into nothing. I ain't interested in bein' no 15-second wonder."

The Devil continued clenching and unclenching Its long fingers then after a time or two, It stopped and offered Its hand again. It managed a brilliant smile as an accompaniment and said, "Trust me, Johnny, I got more to lose than you."

That was it. Johnny was done. Leaning back, shaking his head, he smarted off with, "I'ma take that as no guarantee. And that being the case," Johnny's eyes went dark, his tone unforgiving. "I'ma ask you to leave my house."

The Devil was smart, beyond smart, and knew It'd lost Johnny even before the boy spoke the words. Even if It hadn't learned that from instinct or from the boy's words, It need only look at the stony set of Johnny's face and the boy's body tensed for a fight. The Devil dropped Its hand and lost the smile. It conceded this round, knowing It had not gambled with big enough stakes to shake Johnny loose from his greatest fear. What the Devil understood that Johnny didn't know or couldn't face was the boy was exactly like his father, and his decision to pass on the Devil's offer proved that. He, like his father, was afraid to take big risks. They were men of little faith, willing to sacrifice their dreams for certainty and in doing so guarantee themselves small, unfulfilled lives. The Devil could have given Johnny the big, fulfilling life he wanted. It could have given him the guarantee he'd asked for, but God wasn't the only one who required a little faith, a little trust. So in the end, Johnny had escaped Its trap but had ensnared himself deeper into his own trap of fear, which would only lead to more disappointment, more anger and more frustration—feelings that accompanied dead or dying dreams; dead and dying lives. The Devil stood up from the bar stool, hoping that Johnny never figured out that there were other ways he could break free of his father's mold. It hoped that the boy would continue to attach himself to fear because that would make their next encounter oh so interesting.

The Devil hung Its head, sighed deeply, and when It lifted Its head, It was as friendly as the Devil could be. "Keep the fiddle, Johnny. You earned it. Again."

The Devil took three steps then vanished into air. Johnny missed it. He stared straight ahead, unseeing, damning his father to Hell.

* * *

"Pull over here." Johnny directed Chuck off the gravel to a soft grassy shoulder. Even though it had been a long time, Johnny remembered exactly where his mother lay, would always know.

While Chuck rolled down the windows then shut off the motor, Johnny unfastened his seat belt and reached to the floor mat to pick up the bouquet of purple roses. The salesclerk at the florist shop had told him and Chuck that purple roses symbolized eternal love and Johnny could think of no other woman, or person for that matter—well, maybe Chuck but he'd never tell him that or give him roses—worthy of his eternal love. After stepping out of the car, he opened the back door and grabbed his fiddle case.

As Johnny treaded carefully around the marked places of dearly beloveds, he thought about his last visit here. He'd been on his way out of town and had paused at the cemetery for a visit. He'd played several of his mother's favorite songs and then talked about her choosing death—congestive heart failure so said the doctors, but Johnny believed it had been the years of beatings—as her means of escaping her husband's physical and verbal abuse, and how he had chosen a new life in Atlanta as his means of escape. He'd played a few more songs for her, then re-packed his fiddle and told her he would never return. Twenty-two years later, it turned out he had returned, but only because of Chuck. Chuck had insisted on visiting his parents and siblings before they began a six-month, worldwide tour because, "With planes falling out of the sky and ships falling apart on the seas, ain't no guarantees." Johnny had declined at first but as Chuck kept pushing, he finally admitted he wouldn't mind seeing Aunt Ruby again and eating some of her delicious pineapple upside cake. That had been a lie. His secret reason for giving into Chuck was he wanted to visit his mother and tell her about the good things that had come his way in the last two years. But of course, he'd gone through some grand posturing before finally telling Chuck, "Yeah, sure, but one condition. I don't want to see my father." Chuck had agreed and eagerly made the arrangements, and here Johnny stood in the middle of an ancient cemetery.

Johnny smiled, his heart filling with love as he inspected his mother's well-tended gravesite. It had been important to him that her eternal rest be more beautiful and comfortable than her earthly life had been. Which was why he'd been sending money for years to the caretaker. The man had done right by him and his mother. Lightly colored flowers outlined her plot and an angel, sculpted from marble, hovered over her. Johnny moved to the headstone where a sprawling spring bouquet rested beneath her name. He took time to arrange then re-arrange both flower bundles so that they complimented each other and the gravesite. He talked to his mother as he did this, expressing his never-ending love for her and sharing his life's ups. For in the past two years there'd been a great expansion of his musical career thanks to his exposure on a morning show and a collaborative music project which had birthed four bestselling singles. The CD itself had gone on to sell so many copies that it achieved platinum-level status. The awards and deals had started gushing even before that and hadn't stopped. As he opened his case, rosined his bow, and tuned his fiddle, Johnny told his mother, "I'm living the dream, Mama, I wish you were here to live it with me." She wasn't but he could share his success with her through song. Johnny started with her favorites then launched into his favorites and lost himself in the joy of playing for her, for doing what he loved.

Some time later, he stopped, opened his eyes and smiled down at her. Before he could ask what she thought, a voice behind him said, "You are more than words can express."

Johnny tensed. In all these years, the voice had not changed. He whirled around, expecting to deflect a blow, but there was no physical contact. In fact, there barely stood a man. His father, although in his early sixties, looked thirty years older. Instead of standing tall, he stooped over and leaned to one side. He looked skeletal; his clothes seeming to weigh more than him. One eye looked like it had been stapled shut and part of his upper lip was missing. The rest of his fine features had been crossed out with scars and wrinkles. Instead of harsh words, there was, "You play beautifully, son. Like the angels in heaven."

Johnny saw that he clutched all eleven of Johnny's CDs. His eyes stayed there and when his father noticed where Johnny's eyes lingered, he explained, "I have 'em all. Ever' one. I show 'em to ever'body. Tell 'em, 'that's my son.'"

His father smiled, showing many missing teeth and those that remained seemed perilously close to death. The old man stared at Johnny, studying him, and after a time that one eye misted over and the old man made a slight move as if to reach out. But Johnny flinched and the old man became still. Johnny saw his father's Adam's apple bobbing up and down and the good eye started blinking rapidly and after a short while his father croaked, "I'm proud of you, Johnny. You made it."

The old man stared at him a moment longer, looked down at the fiddle and bow in Johnny's hands, looked down at the grave of his deceased wife, then slowly turned and shuffled off. Johnny watched til there was nothing left of him to see. Then, as if invisible arms had been holding him up and were suddenly removed, Johnny collapsed and cried.

DELILAH

by

Niki Danforth

The bloodied corpses lay dumped on each other as if they've been sorted for the trash. Even with blindfolds covering their eyes, their frozen faces show an unspeakable terror. Two of the teenaged victims appear to have their hands tied behind their backs. The third must have worked out of the rope that's still twisted around one wrist, her other rubbed raw from the binding. Her arms reach around the two girls as if she's pulling them close. Were they already friends before this final embrace?

I click through the next photographs, close-ups of the girls' battered bodies. Their clothes are filthy and ragged, as if they've been held captive for some time.

Other pictures on my laptop reveal the surroundings, possibly a warehouse somewhere in a rundown industrial area. The bleak, abandoned space is light years away from my cozy, safe cottage in Willowbrook, New Jersey, where I complete homework for my Intro to Criminal Justice class.

Warrior, my beloved German shepherd, stirs near my feet on the end of a comfy chaise in my bedroom. This has always been my first choice of where to hunker down with a great book, but at the moment it's where I study these photos.

Suddenly, not wanting to taint my refuge with this Russian mob-related case, I take off my drugstore glasses, sweep up the materials, and head downstairs to the kitchen. I continue reading about this tragic human trafficking case and contemplate whether I'm really cut out for this world of investigative work.

Unexpectedly, the wind picks up. *Crack!*

I jump at the same moment the phone rings and grab it before it can ring again. "Hello? Who is it?"

"Ronnie, it's Will. Are you okay?" his calm voice asks. "You sound panicked."

"I'm fine, I'm fine. A huge noise outside startled me, like a gunshot, but it was probably just a limb that broke off." I pour a glass of pinot noir. "What's up?"

"Do you want to assist me on a new case? I'm swamped—"

"I'd love to, but is it more involved than the gofer work I did last time?" I take a drink. "Not that I don't appreciate the opportunity—"

"It's a cold case in Parklawn, just west of Paterson. It's not that far from you, and you'll have a chance to help a lot in the field," Will interjects. "We'll find out more tomorrow when we talk to the client. Meet me at the diner at eight."

"You're really going to put me in the field?"

"With my close supervision," Will says. "I don't want to see a repetition of your—"

"See you there. Thanks!" I hang up.

I grab my computer and run upstairs to turn in. The wind continues to howl outside, and I pull Warrior's dog nest next to my bed before sliding under the covers. I look at the computer screen, determined to pick up where I left off with my assignment. Outside, the branches creak spookily.

"Who are you trying to kid?" I turn off my laptop. "Enough of the Russian mob for one night."

* * *

Will and I sit in a booth at Angie's Diner drinking coffee, happy to be inside on a cloudy, chilly February morning. Bells jangle when the front door opens and a sandy-haired man in a plaid flannel hooded jacket and heavy canvas work pants enters. He has several folders tucked under his arm, so Will assumes he's the man we want to meet and waves. As the guy walks to our table, I note he looks to be my age, somewhere in his mid-fifties.

"You're Will Benson?" he asks.

"I am." Will extends his hand to shake, and we introduce ourselves. After we order breakfast and make a little small talk, Steve Lyla begins his story.

"Like I told you on the phone, my dad's cousin, Benny Paola, retired from the force over in Paterson where he worked with your dad back in the '80s," Steve says to Will. "He said I should give you a call, that maybe you could help us on a cold case."

"How old is the case?" I blurt.

Will grins at my eagerness. "Start at the beginning, Steve."

"My aunt, Doreen Lyla, was murdered back in 1972, and they never got her killer. Hey, I get it that the police didn't have everything they've got now to track him down." He drinks his coffee. "Parklawn P.D. and detectives in Paterson worked the case long and hard, but they still came up empty."

"So, why now?" Will asks. "It's been more than forty years."

"My old man's got cancer, and we don't think he'll make it."

"I'm sorry," Will and I say almost in unison.

"Pop's dying wish is that his sister's killer be brought to justice," Steve says as the waitress delivers our breakfast.

He gestures toward the folders next to him on the seat. "My dad's cousin gave me his old case files. In his spare time, Uncle Benny helped a guy named Detective Brannigan who ran the Paterson part of the investigation."

"Do those files include a list of people the police talked to back then?" Will asks.

"Yeah, and it's a long one."

"Any witnesses?"

"No, but I was first on the scene—"

I jump in. "How did that happen? You must have been a kid."

"Yeah, I was only twelve. But Mom and I stopped by to drop something off at Aunt Doreen's after basketball practice."

"What do you remember?" Will digs into his eggs, but his eyes are on Steve.

The man looks down and takes a moment. "Mom and I pulled up to the front of Aunt Doreen's house."

"Do you remember what time?" I ask.

"No, but the light was on outside. The door was wide open, and I remember thinking that was weird because it was cold out. Then I noticed something on the landing."

"What did you do?" I ask.

"My mother hadn't even stopped the car when I jumped out and raced over. My aunt was sprawled across the steps. Her eyes were wide open, staring at nothing. I'd never seen a dead person before, let alone someone who'd been murdered." He shakes his head. "It looked like someone had stabbed her over and over and over. I touched her wrist to find a pulse, like they'd taught us in Scouts. There was no pulse, but she was still warm. So I guess it had just happened."

"What an awful memory to carry with you," I say.

"I remember her expression…it was like she couldn't believe that someone wanted to kill her." Steve's mouth goes tight. "I ran inside and my mom screamed at me not to go because maybe the guy was in there. But I had to call the police. Pretty soon, I heard the sirens." He goes quiet, staring at his food.

We give him a moment, and then Will asks, "What happened with the investigation?"

"Like I said, this Detective Brannigan ran it. As the case got colder, Uncle Benny tried to help."

"They didn't come up with anything?" I ask.

"Nothing," Steve says. "Brannigan retired fifteen years ago, and Uncle Benny ten."

"To be fair to the police and detectives, their other work never stops. New cases keep piling up," Will says. "Once the leads dry up in a homicide, it gets pushed to the side for more recent crimes and the case goes cold." Will waves to the waitress for the check.

"Because of Uncle Benny, both the Paterson and Parklawn cops said I can check out their records," Steve says. "That goes for you, too, since I'm hiring you and all."

"I'll email you the paperwork," Will says, "and we'll start right away."

* * *

Back at the office, we lay out Steve's files on the work table.

"I have an appointment in twenty minutes," he says. "It shouldn't take long. In the meantime, take a look at these. Let me know what you think."

"Do you want me to head out to talk to some people who were around when this happened—"

"Not yet. Let me be clear, you're working under my supervision. You're not to set foot out of the office on this case unless you've cleared everything with me." Will's voice is firm. There isn't even the usual flirtatious twinkle in his eye as he talks to me.

"But Will—"

"No buts, semi-Detective Lake."

"Yes, boss." I don't mean to, but I'm certain a discouraging tone sneaks into my voice. Sure, Will's been a private detective for almost two decades, but I'm a good fifteen years older than he is. That has to count for something in experience and maturity. So why do I feel like a bumbling office intern when he tells me what to do?

"Now look, I want you to get some experience while you're going to school for this, but I don't want you in danger." He pauses, and his piercing blue eyes soften. "As we both know, rushing into the field too soon without enough facts can land you in hot water. Remember?"

"Right." I try to keep my voice calm. I've known Will long enough to understand he only wants the best for me. But after last summer's family matter that I tried to investigate on my own, I know I have a lot to learn. Thankfully Will hasn't written me off completely as a detective, and is still game to help me out.

"Look, I just…I want you to be sure about your decision to become a private investigator." The kindness in his voice and the gaze in his eyes makes me want to melt. My face feels hot.

Once Will leaves, I dig in, carefully reading through copies of the autopsy report, various police reports, and Doreen Lyla's death certificate. Next I look at photos of Doreen from that time, and then digest the newspaper articles that Steve's family saved about the murder.

Amazingly, the killer appears to have left no clues so the evidence is slim. The police follow-up back in the seventies yielded very little, but it's hard to believe this may have been a perfect crime.

Doreen was twenty-four at the time of her death and a popular, well-regarded teacher at the local high school. She sang in a church choir, worked out several times a week at a gym, and volunteered at a soup kitchen. The transcripts of the interviews indicate that everywhere she spent time, she left a trail of admirers.

I check out Brannigan's list of candidates who were interviewed, create a shorter version, and then look up contact info. I'm itching to leave the office to investigate, but I don't want Will to fire me before we've even started.

* * *

We meet at a Starbucks around the corner from Will's office. I fill him in on what I've learned so far from the files.

"There were no clues at Doreen's house, nothing from the killer, no prints, no defensive wounds, nothing under her nails. It looks like she turned to walk into the house and maybe he got her from behind." I sip my decaf mocha. "Oh, and none of the neighbors saw anything." I pull a yellowed snapshot out of my bag. "Here's a picture of her house back then."

Will studies it. "Those bushes by the front door were a good place to hide."

"Or maybe Doreen knew the guy and blew him off," I answer. "Then she turned to go inside, and that's when he got her. According to the autopsy report, there were twenty-two stab wounds. They were all over her body, front and back."

"A passionate attack like that, it's a classic sign that the killer knew his victim, meaning he wasn't a pro and there should have been mistakes." Will slowly drinks his coffee. "It's surprising there are no clues."

I pull out another photograph, one of Doreen. "Here." He looks closely. "She was beautiful," I say. "And from what I've read, equally nice."

He nods, pulls out a small pad, and writes a name and number. "Tomorrow morning at eight we'll meet at Parklawn P.D. and spend time going through their cold case files. Give this guy a call. Let him know that Steve hired us, and we'd like to come by in the morning."

"Got it," I answer. "Here's the preliminary list I put together of top candidates to re-interview."

"Go ahead and set up meetings, in person or by phone. Try not to set up any evening interviews unless you have to. And never by yourself at night." Will looks at me with a mixture of tenderness and sternness. "Are we clear?"

"Ten-four, boss."

* * *

After setting up several appointments and leaving voice mails for others on my list, I reread everything Steve left with us, getting lost in the details of Doreen Lyla's murder.

It's late afternoon when I head home. Crosby, Stills, Nash & Young's "Woodstock" explodes from the radio in my red Mustang. Along the way I decide on a new destination, pull over, and reach for my case notes from the back seat. I put the address in my GPS and blast the music even more for the long drive in rush hour traffic.

It's getting dark by the time I arrive, probably close to the time of day of Doreen's murder. I stare at the scene of the crime, an ivory-colored stucco bungalow from the thirties with slate shingles and black shutters.

The large bushes that used to stand sentry on both sides of the front door are long gone. Now, a two-foot-high, neatly trimmed hedge stands in their place. There are lights on inside, and every now and then I see a silhouette run past a window.

I turn up my satellite radio when I hear Megan Trainer singing "Lips are Movin'." My daughter Brooke had shown me the video on YouTube of a pretty, voluptuous blonde with lots of black eyeliner, and I loved the 1960s vibe to her music. I quickly text Brooke that I'm listening to the song again.

I look at the old photo of the house and then glance around the street filled with similar bungalows. It's a quiet neighborhood, perfect for families or a young teacher like Doreen.

A car turns into the driveway and a woman gets out. The light over the door turns on as she runs up the front steps. Before she can open it, a young girl and boy fling open the door and rush to her with hugs. They all go inside.

Wouldn't Doreen's neighbors have heard her cry out when her attacker came at her? The music fades out as I mentally step back to 1972.

I imagine the two large bushes on either side of the front door, tall enough for someone to hide behind. Perhaps Doreen walked up the steps, tired at the end of a long day at school, and pulled out her keys.

As she unlocked the door, she may have heard him behind her, maybe she even knew him.

Before she could fully register his unexpected presence, he grabbed her, covered her mouth, and stabbed her. He cut her again. Over and over, angrier and angrier, he kept stabbing as she dropped to the stoop. This hulking figure loomed over her, continuing to knife her. He didn't need to cover her mouth anymore, because the life was finally out of her and she was quiet.

I snap back to the present where the stoop is empty. The neighborhood is quiet and peaceful, and I drive away listening to another talented blond musician famous for her heavy black eyeliner, 1960s icon Dusty Springfield, singing "I Only Want To Be With You." I wonder if that was what the killer was thinking as he waited here to make his move. And if he couldn't have her, no one else could either.

* * *

The next morning, Will and I walk down several aisles of gray metal shelves stuffed with files, black binders, large brown envelopes, cardboard boxes, and plastic tubs. Parklawn Police evidence tags hang out of many of the files and containers, names written on each of them.

"Are all of these homicide cases?" I know my voice sounds meek, but this room creeps me out.

"Not this entire room—many of these are active but not murders. We're heading to that section over there." Will directs me toward one corner. "This is where they keep some of their cold cases. Parklawn is close to Paterson, so their other case files are over there." He looks for Doreen Lyla's files.

"Do you have to do this a lot?" My voice sounds shaky.

He stops, looks at me, and puts a hand on my elbow. "Are you okay?"

"I will be in a moment." I pause. "It's a little overwhelming."

"Ronnie, when you become a P.I., you'll work all sorts of cases. This one just happens to be a homicide." Will's tone is gentle. "Remember, you're working to see justice for Doreen and her family."

I see a box labeled *Lyla, Doreen*. "There it is." I also see *Lyla* tags on several notebooks and large envelopes.

Will pulls out several files from a shelf where Doreen's case begins. He opens the first file and flips through several pages. "This looks like a master list of what's stored in Doreen's case."

I peer over his shoulder. "Where do you recommend that I start?"

"Make a copy of this list so you can write on it as you go through everything." He pulls a package from his jacket pocket. "Here are some temporary tags. Use them if things are out of order. Make sure the evidence people don't remove them."

Will explains the process of going through the records, writing summaries, and creating a timeline of the crime and investigation. Then he leaves to work on a separate case.

I look around at my bleak surroundings, pull out my laptop, and get to it.

* * *

A day later, after I finish summarizing folders, binders, evidence bags, and boxes, I feel like I've developed a good overview of this case. I've looked through autopsy and incident reports, viewed gruesome photographs of the scene, and I've built the timeline of events.

It's time to tackle the contents of two evidence boxes that grabbed my attention earlier. One contains a pair of bloody white go-go boots that Doreen wore when the killer attacked her. I had a pair just like them back then, and I try to imagine myself in hers. The thought sends a shiver through me.

I reach for a crime scene photograph and study it more closely. Doreen's body is sprawled across the steps. She's on her back, her arms stretched out to each side, her head turned slightly to the right.

She has on the boots and a paisley mini-dress with bell sleeves. Both are blood-splattered...I mean "spattered," as I learned in class. A matching headband pulls her light hair back from her face.

I reach in my bag for a small dome-shaped magnifier and run it over the photograph. I spot a heavy-looking ring on one of Doreen's hands, and what appears to be a charm bracelet on her other wrist.

I root around in the other box until I find clear bags containing the ring and bracelet. On one side of the bag is the form showing the chain of custody, and I see the names of both Detectives Brannigan and Paola.

I flip the sealed bags over and examine the ring first. It's a 1966 class ring from Parklawn High. There's dried blood on it, but is it Doreen's blood from her knife wounds, or did she get a good slug at the killer before she went down? I make a note to check the reports to find out whose ring this was and follow up with Will. Whoever it belongs to, he's never gotten it back. It has stayed locked in a dark evidence room for more than forty years.

I snap some pictures of it inside the evidence bag with my camera phone, wishing I could take the ring out for a better view, but I don't dare.

Next I shift my attention to the bracelet. It's silver, and so loaded with charms that they stick out in every direction rather than lay flat. I touch them through the evidence bag—there are probably a lot of memories tied up in these little objects.

I inspect a heart with two small birds in the middle. It looks like something a child would receive. I spot a silver St. Christopher's medal on an oval baby-blue enamel background, perhaps a gift from a relative to protect her when traveling. A Victorian-era ring with tiny pearls and rubies attracts my attention. Was it maybe from a grandmother?

The bracelet has its share of creatures—an elephant, a turtle, and a West Highland terrier. Maybe she had a small Westie as a child? A silver gumball machine could have been a gift in junior high.

As I flip through the rest of the charms, I almost miss an empty loop that dangles between two other charms on one of the links. I hold the bag very close and see a slight gap between the two ends. That loop's charm must have fallen off.

I check the paperwork on the contents of this evidence box. There's no mention of the empty loop in the description of the bracelet. I take pictures of the bracelet and a few more of the ring.

The master list mentioned a journal that I find in a manila folder. After pulling on latex gloves, I reach in and remove a burgundy leather diary. I carefully flip through it and find its pages filled with beautiful handwriting. Doreen must have received an A+ in penmanship.

The journal is almost three-quarters full. The last date is September 20, 1972, the day before her murder.

Good day at school today. I shouldn't have favorites, but I think mine may be my seniors' creative writing class. The kids seem excited about the course. I love the class discussions, and their writing assignments show me they have a lot to offer. All except for one. There's something troubling about B, and I'll have to keep an eye on him.

Picked up my new dress from Serafina's. It needed a few alterations, and now it's perfect. I'll wear it tomorrow when J takes me out to dinner. First date since K and I broke up...

I close the journal. Never in a million years could Doreen have imagined this would be her last entry. At only twenty-four, she had every expectation of a long life ahead.

I find a summary of the journal and go locate a copier, then spend the next half-hour Xeroxing both the summary and diary. This definitely warrants a thorough reading.

Glancing at my watch, I see that I have just enough time to put everything back on the correct shelves. I gather my things and head out. As I leave, I can almost hear Doreen's voice pleading for me to bring her killer to justice.

* * *

Holding a glass of cabernet, I step into my large porcelain tub in the center of the white tile floor. A tray sits across the tub with my glasses and the copy of Doreen's journal propped up for easy reading. Rather than the usual soft candlelight that I prefer when relaxing, I have the lights on. This particular soak in the tub is going to be a work session.

I slip into the warm water and look up at the huge photograph on the wall. "Hey, maybe you can help me figure this out," I say to the man in the frame as I lean back in the tub with my glass. "This murder happened in 1972."

A classic photograph of Sean Connery as 007 in black tie and holding his gun looks down at me. His expression in this famous picture is definitely inscrutable. Whatever he may have been thinking at the time, his gaze and our one-sided conversations help me unwind.

I look at the official summary of the journal which lists the full names of different people mentioned inside. The list includes her date on the evening she was murdered, the troubled student in her creative writing class, and her ex-boyfriend.

"Okay, James, Doreen was beautiful enough to be a Bond girl, but as a high school teacher she probably wasn't your type. And her life certainly doesn't sound very intriguing from this summary." I sip my wine. "So why would anyone want to kill her?"

I tackle the journal in month-long chunks and flip back to the entry for August 20, 1972. It's literally a day at the beach—a Sunday afternoon at the Jersey shore with her boyfriend. So they hadn't broken up yet, but he'd volunteered for the military and would be leaving shortly for basic training. They'd been together for three years, and she'd been wearing Kenny's ring since the beginning. It's got to be the ring I looked at earlier.

I get to the entries where Doreen prepares for the upcoming school year. At one point she loses Kenny's ring, and she's in a panic to find it. Later she finds it, much to her relief, because she's been terrified to write him that it's missing.

I wonder how much of a temper the boyfriend had. If she's that scared to tell a man three thousand miles away that she can't find his ring, that's probably where I should focus.

I go back to January 1972 and read forward in the journal, looking for clues about Kenny's anger or how he treated Doreen. He definitely comes across as a hothead. Was he ever physically abusive? I can't tell from the journal. Why did Doreen stay with him for three years? I assume the police checked him out thoroughly, but I write a note to make sure.

I continue flipping through the pages and reading. If Doreen had any deep, dark secrets, other than a boyfriend with a nasty temper, she didn't commit them to paper.

A week before her murder, Doreen's brother—Steve Lyla's father, I think, remembering the dying man we're doing this for—gives her an early birthday present. Doreen writes about it in her beautiful script.

Timmy gave me the sweetest gift—he added another charm to my bracelet, a tiny pair of silver boots. He remembered how my friends and I used to play "These Boots Are Made for Walkin'" for hours on end when it first came out. I love it! He really is the best brother a girl could have.

I don't remember a boot charm on Doreen's bracelet in that evidence bag. I glance back at the police summary where anything of note gets a bullet point. There's no entry for 9/14/72 when she received the gift. Detective Vincent Delgado wrote the summary, and in 1972 there was a good chance that everyone involved in the investigation was a man. Most men wouldn't fully appreciate how special charm bracelets were to a girl her age.

By the time I've finished reading 1972 and am considering going back to January 1971, my skin is shriveled from sitting in the tub for so long. I get out and dry off quickly. Warrior's already curled up in his dog nest when I pull on a baggy tee-shirt and crawl under the covers. The last thing I remember hearing is his soft snore.

* * *

The next morning, Will and I go over everything I learned in the evidence room. I pull out my phone and show him pictures of the heavy gold ring and the silver charm bracelet.

"The fact that both were found on her body after her murder rules out robbery," Will says. "I think the '72 investigation confirmed that."

"Yes, it did," I agree. "Will, there's something about this charm bracelet that's got my attention—" I shrug. "Call it a woman's intuition."

"It's our job to look at every possible angle, but I'd focus on the ring and the boyfriend," Will says. "It sounds like the guy's got a temper. Even though he checked out, he deserves a revisit."

We go over the list of prospective interviews I've organized. It's still long, but Will narrows it down to a more manageable size. I'm ecstatic that he wants me to conduct the interviews because he's still swamped with that other case of his.

"Remember, schedule them in public places or take me along," he says. "Absolutely no night-time interviews without me. Are we clear?"

"Got it."

"And when you talk to these people, ask them if they remember anyone strange who might have been stalking Doreen or behaving oddly in any other way, anyone who could have had a connection to her. No matter how obscure, it could be important."

"Ten-seventy," I say, making a feeble attempt at police-talk.

He looks at me funny. "Uh, I don't think you mean 'fire,' which is a ten-seventy. I think you mean ten-sixty-nine, 'message received?'"

"Yeah. Ten-sixty-nine, whatever." My face feels flushed.

A slow grin appears on his very handsome face. "You've got to stop watching all those bad cop shows." He stares at me with penetrating eyes and that look of his that never fails to make my knees go weak.

* * *

I spend the rest of the day calling people on the list and setting up times to meet. Several of them give me an earful about the old boyfriend and what a nasty piece of work he was. They'd all said *good riddance* when he left for basic training.

There's also mention of a couple of other oddball admirers. One was a guy named Sam who taught woodshop at the same school where Doreen taught English. He was drafted and may have died in Vietnam.

The other was a classmate of Doreen's, a pothead named Freddy who ended up working at the local video store.

The biggest surprise? The discovery of a spiteful best friend who turned on Doreen. When Cheri thought her boyfriend was showing too much interest in Doreen, she lost it at a diner where they were hanging out. Cheri made violent threats against her best friend and finished it off by dumping a glass of water over Doreen's head.

The crime scene photos before the body was moved did show a multitude of stab wounds, so it's clear that someone had passionate anger issues toward Doreen. It hadn't dawned on me to consider a woman as a suspect in Doreen's murder, but why not?

I flip through the police files and find several references to Cheri, but the investigators appear to have dropped her quickly from the suspect list. I add her to my short list with the two admirers and that writing student Brian from Doreen's journal.

Doreen's old boyfriend, Kenny O'Donnell, answers my call with a smoker's hack. I introduce myself, tell him why I'm calling, and we agree to try to meet at the end of the week after his chiropractor appointment. Between bursts of coughing, he says he went on disability and retired from the county roads department a couple of years ago due to a bad back.

We chat a bit, but from his tone I'm glad we're not in the same room. Kenny reveals he's on marriage number three. His gravelly voice has a mean edge as he talks about having a couple of kids who don't speak to him much and not seeing his grandkids very often. It sounds like he has more problems than a bad back.

"When I found out somebody knocked her off, I wasn't surprised." Kenny spits out the words as if they have a bitter taste. "Things would've turned out different, better, if Doreen wouldn't have split with me."

"I thought you broke up with her after you left for basic training," I say. "So why was she still wearing your high school ring?"

"She lost hers, and I didn't want to take it with me to 'Nam, just in case something happened...anyway, I told her to keep it. I just made it look like I broke up with her. She was really mad at me because of something I—" He pauses, catching himself. "So I broke up with her before she could do it first."

"Why was she angry with you—"

"I don't wanna talk about that."

"Okaaay," I say, hedging for a moment and waiting for him to explain. He doesn't. "Well, help me out a little bit. Can you think of anybody else I should talk to?"

"Hey, there's a guy you should meet." I can hear from Kenny's voice that he's relieved to change the subject. "He knew everything about everybody back then."

"Who is he, and where do I find him?"

"Richie Cavanaugh. He owns a bar called Cavanaugh's. He's had it for more than forty years. It's where everybody in town goes." He laughs and starts coughing. "It's the only place in town—" Kenny's cough takes over and he can barely breathe. He begins to wheeze.

"Are you alright?"

He answers only with more coughing and wheezing.

"Well, thanks for talking to me—"

He clicks off.

* * *

It's dark by the time I pull up to the tavern and park. On the outside the building has an ordinary brick facade. There's maybe an office or a couple of low-rent apartments upstairs. The name Cavanaugh's is painted in red on a large, lighted sign hanging between the two floors.

I step inside a classic dive bar, the kind of place you stop for a cheap beer. I look around. Two guys are playing pool on one side of the room. The dimmed lights reflecting off the wood-paneled walls and red vinyl booths create a welcoming ambience.

For a weekday evening, there's a decent crowd. I figure little has changed at Cavanaugh's since the place opened in the early seventies, and that's probably why people like coming here.

I walk towards an empty stool and notice the bartender playing dice with a customer. The bartender looks over and nods. I nod back. "No hurry. Finish your game."

I take a handful of peanuts from a wooden bowl and swivel on my stool so I can take a better look at the place. There's a stage on the other side of the room where a tall, skinny guy sets up a karaoke machine.

Behind me, a voice asks, "What'll you have?"

"A Coors Light, please," I answer as I swivel back to the bar. "You must be Richie Cavanaugh?" He smiles, and I stick my hand out to shake. "I'm Ronnie Lake. We spoke on the phone earlier."

"Nice to meet you." Cavanaugh shakes my hand and then reaches in the fridge under the bar for my beer. "That's too bad about Doreen's dad being so sick and all." He pours the Coors into a glass and places it in front of me.

"Doreen's old boyfriend Kenny doesn't sound too well either," I say.

"Yeah. First his back, and now he's on oxygen because of the emphysema. Too many years with the smokes."

"It's a tough habit to kick."

"Kenny was lighting up even back in high school. He played football, and he was huge. Not anymore."

"The three of you go back that far?"

"Sure. But Kenny and Doreen didn't get together until the end of college. I guess they'd been together two or three years when she was murdered."

"Hey, Richie," the karaoke guy calls from the other side of the room. An unlit cigarette hangs from his lips. His mouse-brown greasy hair, combed over to hide baldness, crowns a sunken, unshaven, leathery face.

"We're good to go, it's time," he says to Cavanaugh, looking at his watch. He pushes up the sleeves of an old Yankees sweatshirt, and the glint of a gold chain around his neck catches the light. "Stop flirting, we got a few people asking to sing."

"Yeah, you can start," Richie answers. The guy goes back to the system and starts the first song. The lyrics pop up on the screen, and a woman climbs on stage to the opening bars of Gloria Gaynor's "I Will Survive."

Turning back, I ask, "Who's that guy?"

Richie laughs. "You mean Ted? He was in school with us, too." He scans the place. "A lot of my regulars went to school with us. Ted ran the AV club in high school. Every time I saw the guy, he was pushing a film projector on a cart."

Richie gets a twinkle in his eye. "He had a crush on Doreen back when we were in school. Then again, I had a crush on her, too. Geez, all the guys did. Anyway, Ted ended up running the AV department at the same school where Doreen was a teacher before he went off to Vietnam. That's what I heard."

"Was he drafted? Or a volunteer?" I take another handful of nuts.

"Who knows? We never knew what became of him until one day he showed up here," Richie says. "He was always different, but I gotta believe he saw some really bad shit over there, because he's never been right since. I felt real bad for the guy, so I hooked him up with this job. He comes every evening and handles the karaoke."

All of a sudden, the woman howls one of the stanzas from "I Will Survive," completely off-key, and Richie and I grimace.

"Hey, it keeps the customers happy. You hungry?" he asks.

"How about a burger, medium rare. No fries."

"Got it." Richie goes out to the kitchen to place the order. He comes back and gestures to one of his guys to take over the bar.

"How were they as a couple, Doreen and Kenny?" I ask.

"Hey, I've known him almost fifty years." The bartender hesitates. "I hate to say it, but he was always mean to his women."

"How mean?"

"He'd scream and holler a lot. Really controlling, but I don't think he actually ever beat up a woman."

A guy with a dark crew-cut, tight blue jeans, and a black tee-shirt jumps up on the stage and launches into his version of 5 Seconds of Summer's "She Looks So Perfect." One of his friends joins him, and the two try to get their dance moves synced. They're obviously having fun, and the crowd likes them.

As they wind down, a small group of young professionals—they look like Jersey City financial types—push a lovely mocha-skinned twenty-something toward the stage. She finally removes her suit jacket and rolls up the sleeves of her crisp white shirt. She tosses her friends a smile as she saunters onto the stage.

The first bars of the sax and guitar are immediately recognizable as she sings "What you are..." and wails Aretha Franklin's "Respect." Her voice is amazing.

The short order cook delivers my burger and a sandwich for Richie. He digs into his BLT and says, "I never understood why Doreen stayed with Kenny so long. She was beautiful, smart, had a lot going for her."

"Kenny said his wives all 'got away.' Maybe Doreen couldn't." I take a bite of the burger and drink my beer.

The music starts up again, an old Tom Jones song. Richie raises his voice over the music. "Kenny didn't do it. The police checked him out, and they found nothing."

The karaoke volume goes way up as the performer behind us wails "Deee-li-lah," followed by the rest of the chorus.

I turn around, and that guy Ted is on the stage. He's changed into a tight white shirt that's open to a deep V and even tighter bellbottom trousers that emphasize his unappealing scrawniness. An assortment of gold chains hangs around his neck. It's his sad attempt at replicating what Tom Jones wore on stage decades ago.

It's amazing how the crowd is singing along as he croons into the microphone. "He's really working the room," I say, shocked. I look back at Richie, and he chuckles.

"It's kind of his signature song. He sings it every night."

The next patron hops up on the stage and starts his version of the Rolling Stones' "Satisfaction." Cavanaugh's customers quickly crowd the small dance floor.

Richie spends the next forty-five minutes telling me about other customers in his tavern who were around at the time Doreen was murdered.

"See that guy? Over there?" He points toward a booth near the kitchen. "That's Joey Alberti. He knew Doreen, had a thing for her, too. Back in the day, he used to manage the health club where she worked out. Now he has a sporting goods store." The guy's at least fifty pounds overweight with a shaggy haircut. His brown hair looks like the early mop-tops on The Dave Clark Five.

Joey clinks glasses with a woman sitting across from him. "That's his wife," Richie says. "They come here a lot for their date night."

Joey does look pretty normal, but who knows about back then. I make a mental note to check him out later.

The bartender's stories continue along with the karaoke. Finally, around midnight, Ted shuts down the equipment. People pay their tabs, and I do the same.

"Thanks for all the info, Richie, and the burger."

"Any time."

* * *

I put the key in the Mustang's ignition just as Ted exits the bar and gets into his car. He's silhouetted against the light from the Cavanaugh's sign. I watch him squirm as he changes back into his sweatshirt, jeans, and a jacket. It must be freezing in his car.

Ted peels off the gold chains and throws them on the seat until he gets to the last one. He takes it off, kisses the end of its chain, and hangs it on the front mirror. He stares at it for a moment then touches it. I reach into a tote bag on the floor and feel for my small binoculars.

I'm too late. I focus the binoculars on his car just as Ted leaves. Oh hell, he's weird, and now he's got me curious. I take only a moment to decide to follow. We drive for fifteen minutes then stop at a grocery store. While Ted's inside, I walk over to his car, which fortunately sits in a dark part of the lot. I watch for any sign of him through the front window of the supermarket. When he heads down an aisle toward the back, I lean in for a good look at the chain hanging from his car's mirror.

It's too dark for me to see what it is that's dangling from the mirror. The windshield is filthy. All the other windows are dirty, too. I don't dare turn on my flashlight. I reach into my pocket for my phone and quickly snap a few pictures.

I glance at the big window. No sign of Ted yet, so I walk back to my car in time to see him paying at the front of the store.

I continue tailing him as he drives away—I'm definitely in my dog-with-a-bone mode. Will would be super-pissed at me. He approved the interviews, but not surveillance.

Finally, Ted pulls into a small, dumpy-looking apartment building. He locks his car and goes inside.

My first inclination is to jump out and try to go inside, too, but Will's words come back to me. *You are not to set foot out of the office on this case until you've cleared everything with me.* I think back to last summer, how I was guilty of rushing in before thinking. I like to think I'm capable of learning from my past mistakes, so I resist the urge.

I look up at the apartment building and see a light click on in a third-floor unit. It's got to be Ted's.

I check the pictures I snapped of the mysterious object on the chain. I try to zoom in and focus, but I can't make out what it is. These are useless.

I think about grabbing a few more pictures but his car is again parked in the dark, this time in the lot next to his building. Besides, if I don't get out of here, the boss will fire me for sure.

* * *

It's after midnight, and I'm in my bedroom with a glass of wine and my computer in my lap, swaying to the music and singing along with a YouTube video of Dusty Springfield's "I Only Want To Be With You." As she sings about never wanting to let go, I try to put myself inside the mind of Doreen's attacker. But I'm tired, and my imagination shuts down.

I click over to "These Boots Are Made for Walkin'." Every now and then my adorable Warrior joins Nancy Sinatra with a howl. I give him a kiss on top of his head, jump up, and copy all of Nancy's old dance moves.

Finally, I drop back onto my chaise with a second glass of red. Something grates at me, something way back in the depths of my mind that I can't quite get a fix on. What is it? I shrug and look up old Tom Jones hits. I sing along here and there while Warrior, head between his paws, stares at me with his dark eyes.

I cycle through the greats: "It's Not Unusual," "She's A Lady," and "I Who Have Nothing." He was definitely an amazing crooner with a lot of sex appeal. His wardrobe emphasizes his studliness—the very tight pants, the shirt opened almost to his waist showing a chain with a huge gold cross. He's not my type, but I get why women went for him.

I can barely keep my eyes open, but I find a video link in the sidebar for "Delilah," and I click on it. It's from a 1968 performance where Jones is dressed in black tie. He's young and handsome, and wow, can he sing. I drift off just as he belts out the line "…I felt the knife in my hand."

* * *

I'm in a cold, dark room surrounded by endless shelves that tower over me, overflowing with files and boxes, caging me in. A Tom Jones song reverberates eerily through a sound system, the voice garbled as it plays in slow motion. Where the hell am I?

With my flashlight, I look at a thick file on my lap, and the music changes to Dusty Springfield's voice floating dreamily among the shelves. I frantically flip through the file, searching for something. Exactly what it is I don't know, but I know I have to find it to get the answer. The answer to what? It's hard to concentrate with these strange songs coming at me...

The music changes again, now to "These Boots Are Made for Walkin'." A cold breeze hits me from above and I shine my light on a ceiling fan, turning slowly. A gold chain hangs from its center, teasing me. I stand on my chair to get a closer look, but the ceiling raises higher and higher, pulling the chain further and further away as the blades rotate.

I go back to searching the files. What is it that I have to find?

* * *

I bolt upright on the chaise, shake my head groggily, and glance at my clock. 4:45am. How many bizarre dreams will it take to teach me not to drink red wine right before I fall asleep?

I feel a sudden sinking sensation in my stomach. I know what I was looking for in my dream.

I grab my phone and flip through the pictures of documents from the police station until I locate it. I zoom in, and there it is.

* * *

Will is pissed at me for following Ted without checking in with him first. He grumbles over his coffee at the diner and lectures me about safety. I've heard it all before, but I deserve it. When I try to tell him that I think I may have solved the case, his sarcastic laugh cuts me off. To be fair, an entire police department couldn't solve this murder.

Our breakfast arrives and I tell him about Ted and Doreen, that they'd known each other since high school and later worked at the same school. Next, I click to the document I was searching for in my strange dream.

"The victim's death certificate? So what?" Will sips his coffee.

"It shows her full name."

"Yeah?"

"See? Doreen Evelyn Lyla. Or, D. E. Lyla. See, if you say it a certain way, it sounds like *Deee-lilah*. That's the way Ted pronounces it when he sings 'Delilah' every night at Cavanaugh's. Anyone else would say duh-lilah, but not Ted. Plus, have you ever listened to the lyrics?" I don't give him time to answer. "It's basically the story of Doreen's murder." I switch over to the lyrics from a website to show him the song. "Look."

"Ronnie—" Will shakes his head.

"I know you think it's a reach. I did, too."

"How'd you come up with this far-fetched theory?" Will rolls his eyes.

"Do not eye-roll me, Will Benson. You know I'm a music fanatic, especially classic rock. The music tipped me off."

"What are you talking about?" He looks at me like I'm nuts.

"First, I visited Doreen's old house to get a better feel for the case. While I was there, the radio played Dusty Springfield's 'I Only Want To Be With You.' I wondered about the killer's mindset. You know, that it wasn't a stranger, because there was so much violence. Passion, you called it."

"Okay."

"Next, I read Doreen's journal, the part where her brother gave her a little silver boots charm for her bracelet because she loved that Nancy Sinatra song. FYI, that charm is missing from the bracelet in evidence. Maybe that part's not important—"

"Go on."

"Then I got a tip from Doreen's old boyfriend to drop by Cavanaugh's to learn more about the people who were in her life. The owner knows everybody." I watch Will for some kind of reaction.

"I'm listening."

"And weird Ted got up to sing 'Delilah.' And then it clicked for me."

Will doesn't say anything, he just stares at his coffee.

"It's hard to prove he's the one, but I just know it for some reason," I say. "He'll be at Cavanaugh's tonight, and we should go."

"Slow down, Ronnie," Will says. "You've got my attention. Let's figure out a plan for tonight. And you're going to stick with the script. Understood?"

"Yes." Chastened but grateful that Will wants me to finish the case with him, I drink the last of my coffee.

His next comment throws me for a loop. "But we're gonna have to shock the guy into confessing."

* * *

Will and I arrive at Cavanaugh's and slip in quietly to sit at a table near the bar. A young flame-haired woman cradles the mic in her hands and sings Adele's "Rolling in the Deep" while some of the customers dance. Ted hovers around the equipment with another unlit cigarette dangling from his mouth.

Richie waves and comes over, and I introduce Will. We order beer and burgers. As I take off my coat, both Richie and Will notice my outfit.

"Hey, are you planning to take your turn up there?" Richie smiles and gestures toward the stage.

"No. Why?" I ask. I notice them both checking out my dress. "Oh, you mean my outfit? No, I just love vintage!"

Will shakes his head and mumbles, "Oh, my god." He runs his fingers through his light brown hair.

I smooth my dress, which is very similar to the one Doreen wore when she was murdered. "I just saved a few of my favorite outfits, that's all. Everyone had a dress like this back then."

"Ronnie, I know you." Will isn't buying my explanation. "Remember the plan? Now it looks like you're changing it. If you rush him, spook him, you could blow our only chance."

"Hey, you said to shock him—"

He cuts me off. "I meant 'we,' not 'you.' What else have you got up that flapping sleeve of yours?"

"You'll see." I bat my heavily mascaraed false eyelashes. "Hey, I can't help it if I'm blond and Doreen was blond, and if I happen to remind him of her—"

"Am I going to regret this?"

"Maybe." I smile. "But I hope not."

A waitress serves our beer and then later the burgers. Will digs into his fries with a scowl, and we settle back to watch the singing.

Half an hour later as a forty-something guy wraps up a Bruce Springsteen number, Ted steps out of the back. Just like the night before, he's changed from his old sweatshirt to his Tom Jones outfit. I nudge Will. "Check out all the chains. How many do you count?"

Will looks for a moment. "A half dozen?"

"At least." The opening bars of "Delilah" come through the speakers. "That's my cue."

"Your cue for what?" Will looks concerned. "Ronnie—"

"It's all cool," I say. "Besides, I know you've got my back."

I make it up to the dance floor by the time Ted sings "...flickering shadows of love on her blind..." I don't look up but I know he sees me because he's a half-beat late on the next stanza.

There are only two other couples on the dance floor—the place has cleared out somewhat by this hour on a week night. I do some moves I remember from my past, tamer versions of the Jerk and the Swim.

I close my eyes, sway to the music, and listen as Ted sings the story of Delilah's betrayed lover going out of his mind after watching her in the arms of another man.

Suddenly, he's close, singing directly to me. My eyes flutter open to stare at the look of pure lust on his face, not for me, but for the ghost of a girl he knew. I dip my head and let my blond hair swing over the side of my face—just as Doreen's probably did decades ago—as I turn and continue dancing. Behind me, Will moves in the shadows to get closer to the stage.

Ted tries to dance with me as he sings. He sticks to me like glue, which gives me the creeps, but I lift up my face and smile flirtatiously while fondling the gold chains.

I lift one with a gigantic cross. "These are so cool," I say when the instrumental bridge starts.

"You want to wear it, baby?"

Yuck. I lift one with a peace symbol pendant.

And there it is, underneath the peace symbol—a thin gold chain with a small pair of silver boots.

"This is the one." I lift the thin chain as if to remove it from over his head.

He spots the charm, and freezes. The bridge is finished, and this is the part where he should be singing about watching the other man leave Delilah's house before knocking on her door.

The mic is near his mouth, but he doesn't sing. I look at his face, and his eyes have gone psychotic. He yells at the top of his lungs while pulling the chain away from me. "DON'T TOUCH THIS ONE!"

People stop everything to watch us. The music continues, the part in the song where Delilah laughs and her killer stabs her. Out of the corner of my eye, I see Will turn down the volume gradually so he can hear what Ted says. I keep my hand low, out of Ted's line of sight, and gesture for Will to stay back.

I reach for the necklace again. "Oh, Ted." My voice is soft. "But it was my favorite."

Ted blocks my grab for the chain. He looks confused and something shifts in his eyes as he stares at me in a daze. "I've loved you ever since high school, Doreen. I just wanted to protect you."

I can do this. I can play my part.

"But why the knife, Ted? Over and over with the knife…so much blood."

"Don't you remember?" Ted's voice cracks. "He came out of your house, and he kissed you so long. I tried to warn you about him. I told you he wasn't right for you, not like I was. But you laughed. Why did you laugh?" The volume of his voice rises, and anger creeps in. "You turned your back on me."

"I didn't laugh, Ted." I smile and turn my back on him. He grabs my arm and swings me around.

"How dare you turn away from me, like I was nothing?" He spits out the words. "I loved you! I had to keep you from him." I try to step back, but he doesn't let go. Ted has a strong grip, and I see Will moving in slowly from the side, out of Ted's line of vision. With a small wave, I warn Will away again.

"He was gonna hurt you, but you wouldn't listen, Doreen! And when you laughed at me, I couldn't stand it. I had to stop you."

"How could you stop me?" I ask, taunting him.

"With my knife!" Ted screams at me like a wounded animal and then comes at me, using the microphone like a knife to stab at me over and over. I use my arms to shield myself from his repeated forceful blows.

Will is on him in a flash, pulling him off me, but Ted is completely out of it and screaming at me. "I had to kill you, Doreen!"

Ted crashes to the floor, mumbling incoherently with Will on top of him. Will reaches into his pocket and pulls out zip ties to secure Ted's wrists behind him. Sounds rise from somewhere deep inside this tortured man, growing into shrieks of suffering like nothing I've ever heard before.

"Doreeeeen," Ted wails at me. "I had to kill you. I thought I'd lost you." He breaks down sobbing. "I'm so sorry. Please don't leave me."

I hear sirens in the distance.

Will and I look at each other and then at Ted, who's still wailing Doreen's name.

* * *

Later that night, I soak in the tub to erase the feeling of creepy Ted's body pressed against mine. I take solace in knowing that Will and I have helped the Lyla family find peace. I also think of my own two daughters who are close to Doreen's age when she died.

I look up at the huge photo of James Bond and offer a toast. "Here's to the memory of a lovely young woman with so much promise, one who had her whole life ahead of her."

Beside me, my phone rings and Will's number shows on the caller ID. I answer, and can't hold back a grin when his quiet voice says, "Good job."

"I didn't offer much besides a little intuition and a whole lot of luck," I answer truthfully.

"I would have missed this one, Ronnie. It would have taken me much longer to finish this case, if I ever caught it at all, and Steve's father doesn't have much time. Your work made all the difference."

"Thanks, Will. That really means a lot to me, especially coming from a pro like you."

"You know, you might turn out to be a *private* eye after all," Will says, emphasizing the word "private" in a way that could easily be taken wrong by the right woman.

"Will Benson, I just said you were a professional! You never struck me as the kind to make a dick joke!"

He doesn't say a word, and I can envision the open-mouthed look of shock on his face. I laugh and tell him goodnight before hanging up the phone.

ANGIE BABY

by

Terri Reid

Chapter One

The windows of the small house glowed bravely in the darkness of the autumn night. Large, bare branches of ancient oak trees that waded in the season's gathering of leaves, waved provocatively in the wind, coaxing any who saw them to come closer with their gnarled and bent fingered twigs. However, the woodland creatures that inhabited the woods just beyond the white picket fence were not tempted; instead they huddled in dens, burrows and hollows, hiding from the terror they sensed on the wind. A wind that whispered and warned all who knew to listen.

The front door of the little house was locked and bolted for the night. Beth Wisnewski knew her husband's truck route would keep him out of town until mid-morning the following day and they had no friends or family, so she wasn't expecting visitors.

Watching the evening news in her faded, flannel nightgown and worn-out slippers, Beth sipped the cup of tea her midwife had promised would help protect the tiny embryo she had growing in her womb. This time her husband, Paul, had decided they were going to use a midwife because the doctors in town hadn't been able to do anything to stop her last four miscarriages. And, perhaps even worse, they hadn't been able to tell them why they were happening. She knew, deep inside, that Paul blamed her. All the solicitous comments and thoughtful gestures didn't disguise the suspicion in his eyes when he looked at her.

Draining the last dregs of the disgusting brew, she rose from the sofa to rinse the empty cup out in the sink. Immediately a sharp pain in her abdomen had her crying out and doubling over in agony. "No!" she screamed, all too familiar with the initial symptoms of losing a child.

He won't believe me, she thought frantically. *He'll think I killed the baby on purpose. None of them believe me; they all think I'm a murderer.*

The pain subsided and she was able to release her hold from the arm of the sofa. She straightened and took a deep breath. Perhaps it was nothing. Perhaps it was an early contraction, that's all. Perhaps it was just indigestion.

Walking tentatively, she crossed the room and entered the bathroom. Telltale splotches of blood stained her undergarments and she knew it was going to happen again. Ripping the offending garment from her body, she threw it across the room into a small, white, plastic, trash container and watched in horror as it slipped down the side, leaving a dark, red streak in its wake. A primeval sob rose from her gut and exploded from her mouth in a guttural groan. "Not again," she wailed, burying her head in her hands as she felt the now subtle contractions move through her body. She sat up and wrapped her arms around her abdomen, trying to frustrate the machinations of her own body that were destroying the tiny life inside.

"I need to save my baby," she sobbed, pushing herself up from the toilet. "I need to save her."

She stumbled from the bathroom, her eyes wide with manic resolve, and then down the hall to the kitchen, frantically searching for something, anything that would stem the blood. She opened cabinets and drawers, throwing useless items to the side, searching for a way to save her baby. Tossing a pan lid over her shoulder, she froze when she heard it bounce against the wall, followed by a resounding, shattering, crash on the old linoleum floor.

"No," she cried, turning to see her porcelain crucifix lying on the floor in pieces. Kneeling down, oblivious to the small shards of glass on the floor, she tried to piece the cross back together, but her trembling hands scattered the pieces even farther apart. "Oh, Lord," she prayed frantically. "Please forgive me. Please forgive me and send me a sign. Show me how to save my baby."

A fierce wind blew against the house and rattled the back door and windows, drawing her attention. An oak leaf slapped against a window pane and was stuck for a moment, holding tightly, until the wind shifted and blew it on its way.

"I should go," she gasped, her face now covered in a sheen of perspiration. "That's the sign. I should go into the woods. I'll be safe in the woods."

Grabbing the knob with both hands, she pulled the door open and then released it, letting it slam against the inside wall with a bang. She pushed away the wooden screen door and staggered forward, a trail of blood splatters behind her.

The white gate lay open, inviting her into the dark woods and she went, one hand on her abdomen, the other grasping saplings for support as she wove her way into the depth of the trees. The wind was quieter, muffled by the density of the forest. She moved forward, drawn to a familiar place, her sanctuary, deep in the hollow of the woods. Somehow she knew it was where she needed to be.

Once she reached the border of the tiny clearing, with its softly babbling creek, she shuddered with relief and wiped some of the moisture from her face. This was where she could save her child. She stepped forward onto the carpet of thick leaves and then screamed as another shooting pain knifed her belly. She dropped onto the ground, the leaves blanketing her body, and curled herself into a fetal position. "No," she whimpered, as she felt the child move through her body.

The physical pain lasted for only a few more moments. She knew that the embryo lay at the very edge of her body and if she moved, it would fall out. The distant voice of sanity still remaining in her muddled brain reasoned that there was no life left in the tiny baby. But she could not, would not, allow her movement to be the deciding factor between life and death.

Then suddenly, everything changed. The darkness of the woods evaporated with a light so blinding it caused Beth to shield her eyes against it. She tried to look for the source, but it encompassed the entire clearing. She heard a soft whirring sound, almost like the noise an owl makes as it swoops by, nearly silent, in the night sky. There was a movement of air, a gust of warmth and the clearing was dark once again.

"God, if that was you," Beth prayed. "Come back and take me with you. I don't want to live in this world anymore. I don't want to be anywhere without my baby."

Tears slipped down her face, over her nose and landed on the leaves surrounding her face. "Please God, I want to die."

She paused when she heard the noise. A scattering sound underneath the blanket of leaves, too small to hear actual footsteps, only the movement and rustle of the leaves all around her. She lifted her head; careful she did not disturb the lower part of her body.

The woods were dark, but the half-moon shone onto the clearing and reflected against the thick ground cover. She watched, mesmerized, as the burnished leaves caught and then lost the moon sparkle as they slowly shifted their positions from the creature beneath. Beth felt around under the leaves and finally grabbed hold of a thick stick. She pulled it from beneath the pile and held it in the air. "You stay away from me," she screamed. "You stay away from my baby."

The movement paused for a moment and Beth breathed a sigh of relief. She had frightened it, she reasoned. Like most woodland creatures, it was afraid of human beings. She was about to lower the stick when the creature darted forward. Leaves lifted as it came forward, marking its path directly towards her. She slapped the stick on the ground, over and over again, trying to protect herself. "No," she screamed. "Stay away."

She froze and gasped in terror when she felt it climb onto her legs. She swiped at the leaves on her legs, trying to knock it away, but it avoided each blow, moving up her legs. "No!" she screamed, still keeping her lower body still. "Please no!"

She felt the invasion, the slippery entrance of the creature through her own blood and up into her womb. She screamed as heat infused her body and her abdomen glowed bright red. Finally she fell unconscious into the layers of leaves.

Chapter Two

sixteen years later...

"Come on Angie," Dr. Feinstein, the school psychologist, coaxed. "Just take the ear pods out for a moment, so I can check your hearing."

The teen-aged girl clapped her hands over her ears and shook her head. "No," she yelled, her voice sharp and defiant.

"Doctor," Beth Wisnewski, Angie's mother said, placing her hand on the doctor's arm. "Perhaps it would be better if we just didn't check her hearing."

"Damn it, Beth," Paul Wisnewski, Angie's father, exclaimed. "The girl's sixteen years old. It's about damn time she took those ear pods out of her ear and lived in the real world."

Beth turned on her husband, her face red with embarrassment. "I'm well aware of the age of our child," she said softly, "And perhaps if you were home more often you would understand that she needs the music to be calm."

The doctor discreetly closed his eyes for a moment, wishing away the headache that always seemed to appear when the Wisnewskis came for a visit. "It shows on her chart that she hasn't had her ears examined for several years now," he said gently. "And if we are to continue to allow her to wear ear pods in school, I need to do a basic auditory exam to confirm they aren't damaging her hearing."

But the thoughts going through his mind were quite different. *Rip those idiotic things out of her ears and be the parents, for once in her life.*

Angie met his eyes and a quiet smile formed on her lips. *Little brat,* he thought. Her smile widened.

"Dr. Feinstein, my wife and I need to have a little discussion," Paul grumbled through clenched teeth, his hand clutching his wife's arm in a death grip. "I'm sure everyone will be more cooperative in just a few minutes."

Dragging Beth by the arm, Paul slammed the solid wooden door behind him. But not before his words echoed back into the office, "Dammit Beth, don't make me get angry with you…"

Sighing, Feinstein leaned back against his desk and slowly shook his head. "You know, life would be much easier for your mother if you would just cooperate with me," he said. "Your father would not be mean to her, if you weren't so rebellious."

She stared at him through large, blue eyes and studied him intently. He studied her back, meeting her glance for glance. She was one of those rare human beings whose beauty made you stop and take a second look. Her hair was platinum blonde, her face porcelain white and her cheekbones were high and defined, giving her an aristocratic appearance. She was tall, taller than both of her parents and her body was fluid and graceful. *Yes, she had it all,* he thought, *a throwback to some ancient royal relative. Too bad she's certifiably crazy.*

"Do you want to dance with me?"

He shook his head in amazement. This was the first time she had directed a question at him in all the years he'd been testing her for the school district. Perhaps he was having a break-through. "What did you ask, Angelina?" he asked.

"Angie," she said. "My daddy said you need to call me Angie."

"I'm sorry," he said with a smile and an acknowledging nod of his head. "What did you want, Angie?"

She slid from her chair and stood up next to him. "Do you want to dance with me?" Her body already undulating in time to the inaudible tunes.

He knew he shouldn't. Knew it would break every rule, every code and every oath he'd taken as a physician. And yet, there was something about her, something about the way she looked at him...

"I shouldn't," he said, taking a small step back.

She followed him and slid her hands onto his shoulders. "I'll let you listen to my music," she whispered into his ear.

Gulping audibly, he felt his body react in a way that was strictly forbidden by the school code of conduct. Her scent, like a hot summer night, was enveloping him, causing his body to burn. "Angie," he began.

She pulled the ear pods out of her ears and placed them in his. "Dance with me, doctor," she insisted softly, slipped her arms around his neck and moved her body against his.

For a moment he hesitated. For a moment he tried to remember who he was and why this wasn't a good idea. But the moment passed quickly and then he was lost.

Chapter Three

"You're hurting me, Paul," Beth cried, trying to pull her arm away.

"You're hurting yourself," Paul replied. "And if you don't stop pulling away, I'm going to slap you."

She immediately stopped and allowed herself to be pulled into a deserted classroom at the end of the hall. Once the door had closed, Paul yanked her around and threw her against the chalkboard. "Don't you ever embarrass me like that," he yelled. "Don't you ever contradict me or question me. Do you hear?"

"Yes, Paul," she whispered, holding back her tears. "But you are gone from home so much, people are..."

"Yeah, what?" Paul demanded.

"They're starting to talk," she said. "They're starting to say you're stepping out on me."

A spiteful chuckle slipped from his lips. "And so what if I am?" he asked. "Face it, Beth, you ain't had nothing to lure a man for years now."

"We're married, Paul," she stammered, tears filling her eyes. "We made a vow."

"Yeah, well, that vow didn't include crazy bitches who think their brats are angels," he threw back at her.

"Angelina is an angel. She's a miracle. She came to me from the sky," she insisted.

"Yeah, you decide to experiment with drugs while you're pregnant and I'm stuck with a looney kid for the rest of my life," he spat.

"I didn't do no drugs," she whispered fervently. "You know I wouldn't do nothing like that. You know it would be a sin."

"Oh, so we're all religious and holy now," he taunted. "You weren't so damn religious when you climbed into the back seat of my car on prom night and spread your legs, were you? Weren't so damn religious when you walked down the aisle in white, but we both know it should have been red."

"But you loved me," she insisted, tears streaming down her cheeks. "You told me you loved me."

"Yeah? Well I guess that makes us both liars," he replied easily, enjoying the pain in her eyes.

"I guess you'll want a divorce then?" she replied, surprised that she was actually hoping he'd say yes.

"Hell no," he yelled. "There's no way I'm gonna let you keep all that nice government money we get for having a crazy kid." He moved forward and grabbed her chin, squeezing it tightly. "No, baby, you and me, we're in this one together."

He pushed her up against the chalkboard. "Now, nod and say 'yes baby,'" he commanded.

She hated herself for her weakness, but she nodded slowly. "Yes baby," she whispered.

"Good. Now you come back in that office with me and you follow my lead," he said, releasing her chin. "You don't say nothing unless I ask you. Got it?"

"Yeah," she said, nodding again. "I got it."

Chapter Four

Paul pushed the office door open, lumbered inside and glanced around the room. "Where's the doctor?" he asked his daughter who was sitting right where she'd been when he and Beth left the room.

Angie shrugged insolently. "I guess he had to go," she said, meeting her father's eyes for only a moment and then moving on to stare at the school scene beyond the window. "Mama, I don't feel so well. I think I need to go home."

Beth squeezed into the room behind her husband. "Well, of course, dear," she agreed. "If you're not feeling well, there's no reason for you to stay at school."

"Course there's a reason, a damn good reason," Paul interrupted. "If she misses any more school, we don't get all the money coming from the government." He walked over and stood in front of his daughter. "Listen, baby, you have to stay here for the day.

"None of the kids are nice to me," she replied. "No one talks to me."

"Well that's your mother's fault," he said indulgently. "She insists on keeping you away from the other kids. She's the one who makes them teach you with a tutor, instead of letting you interact with the other kids."

Angie turned her head and looked at her mother. "Why can't I be with the other kids?" she asked.

"Because you're too special," her mother replied, smiling and walking towards her child. "We want you to have a teacher all your own, not have to share with the other children."

"Don't lie to the girl," Paul inserted. "You didn't trust her. You didn't trust your own daughter. You thought she would hurt the other kids."

Beth shook her head. "No," she stammered. "No, I never..."

"Sure you did," Paul said, smiling with glee. "Ever since that little incident in kindergarten, you made them keep her away from the others." He turned to his daughter. "I would have trusted you, Angie. I've always trusted you, baby."

"What happened in kindergarten," she asked her mother, cocking her head slightly to one side. "What did I do?"

"It was nothing, really," Beth reassured her. "And I'm sure the little boy did something to you first."

Closing her eyes, Angie leaned back in her chair. "I remember now," she said, her voice soft and wistful. "He wanted to take my music. I told him no, but he wanted to take my music."

"See, I knew he'd done something to you," Beth said.

Angie shrugged casually. "So, I wanted to stop him," she replied.

"Stop him from taking your music," Beth added.

Angie looked up at her mother, smiled and shook her head. "No, stop him from breathing."

"Well, that was a long time ago," Paul said, his voice a little less confident. "And you know that stopping people from breathing is not a good thing to do. Right?"

Angie nodded dutifully. "I don't want to stop people from breathing anymore," she agreed. "I just want to dance with them."

Paul looked over his shoulder at his wife with a triumphant smile. "And I think dancing is good. Not like your mother who would punish you for something you did a long time ago," he said. "Your mother doesn't trust you the way I trust you."

"Paul, don't do this," Beth begged softly.

"Shut up, Beth," he exclaimed. "I know what's best for my daughter and I'll prove it."

He pulled open the office door and looked up the hall at the reception area. "Hey, we need someone in here who can change

Angie's class schedule," he called to the student aide sitting near the main desk. "And we need them in here right away."

He looked back into the room at his daughter. "See, this is the way a loving parent takes care of things."

A half-hour later, the assistant dean of the high school entered Dr. Feinstein's office with a print-out in her hand. "I still can't apologize enough for Dr. Feinstein just leaving you like this," she said. "But if he approved Angelina for streamlined classes, then we can get her started right away."

"She still needs to wear her headphones," Beth inserted. "It keeps her calm."

"I'm sure we can work with that," the administrator said. "And I'll make a note of it on her class schedule, so the teachers are aware of it too." She turned to Angie and smiled. "It's so exciting for all of us that you are going to be with the other students. Are you excited?"

Angie studied her for a moment, her blue eyes intent on the woman's face. Then suddenly, she smiled. "Would you like to dance with me?" she asked.

"No!" Beth exclaimed, rushing forward, aware of the surprised looks she was getting from the assistant dean and her husband. She took a deep breath and modulated her tone. "I mean, it's not time for dancing right now, Angie. You need to go to your new classes."

Angie smiled at her mother. "I'm glad I get to be with the other children," she said.

Beth nodded, a sheen of nervous perspiration on her forehead. "Well, you be a good girl, hear," she replied, looking meaningfully in her daughter's eyes.

"Of course, I will," Angie replied easily. "I'm always a good girl."

Chapter Five

"Hey, what's the psycho doing in with the rest of us?" Bobby-Joe Meyers called out from his seat in the middle of English Composition when Angie walked in the door with the assistant dean.

"I don't believe I asked for your opinion," the teacher said, before walking over to the door to meet the new student.

"This is Angelina Wisnewski," the assistant dean said. "Angelina, this is Miss Baker, your new English teacher."

"My daddy said to call me Angie," Angie replied.

"Of course, Angie," Miss Baker replied. "Welcome to our class."

"Angie is being streamlined," the assistant dean said, stressing the last word. "So, she might need a little help getting acclimated to having other students around her."

Miss Baker's eyes widened slightly. "Is she dangerous?" she whispered into the assistant dean's ear.

The administrator stepped back and shook her head. "Oh, no, of course not," she replied. "Dr. Feinstein just tested her and gave her glowing reviews. She is a district success story."

Miss Baker nodded and then put her hand on Angie's shoulder to guide her into the classroom. Angie froze and stared at the woman. "Do you want to dance?" she asked, slightly confused.

"No, Angie," the assistant dean inserted. "Miss Baker just wants you to take your place with the other students."

Miss Baker nodded. "And if you'll just remove your headphones," she added.

"Oh, no," the administrator replied. "Angie needs to keep those on for now. They help to keep her calm."

"Well, okay then," Miss Baker said with a quick sigh. "I see this is going to be an interesting experience. Please, Angie, take a seat there in the first row."

Angie slowly walked from the door, across the front of the class to her assigned seat. Once she sat down, students on all sides of her scooted their own desks just a little further away.

Jared Hood, a fairly new student at the school, watched the scenario unfold with rapt interest. He leaned forward and tapped the shoulder of the girl seated in front of him.

"Hey, what's the deal with her?" he asked.

Lindsey Markum swung her long blonde hair around, a movement that Jared had noticed she did at least twenty times per class, and turned in her seat. "That's Angie Wisnewski," she said, her eyes twinkling with excitement. "She almost killed another student."

"Wow. When?" he asked.

"When we were all in kindergarten," she replied.

"What the heck?" he replied. "I stuck a pea up Patrick Perkins nose when I was in kindergarten and no one is still blaming me for it. What's the issue here?"

"Well, she was taken out of class and never allowed to interact with the rest of us," Lindsey replied with an uninterested shrug. "So, I guess she must be better now."

"Sounds like a lonely life," Jared said softly.

"What?" Lindsey asked.

"Nothing. Nothing," he answered, searching for something to say. "I mean, I think she's hot."

"Yeah, well, if you like that type," she replied, flicking her hair once again and turning around to face the board.

Jared nodded slowly. "Yeah, I could like that type."

The rest of the class passed without a problem. Angie sat quietly, staring at the blackboard, listening to her music and rocking back and forth in her seat. The bell rang and all the students, except Angie, jumped up and rushed for the door.

Stopping at the door, Jared noticed that she hadn't moved and walked over to her chair.

"Hey, I'm Jared. Hi," he said.

Angie looked up and studied him for a moment. "Hi," she finally said.

"Um, do you know what your next class is?" he asked.

She pulled the printout from her folder and handed it to him. Scanning it quickly, he noted that she was scheduled to be in his next class, Algebra. "Hey, cool," he said. "You're in my next class. Want me to walk you?"

Once again, his response was met with silence and large curious eyes. "Walk me?" she asked, a slight smile on her lips. "Like I'm a dog?"

He chuckled and shook his head. "No. No, you're right," he replied. "I would like to accompany you to the next class."

The smile widened. "I would like that," she said, slipping out her seat and standing next to him.

"Great," he nodded. "Great, let's go."

He walked next to her through the crowded halls, helping her to maneuver away from the known danger spots of any high school; the jocks, the mean girls and the dean. He realized that she was easy to guide, never once questioning where they were going. "Hey, you know, you shouldn't be so trusting," he said. "Not all the guys in school are on the up and up."

"The up and up?" she asked, turning to him.

"Yeah, they're not all your friends," he said.

She thought about that for a moment and finally nodded. "Are you my friend?" she asked.

"Yeah, well, I'd like to be," he replied with a quick smile at her.

She smiled back. "Do you want to dance with me?" she asked.

He shook his head. "I suck at dancing," he replied. "But maybe we could go to the movies some time."

She nodded eagerly. "That would be nice."

Chapter Six

Beth paced back and forth across the living room waiting for Paul to return from picking Angie up at school. He had argued that she could take the bus, now that she was streamlined, but he finally relented when the school called and told them it would take a few more days to make the changes in the bus routes. But that only bought her a few more days. Could she risk Angie at school for a few more days?

The old, maroon Pontiac sedan pulled into the drive and Beth breathed a sigh of relief. Beth hurried to the door and pulled it open before Paul had a chance to walk across the driveway.

"What the hell are you doing with the door open?" he yelled. "You trying to heat the whole outdoors?"

Beth, huddled in a thin cardigan sweater, shook her head. "I'm just excited to hear about my baby's day at school," she said.

"Well, me and Angie had a conversation about it on the way home," he said, barreling up the front stoop and standing in front of her. "We both think you need to back away from her and let her grow up a little. Your molly-coddling has already cost her years of normal schooltime."

"But, I only..." Beth stammered.

"I don't want to hear it," Paul interrupted. "You can cook our dinner and then I want you to spend the rest of your time in the bedroom. We don't need to see your sniveling little face while we enjoy our evening."

Beth shook her head. "No, you can't mean it."

Paul raised his arm and Beth crouched defensively. Laughing at her, he lowered his arm to his side. "Yeah, I mean it," he said. "Now get away from us."

Beth hurried to the kitchen, but not before she glanced back to see her daughter enter the house with a smile on her face. *It must have gone well*, Beth decided with a frisson of relief coursing through her body. *Maybe she had been wrong all along. Maybe Angie could handle being with the other children.*

Dejected and questioning her own decisions, she quickly prepared a casserole and slipped it into the oven. Then she washed the dishes and set the table.

"You done in here?" Paul called as he entered the kitchen.

"I'm just setting the table," she explained softly.

"Why the hell are there three plates?" he asked, stepping forward and picking up a dinner plate.

"Because...because...I thought..." she began.

Paul threw the plate against the kitchen wall, causing it to explode into shards of floral printed glass. "I told you we didn't want you around us," he screamed. "What does it take for you to understand, woman? You ain't wanted!"

Sobbing, Beth started to run from the room, but Paul grabbed her by the back of her sweater and swung her around. "Oh, no, you got a mess to clean up," he yelled, tossing her in the direction of the broken glass. "And only after you clean that up, you can go."

He stormed out of the kitchen, slamming the door behind him on the way out. Beth hobbled over to the corner of the room and picked up the broom, her body aching from the abuse it had suffered from Paul's hands that day. She turned and a soft hand was laid over hers.

"I'll clean it up, Mama," Angie said, taking the broom from her mother. "You go and sit on the chair."

"No," Beth whispered urgently, pulling back the broom. "If your father finds out…"

"Mama, does Papa hit you because of me?" Angie asked.

"What? No, of course not," Beth replied instantly. "Your father has a lot of stress in his job and he just needs to vent sometimes."

Angie cocked her head slightly and studied her mother for a few moments. Then she shook her head. "He shouldn't hit you," she said simply and then walked out of the room.

Chapter Seven

The house was quiet and Paul was enjoying a comfortable evening watching the television. A bottle of beer hanging casually from one hand, he used the other hand to aim the remote and switch channels from one sporting event to the next to gather scores and highlights. He yawned widely and then burped loudly. He had to admit, Beth was a damn good cook, even if she couldn't manage anything else. He looked through the open kitchen door at the mess still on the table. Maybe he'd let her come out so she could eat a little supper and clean things up. He hated when the house was messy.

He climbed out of his chair and started to walk towards his bedroom when he heard a noise from Angie's room. Glancing at the clock, he saw it was nearly midnight. Far past the time Angie should have been in bed. Changing direction, he walked down the opposite hall to the girl's room and knocked on the door. "Angie, you okay in there?" he asked. "Time to go to bed. Time to turn off your music."

"Papa," Angie called back through the door. "Papa, I need you."

Paul heard the theme song from the sports channel announcing the game was starting and he huffed impatiently. "Listen, little girl, I don't have time for this right now," he said. "The game's starting."

"But Papa, I need you," she called back.

He grabbed hold of the door and pushed it open. "What the hell do you want?" he yelled.

She stood next to the window, her ear plugs on, slowly moving to the silent notes. Moonlight filtered in and washed her body with light, causing her thin cotton nightgown to become nearly transparent. Paul felt a sexual pull immediately.

"You need to put a robe on," Paul growled, upset that seeing his daughter like that would cause such an instant physical reaction. "Shouldn't be standing in front of a window like that. What are the neighbors going to think?"

She slowly turned away from the window and walked over to him, studying him silently.

"I don't know how many times I've told you little girl," he exclaimed. "It ain't right to stare at people like you do. It gives 'em the willies."

Still silent she stopped in front of him and raised her arms. "Papa, will you dance with me?"

"What the hell?" he asked, but found himself moving towards her.

"I'll let you listen to my music," she said, slipping an ear pod from her ear.

"Angie! No!" her mother cried from the doorway. "You do not dance with your father."

Shaking his head, Paul immediately stepped back. "What the hell?" he yelled and then, feeling guilty for being caught in a potentially compromising situation, turned his emotions on Beth. "What are you doing out of your room? Who the hell do you think you are?"

But this time, Beth wasn't cowed by his anger. She stood in the doorway calmly and met his eyes. "Paul, we need to talk," she said and then turned around and walked down the hall.

Paul turned to his daughter. "Get some clothes on," he yelled. "And then go to bed!"

He stormed after Beth, caught her by the arm next to their bedroom and spun her around. "You don't ever order me around," he yelled.

"This time I do," she said. "This time you have to listen to me or you will die."

She said it with such complete calm that it chilled his body to the bone. "What are you talking about?" he asked, his voice shaky and unsure.

Beth walked over to her dresser, opened the top drawer and pulled out a small ledger. "She's been doing it since she was three," she said, opening the book to the first page.

"Doing what?" Paul asked.

Beth ignored him. "The first time was with the little kitten you bought her for her birthday," she continued.

"The one you let get away," he replied, his voice a little stronger.

She looked up and met his eyes. "No, I didn't let it get away," she said. "Angie…" She paused, searching for the words and finally she just shrugged. "Angie danced with it."

"What?" Paul asked, clearly unconvinced.

"She danced with it and it disappeared," she said. "I didn't know what to think at first, but then, after a few times, I realized that somehow she transports people or absorbs people or, well, I don't know the science of it. I just know that if someone dances with Angie, they ain't around anymore."

Paul stared at her and shook his head.

"You've got to believe me, Paul," she insisted, shaking the ledger book at him. "I've got them all recorded, all of them that I know of, from the kitten to Dr. Feinstein."

"Dr. Feinstein, you blaming her for that?" he asked, disgust on his face. "What? Are you jealous of your own daughter? Are you jealous because she is more beautiful that you could ever hope to be? Are you jealous that I think she's attractive?"

"Paul, she's your daughter," Beth replied, shocked at his confession. "What are you thinking?"

He grabbed the ledger from her and threw it across the room. "I'm thinking it's not my daughter who's the looney, it's my wife," he yelled. "And it's about time I got to know her a little better."

"Paul, no!" Beth screamed.

"Shut up, bitch," he yelled, slapping her across the face with enough force to knock her backwards onto the bed. "I'm going to go and dance with my daughter."

Chapter Eight

Sheltered behind the corner of the high school, Bobby-Joe Meyers watched Angie climb out of the old Pontiac her mother drove, gather her books and begin the walk across the campus toward the school building. She'd been going to class with the rest of the students for several weeks and he'd been watching her, waiting for his chance to make a move. *Yeah, she's a crazy bitch*, he thought, *but she's also one fine piece of ass. Maybe crazy Angie and I need to have a little party time.*

Pushing himself from the wall, he casually strolled toward the same door she was heading towards and managed to meet her just before she walked in. "Hey Angie," he said. "Let me get the door for you."

She stopped and stared at him for a few moments, making him feel uneasy. Then she smiled and nodded. "Thank you," she finally said, moving past him into the school. He easily caught up with her and fell in line as they moved down the hallway.

"So, what are you listening to?" he asked.

"Music," she replied innocently.

"Yeah, well, damn, I know it's music," he said. "But what kind of music."

She shrugged. "My music," she said.

This girl is thicker than a brick, he thought and then he glanced down at her. Her shirt was cut just low enough to display a glimpse of her cleavage. *Damn, I need me some of that.*

"So, it's your music," he said nodding. "Yeah, I get that. You know, you and me, we got lots in common."

She glanced over at him, confusion written on her face.

"I mean, we should get to know each other," he inserted. "You know, I heard your daddy ran out on you and your momma and there ain't no man around the house to protect and, you know, do stuff."

"My daddy went away," she said with a smile.

"Yeah. Yeah, I know," he replied. "So, I'm thinking that I should maybe come on over to your place. You know, when your momma ain't home and I can show you some stuff."

"Show me?" she asked.

He smiled down at her and nodded. "Yeah, show you some stuff that will make you feel good," he said. "Real good."

She stopped abruptly in the middle of the hall and stared at him for another few moments. "Do you want to dance with me?" she asked.

His nodded his head and slowly licked his lips. "Oh, yeah, baby, that's right," he said with a grin. "I want to dance with you. I want us to do the horizontal cha-cha."

Confused again, she shook her head. "Do you want to dance with me?" she asked.

"Yeah, I do," he said. "Real bad. When can I come see you?"

She smiled at him. "My momma's gotta work," she replied. "Wanna come tonight?"

"Oh, baby, I wanna come tonight for sure," he mocked. "How about I'll be at your place at six?"

She nodded. "Momma leaves at five," she said.

"I'll be there at six," he said. "And we are going to have a good time."

He nodded with satisfaction and then turned away from her. "I'm gonna get me some tonight," he yelled out loud to the delight of his friends gathered around their lockers.

Angie just turned and continued down the hall to her first class.

Chapter Nine

Sweat, steam and laughter filled the boy's locker room as the football team finished their practice and were changing back into street clothes. The conversations ran from diagramming a new play, the weaknesses of the team they were going to play on Friday and the cup sizes of the cheerleading squad.

Jared Hood pulled off his helmet and laid it next to him on the wooden bench between the two rows of lockers. He bent to unlace his shoes when another classmate sat down next to him. "Hey, if coach asks, you didn't see Bobby-Joe today at school, okay?" he whispered.

Jared shrugged. "Sure, no big deal," he replied. "Why didn't he make practice?"

The boy snickered. "He's going to be doing Crazy Angie."

"What?" Jared asked, lifting his head up and looking at the boy's face. "What did you say?"

"Angie's mom works tonight, so Bobby-Joe talked her into letting him come over," he replied with a snicker. "She thinks he's coming over to dance with her. She's a little weird about that. But Bobby-Joe's says he's gonna show her how to have a good time."

"I didn't get the feeling she was into that kind of thing," he replied, picturing the shy girl who barely spoke during class.

His teammate shrugged. "That won't matter to Bobby-Joe," he said. "He's got ways to make a girl give him what he wants, even when they're saying no."

"When were they supposed to meet?" Jared asked.

"I don't know, like six I think," the boy replied.

Jared glanced up at the clock, it was a quarter to six. "Why didn't he come to practice?" he asked, pulling his cleats off and throwing them in his locker.

"He could've come, I guess," the boy said. "But he said he didn't want to inhibit his performance."

Jared ripped his jersey over his head and threw it on top of his shoes. Then he quickly removed the rest of his gear, tossing it haphazardly into the locker.

"Hey," the boy said, watching him. "Coach ain't going to be really happy with how you treating the equipment."

Jared pulled his jeans on and slipped his feet into his shoes. "Well," Jared said, pulling his sweatshirt over his head and kicking his locker closed with his foot. "I guess I'll just deal with that later."

He ran out of the locker room into the empty hallway and ran down the hall to the door. His car was at the end of the parking lot. But even if he hit all the lights, he knew he couldn't be at Angie's place until after six. He hoped Bobby-Joe planned on a at least a little romancing before the main event.

Pulling the car out of the parking space, Jared threw it into drive and sped across the parking lot. He turned right onto the street and headed towards the outskirts of town. The lights were working against him and his anxiety increased as he had to wait for each red to turn to green. For a moment he considered calling the police, but Bobby-Joe's family was positioned high in the political echelons of the community and he didn't think the police would even respond.

The light turned green and Jared floored the accelerator pedal, increasing his speed from the tepid thirty-five miles per hour allowed in town to the fifty-five plus permitted for country roads. He took the next turn at sixty-five and increased his speed another five miles after that. He could finally see Angie's house in the distance and his heart sank when he saw Bobby-Joe's red pickup truck parked in the drive.

"Hold on, Angie," he said, bringing the speedometer to its limit. "I'm coming."

He swerved into her driveway and threw the car into park before leaping up and running to her front door. With a closed fist, he pounded against the wood. "Angie!" he yelled. "Angie! Open the door."

A moment later the door opened and Angie stood in the doorway, studying him.

"Are you okay?" he asked. "Did Bobby-Joe hurt you?"

She smiled at him and shrugged. "Bobby-Joe went away."

He released an audible sigh of relief and leaned against the doorframe. "So, you're okay?" he asked again, needing to be reassured.

She nodded. "Yes, I'm fine."

He smiled at her, still catching his breath. "That's good," he said. "That's great."

She just stood in the doorway serenely watching him.

"Listen," he finally said. "I guess I didn't realize how important it was to you, but, you know, if you really want to dance. I'd be happy to dance with you."

She cocked her head to the side and studied him quietly. Then she stepped back, silently inviting him into her home. He walked in and looked around. "Hey, this is a nice place," he said.

She nodded.

"So, do you want to dance with me?" he asked.

She smiled up at him. "No, you suck at dancing," she replied. "Let's watch a movie instead."

MAGGIE MAE

by

Sharon Love Cook

As a child, Benjamin Putnam had been curious about the Weidermans. They lived in a sprawling stucco house on Bridal Path Lane. Ben's house, across the street, sat in a row of split-level and Cape-style homes. Each had a small lawn with neat shrubs and hedges.

The Weidermans' house, on the other hand, sat atop a high rise. The surrounding land, a tangle of bushes, trees and vines, had once been a thriving apple orchard. In the fall, old Mr. Weiderman invited the neighbors to help themselves to the fruit.

Ben remembered accompanying his mother into the orchard. He was fascinated with the gnarled old trees and the intoxicating scent of rotting apples. Carrying their buckets home, Ben's mother warned him not to visit the Weiderman property alone.

"Why not?" he asked.

"Just do as I say. " Immediately regretting her sharp tone, she added, "I heard there's a bobcat hanging around the orchard. It's not safe."

Instead of frightening Ben, it stirred his curiosity. He'd never seen a bobcat. One afternoon he crept across the street. He went up the long driveway, concealed behind a row of evergreens. Inside the orchard, he heard voices and peered through the branches of an apple tree. It was the three Weiderman sisters: Tessa, Nora, and the youngest, Margaret Mae. The girls were rarely seen in town; they attended a boarding school. Nonetheless, they accompanied their father to St. Rupert's Christmas Eve service. The family looked like visitors from another era in their dark capes and buckled boots.

Now peering through the hedge, Ben studied them. The two older sisters sat under an apple tree reading aloud from a book while Margaret Mae was a whirl of activity. Ben watched her swing from branch to branch like a lemur. When she moved deeper into the orchard, he followed. She hung from limbs, spinning from tree to tree. Her skirt rose high on her pale thighs. She didn't bother to pull it down. Ben watched, enrapt.

It was getting dark when Ben finally stole away from the orchard. A neighbor spotted him scurrying down the Weidermans' driveway and reported this to Mrs. Putnam.

At the dinner table that night, Ben's mother announced he'd been seen leaving the Weidermans' property. Ben stared down at his plate. "If you go over there again we'll take your bike away," she said. "I've warned you not to go over there."

"I was just playing in the trees," he said. "It's fun. "

"That's not the point," his father said. "We don't want you on their property."

"Why?" he said. "I didn't see any bobcat."

His older sister Rebecca, who rarely bothered to join the dinner table conversation, spoke up: "It's because crazy Mrs. Weiderman might grab you."

"That's not nice, Rebecca," Mrs. Putnam said. "Mrs. Weiderman isn't crazy, she's … got a nervous illness. I doubt if she's even at home."

"She is," Rebecca said. "I saw her getting out of a long black car. Two men in scrubs helped her into the house."

"I feel sorry for Mr. Weiderman," Ben's father said, "a sick wife and three daughters to raise."

"The Weidermans can afford plenty of help," Ben's mother said in a disapproving tone.

"But they can't keep their help," Rebecca said. "I was talking to the lady who runs Cafe Le Mer, downtown. She used to cook for the Weidermans. She said the cleaning ladies didn't last a month because of Margaret Mae. She was always doing weird things, like burning black candles and chanting in her room."

"It's not nice to gossip about one's neighbors" Mrs. Putnam said. "I'm sure young Margaret is going through an adolescent phase." Ben's mother, a senior clerk at the city hall records department, had a proprietary view of the town's residents.

"Burning candles in her dorm room was one thing," Rebecca said. "Sleeping with the rowing coach got her expelled from school."

"That's enough, Rebecca," Mrs. Putnam said, glancing at Ben.

"Was he a local man?" Mr. Putnam asked.

"Let's just drop the subject," Mrs. Putnam said.

"Fine," Rebecca said, "but I doubt the Weidermans care. Living high on that hill, they barely know we exist."

"I still think it's a shame the way Mr. Weiderman let those trees go to ruin," Mr. Putnam said. "The orchard was his old man's pride and joy. It was a paradise when I was a kid."

"Apparently the family has little respect for ancestry," Mrs. Putnam said with a note of satisfaction.

Nothing more was said about the Weidermans, yet it had been enough to fire Ben's curiosity. He was particularly keen about the teenage Margaret Mae "sleeping" with the rowing coach. Ben had learned the facts of life from health class: how a sperm fertilizes an egg, leading to the development of a baby. Yet when he thought of Margaret Mae and the rowing coach, he didn't associate their behavior with his textbook. Instead he pictured the pair on a narrow cot in a dark, shuttered boathouse. Outside would be a tangle of overgrown trees and vines, much like the Weidermans' property. Ben remembered Margaret Mae's firm thighs glimpsed through the branches of the apple trees. His face burned.

* * *

At age fourteen, Benjamin finally met Margaret Mae Weiderman. Three days a week he worked after school at Save 'n Rave. The supermarket was medium-sized, its customers mostly elderly shoppers who lived downtown. They trudged the aisles, slumped over their shopping carriages as if the effort of standing upright was too burdensome.

Ben became friendly with Evan, another part time employee his age. During breaks, Evan smoked cigarettes behind the dumpster. He adopted a world-weary attitude, referring to Save 'n Rave as "the boneyard."

One afternoon, as Ben knelt on the floor stocking cans of vegetables, he felt a prickling along the back of his neck. He glanced at the entrance where Margaret Mae Weiderman, in a long, dark cape, strode into the store. Without hesitating, she headed straight for Ben.

He clamored to his feet, tripping on his long white apron, watching her move up the aisle, her cape swaying. The bright autumn light was at her back, throwing her face in shadow. Her question surprised him: "I've been looking everywhere for persimmons, Benjamin," she said. "Where can I find them?"

"Persimmons," Ben repeated, his mind in a whirl. He had no idea what a persimmon looked like and he doubted Save 'n Rave carried them. "Um, let me go and ask the manager, okay?"

With great effort he managed to not break into a run as he headed to the fruit section. He couldn't believe Margaret Mae knew his name. If that wasn't enough, she was waiting for him in aisle five.

Mr. Zagrobski, the store manager, snorted upon hearing Ben's inquiry. "We don't even carry canned persimmons," he said. "No call for them. Tell the customer to use cranberries."

Ben raced back, slowing as he reached his aisle. Margaret Mae stood waiting. Before he could speak, she said, "Cranberries? I'm afraid that won't do." Ben wondered how she knew about Mr. Zagrobski's suggestion. Their conversation had taken place on the other side of the store. Seeing his confusion, she laughed. "You're wondering about me, aren't you, Benjamin? For instance, how do I know you work here?"

Ben nodded, his cheeks flushed. He couldn't believe he was having a conversation, however one-sided, with Margaret Mae Weiderman.

She leaned down so they were at eye level. "It's because you and I have unfinished business," she said quietly. "Are you aware of that?"

Once again Ben nodded. He had a glimmer of understanding, and he involuntarily stepped back.

She winked and turned, moving across the floor tiles with long strides. When she swept out of the store, Evan joined Ben. "Do you know *her?*"

"Who?" Ben said, not wanting to share the moment.

"Maggie Mae Weiderman, dummy. She was talking to you."

"She's a neighbor," Ben said with a shrug.

"If she were *my* neighbor, I'd be at the window with binoculars. She's beautiful," Evan said. "I mean, for an old person."

"She's not that old—maybe ten years older," Ben said, although it was a lifetime to him. "How do you know her?"

"She went out with my brother Spencer years ago."

Ben felt a hot stab of jealousy. "Yeah?"

"He worked at the gas station downtown. Spencer was captain of the football team. He had no trouble getting chicks. Maggie drove up in her old man's Town Car and he asked her out. Eventually he learned she was only fifteen years old. She didn't even have a driver's license. Didn't bother her a bit. My brother said she's crazy."

"He probably said that because she dumped him."

Evan laughed. "You got that right. Spencer admitted he was out of her league."

* * *

In case Margaret Mae visited Save 'n Rave again, Ben kept a roll of breath mints in his pocket. Mornings he dabbed on his dad's aftershave lotion. When she didn't appear in the store, he tried putting her out of his mind. It was a stupid crush, he admitted. She was just teasing him.

Getting over Margaret Mae became easier after Ben got to know Alyssa from his computer class. She sat in front of Ben, her long blond braid hanging down her back. One day she turned and asked how he'd done on a test. Ben confessed he was barely passing the class. "English is my best subject," he said.

Alyssa claimed she had the opposite problem. "I'm a geek, yet I can't put two paragraphs together." They agreed to help each other. During the next few months, their friendship grew stronger. Ben liked Alyssa's friendly, open manner. She said Ben made her laugh.

* * *

In March, spring showed no sign of arriving. Residents of Bridal Path Lane had barely gotten shoveled out from the last storm when a blizzard dropped another six inches of snow. Mr. Putnam came home early from his job in the city. He put on his woolen hat and fur lined gloves and grabbed a shovel from the garage. Ben helped his dad clear the driveway.

As they got underway, Mrs. Putnam beckoned to them from the side door. Pulling her sweater close, she said excitedly: "Helen from the police dispatcher's office just called. Mrs. Weiderman was found this morning in the apple orchard, frozen stiff in her nightgown." She continued: "She'd just been discharged from the hospital. No one heard her sneak out of the house. The nurse who was supposed to be watching her had fallen asleep."

"As a matter of fact," Mr. Putnam said, "as I was walking to the train this morning, I saw a couple of cruisers heading for their house. I figured it was bad news."

"We'll have to attend the funeral," Mrs. Putnam said, "to show neighborly support."

"I can't take more time from work," Mr. Putnam said. "You go with Ben."

Ben nodded and looked up at the Weiderman house, surrounded by tall evergreens. He would have attended the funeral even if it meant sneaking into church. He wanted to see Margaret Mae again.

* * *

The obituary for Charlotte Collier Weiderman appeared in the local newspaper. The accompanying photo showed her as a young woman with thick dark hair and luminous eyes. According to the write-up, she'd attended Wellesley College and had been wardrobe curator at Boston's Museum of Art before her marriage to Horace Weiderman.

The day of the funeral was sunny and cold. Ben yanked at the sleeves of his wool blazer; they were an inch too short. His mother, in a long tweed coat, took his arm as they approached St. Rupert's Church. A row of long black cars lined the street. As they climbed the concrete stairs to the church entrance, a black limo stopped behind them. The driver hopped out and opened the back door. Ben spotted the Weiderman sisters inside.

"Don't stare," his mother hissed, tugging his arm.

Inside the chapel, Ben looked around. Outside of a few neighbors, he didn't recognize any of the well-dressed mourners. "New York people," his mother whispered, scanning the rows. "Old money." The church was lit with more candles than Ben had ever seen. Likewise, masses of flowers covered the altar and the steps leading to it.

Before long the double doors opened and the choir, wearing maroon velvet robes, moved down the center aisle singing. They were followed by a gleaming casket carried by dark-suited pall bearers. The Weiderman family walked behind them. The recently-married Nora held the arm of a balding man. Margaret Mae and Tessa flanked their father. Gray-faced, he walked unsteadily forward.

After the congregation was settled, Reverend Mumford, resplendent in robes of gold and white said: "In the midst of life we are in death." At this, Ben's mother pulled a tissue from her pocket and sobbed. Ben leaned forward, attempting to get a glimpse of Margaret Mae through the tangle of bodies surrounding him.

It was not until they stood to sing "Morning has Broken" that he was rewarded. Margaret Mae, taller than everyone in her row, slipped off her coat, letting it fall behind her. She wore a bright scarlet dress that hugged the contours of her long body. Amid the rows of dark suits and coats, the dress was a brilliant flame. Ben sucked in his breath. The sight made him dizzy and he clutched the back of the bench.

The service ended with the choir singing "How Great Thou Art" as they moved down the aisle. The Weidermans rose. Margaret Mae and Tessa assisted their father from his seat. The family followed, accompanied by the choir's majestic singing. Ben's mother sobbed anew while at the same time studying the procession. As the Weidermans passed, Margaret Mae turned. Looking directly at Ben, she smiled.

"You see that?" Mrs. Putnam said, stuffing tissues into her pocket. "She appreciates us being here."

* * *

During the next two years Benjamin had glimpses of the Weidermans coming and going from their house. Tessa Weiderman, he heard his parents say, was now married and living in Connecticut. Margaret Mae, still single, was in Boston. "Louisburg Square, don't you know," his mother said. "She comes home now and then to see her father, the poor man."

Mr. Weiderman, according to the neighborhood grapevine, had developed congestive heart. Home health aides arrived in shifts. Periodically the quiet of Bridal Path Lane was broken by the wail of an ambulance. "He can't keep that up for long," Ben's mother said, watching from a window.

Ben still experienced a thrill whenever Margaret Mae's name was mentioned. However, he was no longer consumed with curiosity about the Weidermans. He was involved in high school school activities, particularly theater. He'd written a two-act play for the drama society.

When he wasn't working at Save 'n Rave, he was with Alyssa. The two marveled at how much they had in common. Ben felt comfortable visiting Alyssa's house. Her parents approved of his respectful attitude and work ethic.

Additionally, once a week he took driving lessons. He secretly hoped he and Alyssa might experience a deeper intimacy once he got his license and they could be alone. At the same time, he feared his lack of experience would prove humiliating. At night, he furtively scanned sex sites on the Internet, looking at the free "teasers." There was plenty of activity, but no step-by-step instructions for novices. Watching the couplings, however exciting, made Ben feel inadequate. He never mentioned his yearnings to Alyssa. Although she appeared to enjoy the clandestine kissing and fondling sessions on the family couch, she set firm boundaries.

One December weekend, Mr. and Mrs. Putnam made plans to stay overnight in Rhode Island. Ben's sister Rebecca had an apartment in Providence. She'd encouraged her parents to visit.

On Saturday morning, their departure day, Ben's mother watched the weather channel for news of an upcoming snow storm. "Why don't we go next weekend?" she again asked her husband. "I don't want to leave Ben alone."

Mr. Putnam had come into the house after loading the suitcases into the Subaru. "Don't be silly," he told her. "Rebecca made reservations at a restaurant she wants to try. Besides, next weekend I'm helping at the church blood drive."

Mrs. Putnam slipped into her coat. "You'll call if anything goes wrong, won't you, Ben?"

Before he could respond, Mr. Putnam said, "Ben's fine. Let's get moving. If we leave now, we'll be there before the first flakes."

Ben walked his parents to the car. After hurried last minute instructions, they drove away. Ben turned back to the house, glancing at the leaden sky. The air had the metallic smell of snow. He went inside, happy to be alone and free. He wished Alyssa could come over, but she was babysitting.

He made popcorn in the microwave and carried it into the den where he stretched out in his dad's recliner. He clicked the TV remote and settled in to watch a Celtics game. Before long his eyelids drooped; the room was warm. He contemplated turning down the thermostat. Before he could rise, his eyes closed and he slept.

Ben woke to the shrill ring of the kitchen phone. Darkness had fallen while he'd been asleep. In the dim light he stumbled to the sound. He figured it was his mother calling, anxious about her son's welfare. Thus he was shocked when the caller spoke: "Benjamin, it's Maggie Mae Weiderman. Our handyman had to leave early and the snow's piling up. I wonder if you'd help shovel us out."

Ben pulled the curtain away from the window. The snow had fallen fast. It covered the salt marsh behind his house. *A winter wonderland,* Alyssa would have said of the freshly fallen snow.

"Sure, I can come over," he said. "Let me get my boots on."

"You're an angel of mercy, Benjamin."

He sat to pull on his boots, aware that he was breathing fast. *Calm down,* he told himself. *You're just helping out a neighbor.* She probably wants the snow cleared in case the old man has to go to the hospital. Before leaving the house he brushed his teeth, rinsing with mouthwash.

Ben opened the garage and grabbed a shovel with a wide, shallow scoop. Carrying it over his shoulder, he began to climb the Weiderman's hill.

A light was on over the side door. Ben glanced through a window in the garage that had once been a stable. Now a long black car and a gleaming BMW convertible were parked inside. He had spotted Margaret Mae driving the BMW, roaring out of the long driveway with barely a glance at the street traffic.

He turned and faced the side door, aware that he was stalling. At that moment Margaret Mae appeared. She wore black pajamas of a silky material that reflected the light. Her dark hair was loose, falling to her shoulders. Her feet were bare. "Do you want a shovel from the garage?" she called.

"I brought my own," he said. "Do you want me to do the area outside the garage and then a path to the door?"

'That would be wonderful." She looked up at the sky. "We're not supposed to get much more." Before closing the door she said, "Let me know when you're through."

Although Ben had been tired earlier, he felt a renewed energy. The snow was light and he made good progress. From time to time he stole glances at the big house, watching for movement at the windows. Finally he was finished. A wide, neat path led to the side entrance while the garage area was cleared. He looked around, pleased with his work. As he debated knocking on the door, it opened. "Come in Ben," Margaret Mae said, beckoning to him. "I've got a check for you."

"That's okay, Ms. Weiderman. I'm glad to help a neighbor."

She laughed. "I insist. I made hot apple cider to warm you."

Ben stuck the shovel in the snow and headed to the house, feeling a mixture of anticipation and apprehension. Inside, Margaret Mae chatted casually about the storm as she ushered him to a room at the rear of the house. A huge fireplace made of rough granite blocks occupied one wall. Facing it was a long sofa with fat cushions. On either side were overstuffed chairs covered in worn leather. Colorful woven rugs lay scattered on the old wood floor.

"This is nice," Ben said, looking around.

"Get comfortable while I pour the cider." She knelt before the fireplace, her back straight, and lit a match. Immediately the neat pile of logs and kindling burst into flames.

"Wow," Ben said. It was like a movie setting. He lowered himself onto the sofa.

She pointed to his boots. "Better take those off. Put them on the rug to dry."

She swept out of the room and returned with a tray and two pewter mugs. "This is the last of the apples," she said, handing Ben a mug. "I added lots of sugar and spices because they were a little tart." She joined him on the sofa.

Ben took a sip. His mouth puckered. The cider tasted medicinal. Nonetheless, it warmed his stomach. "Is your dad okay?" he asked politely.

"He's at the hospital. Periodically they have to drain the fluid around his heart."

"Oh." Ben had gotten the impression that Mr. Weiderman was at home. He was aware she was watching him. To cover his self-consciousness, he blurted out, "I'm sorry about your mother. I mean, about what happened to her."

She reached over to touch his hand. "You were sweet to attend the funeral. I knew you would come."

He stole a glance and discovered she was watching him, her cheek resting against the sofa. "Neighborly support," he said, echoing his mother's words.

"Have you forgotten what I said, Benjamin? That we have unfinished business, you and I."

He felt his cheeks burn. Not knowing how to reply, he said, "Were you the one who found your mother, I mean, in the snow?"

She nodded. "I found her earlier that night and didn't want to disturb her. She looked so peaceful lying there, the snow glistening in her hair. I thought it a shame to rouse her." While Ben mulled this over, she added, "My mother was tormented by her demons. She didn't know how to master them." She peered into the flames. "You have to take control or they'll rule you."

Ben took a gulp of his cider. He felt a boldness and wondered if she'd put something in it. "Do you mean when you found your mother she was—"

"Freezing to death is a blissful way to die," she said, her voice dreamy. "It's like a long, lovely sleep."

"Uh huh." Ben sat for a moment, transfixed by the flames. Then he finished the last of his cider and set the mug on the coffee table. He leaned forward but when he attempted to rise his legs felt rubbery. He tried again and finally sank back onto the cushions. When he turned to Margaret Mae, her face was close.

"Benjamin," she said, her voice barely audible in the big room, "do you realize that destiny has brought us together?" Her breath smelled like apples. The room tilted and he opened his mouth to speak but nothing came out. He closed his eyes.

* * *

Ben woke sprawled on the sofa. The room was cold and dark, a faint light coming from the fireplace embers. He struggled to a sitting position, closing his eyes against the pain in his head. He reached for his boots and pulled them on with great effort. Holding onto the sofa's armrest, he got to his feet. A light was on in the kitchen and he slowly made his way to it.

He let himself out the side door. Breathing deeply of the cold night air, he headed down the hill, the snow crunching under his feet. A full moon cast purple shadows on the drifts while the evergreens, their boughs heavy with snow, creaked in the wind.

Inside Ben's house, the only sound was the ticking of the kitchen clock. It was three in the morning. He kicked off his boots and stumbled up the stairs to his room. There he pulled off his clothes, letting them drop to the floor. In his pants' pocket he found a folded piece of paper. He turned on a lamp. It was a check for three hundred dollars from Margaret Mae Weiderman.

* * *

During the next two years, Ben caught glimpses of the Weiderman sisters coming and going from the house. The old man, Ben's mother said, was due to move to a private nursing facility; most likely the house would be sold.

During the spring of Ben's senior year, he took a trip to Spain with the high school Spanish department. One afternoon in Barcelona, the group stopped for lunch at a tapas bar. The students sat at a long wooden table drinking *tinto* accompanied by plates of cheese and olives. Ben suddenly felt cool hands on his shoulders.

"*Hola* Benjamin," Margaret Mae said in his ear. Her long hair caressed his cheek. He turned, too surprised to say anything. As quickly as Margaret Mae had appeared, she slipped away. He watched her cross the room, her heels clicking loudly on the hard tiles.

"Got a secret girlfriend?" one of the male students said. "Who is she?" another asked. Ben mumbled that he wasn't sure. His face reddened. The group laughed. Ben was relieved when their food arrived and conversation turned to other topics.

Nonetheless, for the remainder of the trip Ben looked warily around, expecting to see Margaret Mae in a hotel lobby, on a city street, or in a crowded shop.

* * *

During their last year of high school, Ben and Alyssa drifted apart. Ben was sure it was for the best. After all, they'd be attending different colleges, Alyssa heading to New York and Ben to Boston.

At Emerson, he took advantage of the creative opportunities the school offered. However, rarely did he attend social activities. He told himself he liked being a loner. However, during the fall of his junior year, he decided to take in one of the city's most popular offerings: the Head of the Charles Regatta. The October event attracted students from the greater Boston community.

On a brisk fall day Ben sat on a bench overlooking the Charles River. As he idly surveyed the crowds, he spotted a familiar blond braid among the masses of young people lining the riverbank. He got to his feet and moved closer. It was Alyssa and her younger sister Amy.

After hugs and expressions of delight, the three returned to the bench to talk. Alyssa was visiting Amy, a student at Simmons. The following day she had an interview at MIT; she hoped to transfer there. "I've got a full scholarship to Rensselaer, but MIT has always been my dream."

"You'll get accepted," Ben told her. "You always were a techno genius." He was happy to see Alyssa and realized how much he'd missed her company. Thus he was pleased when she suggested they get together during the Thanksgiving holiday.

Before long Ben was welcomed back into Alyssa's family. He felt as if a big part of him had been restored. For the remainder of the college semester, Ben and Alyssa got together whenever they could. Sometimes she made the drive from Troy to Boston. "I can't wait until February when I'm at MIT," she said, "and you'll be right across the river."

One December night they stopped for pizza following a movie. They hadn't talked much about their earlier breakup. Now Alyssa brought it up over mugs of beer: "You changed, Ben, almost overnight. You acted remote, closed off. I felt shut out."

He squeezed her hand. "I won't let that happen again, I promise."

That spring, Ben took Alyssa for a ride on the Swan Boats in Boston's Public Garden. As they passed under the arched bridge, he asked her to marry him. Alyssa hugged him with such enthusiasm they almost capsized the boat.

It was a hot July morning when Ben and Alyssa stood on the curb of Tremont Street holding hands. They were headed for the jewelers district on Washington Street. The pedestrian light flashed and Alyssa stepped off the curb. Ben yanked her back as a navy BMW convertible came to a stop at the lights, its brakes screeching. Margaret Mae Weiderman sat behind the wheel, a long silk scarf around her neck.

"Hello Benjamin," she called. "Sorry."

He nodded. Gripping Alyssa's hand, they crossed the busy street. Ben was conscious of the woman's eyes upon them. When the light turned green, Margaret Mae roared away, her scarf fluttering in the breeze.

"Who's *that*?" Alyssa said, turning to stare.

"Just a neighbor," he said.

"Some neighbor."

In August, Alyssa moved in with Ben while her Cambridge apartment was being painted. Early mornings she got up to run along the Charles, leaving Ben in bed. "I hope you're not going to continue this when we're married," he said, yawning.

"Nope, I plan to stop all activity and get fat and lazy." She bent to kiss his forehead. Slipping her keys into the pocket of her shorts, she closed the door behind her and skipped down the stairs.

When Ben awoke three hours later and Alyssa hadn't returned, he called Amy. "Did Alyssa stop to see you?" he asked.

Amy hadn't seen her. "She might have sprained her ankle or something," she said. If that was the case, Ben said, then why hadn't she called on her cell phone? He had to leave for his tutoring job. He told Amy to call if she heard from Alyssa.

All through the morning, Ben couldn't keep his mind on the subject. Every few minutes he glanced at his phone. He cancelled his afternoon tutoring sessions and went home.

Just as he feared, the apartment was empty with no sign of Alyssa. He called Amy, who told him to call the police. "I will," he said. "Don't tell your parents. Alyssa's probably at a local hospital. No sense in alarming them until we know more." It was with a sense of dread that he called the Boston Police.

The woman who answered said, "You say she's been missing six hours?" Ben was told the police wouldn't do anything until the missing person was gone for more than twenty-four hours.

Ben stayed at the apartment throughout the afternoon. Amy came over. They called the local hospitals. Later they walked to the Charles River and searched the area where Alyssa ran. Rows of maple trees lined the concrete path that meandered along the river. Ben collapsed onto a bench. "Why did I let her go alone?" he said, his voice breaking.

"Alyssa liked to run alone," Amy said. " Don't worry, we'll hear from her."

Ben merely shook his head.

Around the time the police got involved, Alyssa's body was discovered floating near a stone embankment. The coroner said she'd been hit from behind with a heavy object that fractured her skull. Her body had been dragged into the river. Alyssa's picture appeared on TV news stations along with warnings to "buddy up" when running in the city.

* * *

The crowds at Alyssa's funeral filled the pews of St. Rupert's Church. Ben walked alongside Amy in the procession, behind her parents. He sat numbly during the service, not believing what was taking place. How could someone so young and vibrant be lying lifeless inside the wooden coffin?

When the service ended, the family made their way down the center aisle as the choir sang, "How Great Thou Art." Ben, his head lowered, put an arm around Amy, who sobbed quietly. When the procession reached the entrance doors, sunlight poured into the church. Ben shielded his eyes from the sudden glare. From a corner of his vision he spotted a kneeling figure in the last row, dressed in black. He turned his head to look, although he instinctively knew who it was.

Margaret Mae lifted the black lace veil that covered her eyes and smiled.

EVERY BREATH YOU TAKE

by

A.T. Reid

Prologue

The beam from the headlights failed to cut through the fog, but the car continued steadily along the road that ran through the middle a dense forest. Brad leaned his head closer to his windshield and squinted. From the corner of his eye, he saw a bright light pierce through the mist. He quickly did a double take, only to realize it was just a road sign warning him of oncoming deer. *Come on, Brad,* he thought. *You're just scaring yourself. This road isn't that bad.*

Not entirely convinced, he turned on his high-beams and was rewarded with a blindingly white reflection. He swore as he turned the lights back to normal. "Well, I guess I'm stuck with the slightly dim and totally creepy lights," he confirmed to himself, finding the sound of his own voice better than nothing. He checked his side mirror to see behind the car. There was nothing else in sight except empty road and fog. *If there's no one behind me,* he thought to himself, *then why do I feel like I'm being watched...*

Brad risked a glance at the box on the passenger seat. A smile touched his lips as he thought about the reaction Stacy, his girlfriend of two years, was going to have. He allowed his heart to soften as he thought about everything he and Stacy had been through these last two years, the good and the bad.

Taking a brief look in the review mirror, a flutter of panic washed over him. "Crap, crap, crap..." he muttered as he licked his finger tips and smoothed the tuft of hair that was rebelliously sticking out from the side. "There," he said, as he smoothed the troubled tuft to his satisfaction. He then wiped the spit off of one hand onto his jeans, followed by wiping the sweat he'd accumulated on his other palm onto his jeans. He let out a shaky breath as he placed both hands on the wheel.

He didn't realize he was going to be this nervous. What if she didn't like the gift? What if it made her feel uncomfortable? Was he giving it to her too soon? Was he giving it to her too late? He trembled when he thought about how she would react if he did anything wrong. Tonight had to be perfect.

He checked his digital clock and swore out loud. "I should have gone through the city. Maybe then I wouldn't be in all this fog. But this damn road is just too bad to go fast. I can't speed in this weather. That would be stupid."

He checked the clock again and let out a huff of air. "Well," he resolved, "I guess I'm going to have to be a little stupid."

He accelerated a bit above the speed limit and hoped his memory of the road would serve him well. He had gone down this road many times. It was the back road to get to Stacy's house and he used it to travel without fear of getting pulled over for speeding, seeing as he tended to be a bit late. He checked the time again and pushed the accelerator down a bit further.

Suddenly, something leapt from the side of the road. Brad only caught a glimpse of a large white blur before he slammed on the brakes and pulled the wheel sharply to the left to avoid the creature. The car fishtailed and he lost control. He panicked as he sped toward the ditch and jerked the wheel to the right, just as the front tires hit the edge. His small car tipped and rolled toward the trees. With regret, Brad watched the box as it sailed from the passenger seat and flew toward his face.

That's why he didn't see the tree coming closer to him from the other side.

The creature whose life Brad had attempted to save stepped out of the fog into the beam of the headlight, now pointed haphazardly into the forest. The light shone upon its frame, tall and thin, as it moved toward the car on two spindly albino legs that were more akin to a flamingo's legs than that of a man. Its face was nearly a blank oval, with a bald head that shone in the moonlight and two slits where its nose should be. The illumination from the headlights cast shadows into where the eyes should be, but none were to be found. The thing parted its lips into what can only be described as a smile, displaying its too many long and pointed teeth, yellowed with age.

It sauntered over to the car, bent over, and peered into the passenger window. A trickle of saliva fell from its lips as it sniffed the upholstery. Hunching its back and getting down to all fours, it let out an earth-shuddering howl before tearing back into the woods.

Brad was never able to give the gift to Stacy.

Chapter One

A year later...

The nightmare was always the same.

Stacy looked from her plate of spaghetti over to her loving boyfriend. She smiled as she brought the cup of wine to her lips. The air smelled of Italian spices and there was soft instrumental music playing under the chatter of others who were in the restaurant. However, she didn't notice anyone else. To her, it was only she and Brad. She stared into his deep, blue eyes and said nothing. She didn't have to. She knew how great their love was.

A sudden look of panic tainted his piercing eyes and his smile faded. He looked past Stacy's shoulder and brought a napkin to his mouth. Stacy looked over her shoulder to see what he was looking at, but could only see a few more couples laughing and dining.

"Stacy," Brad said, bringing the napkin down, "I need to use the restroom. I will be right back." He smiled at her. "Stacy, I love you so much."

She saw his lips move as those last words were spoken. She saw him articulate and she knew he said them. But, there was something about the voice that sounded wrong. It was just a little too soft, just a little too light.

She wanted to stay put. She wanted to believe that he was coming back. She loved him so much, she wanted to trust him. But, something was bothering her. A feeling. A fleeting memory.

She stood up slowly and started walking over to the bathroom. The noise and laughter grew quiet and she had the distinct impression that the room was watching her. However, she wouldn't be deterred. She pressed on, walking toward the bathroom. The walls melted around her and the sweet, soft sound of music was replaced by the distant noise of radio chatter and the rush of the wind outside. She continued walking. The hallway to the bathroom crumbled and behind it was a car that was flipped on its roof. Gasping, she recognized Brad's car. She wanted to stop. She didn't want to see what was waiting for her on the inside of the car. But, her feet didn't allow that to happen. One step at a time, she finally made it to the driver's door.

She bent over to look inside.

Brad stared into the darkness, piercing blue eyes focusing on nothing. His mouth hung limply open and blood oozed from a gash on his forehead.

She tried to look away. She wanted to look away. She tried to scream, but she couldn't move any air.

The blue eyes suddenly shot right back into Stacy's. She watched as he tried to speak, but couldn't. Fear crept into his face as all that he could do was wail and groan.

Then a serene mask covered his fear and a voice crept out of his throat. Without moving his lips, a voice that was too soft said, "Stacy, I love you."

* * *

Stacy woke up in a cold sweat. She shot into a sitting positon as she tried to pull herself out of the dream and remember where she was. Breathing heavily, she wiped the perspiration off her brow and put her arms around one of her knees. It took several moments for the pounding of her heart to quiet down.

She closed her eyes and let out a breath of air. Then, looking for comfort, she grabbed the purple teddy bear that was lying at her side and hugged it. Holding it there for several moments, she let the memories of good times sweep through her.

She pushed the button on the paw of the teddy bear and heard Brad's last words to her. "Stacy, I love you."

A stray tear slid down her cheek only to be absorbed by the teddy bear.

Hesitantly, she put the teddy bear down as she decided that she should get ready for the day. That was when she looked at her clock.

It read 6:30.

"Well, crap," she huffed, disappointed at her lack of sleep. "It's not like I could go back to bed if I wanted to."

She swung her legs over the side of her bed and let her feet drop to the carpeted floor. She looked at the sun, just barely peeking over the horizon through the tiny opening in her curtains.

Running her fingers through her hair, she stood up and walked over to the door. She flipped the switch and the room burst into light and color.

Stacy flinched away from the new light and shielded her eyes with her hand. "Damn these lights," she cursed, squinting her eyes to block out as much light as possible. The superintendent had recently installed new lights that were much brighter than Stacy was used to. She closed her eyes for a while longer, and then opened them again. Her eyes adjusting, she now looked at the window, and leaned against the wall as she admired the view of the sunrise. A smile touched her lips as she tried to reason that life could be worse. Her eyes slowly left the window and made their way to the bed, where her teddy bear was smiling back at her with its stitched mouth. A twinge of pain struck her heart as she looked at Brad's last gift to her. The one the police found in his car on the night of the accident.

She closed her eyes and forced herself to look away. *No*, she thought to herself. *Don't think about it. You don't need to think about him anymore.*

She turned away from the purple teddy bear and forced herself to get on with the rest of the day.

Chapter Two

The rest of the morning was uneventful. It was a Saturday, so Stacy didn't have work. The majority of her day was filled with watching TV and eating cold leftover pizza.

Around two o'clock, however, her day became a bit more interesting than she was hoping for.

She was lying on her old and overused couch watching another house rehabbing show when her phone rang. She tilted her head up and looked at her cellphone, which was lying on the small coffee table a couple of feet in front of her, just to make sure she hadn't imagined it. Sure enough, the phone rang a second time.

Stacy sat up and grabbed the phone to see who was calling.

The caller ID read Amber Hill.

She pressed the "accept" button on the screen and put the phone up to her ear.

"Hello?" Stacy said, bewildered. Why would Amber be calling her now? It was a Saturday afternoon. Doesn't she have other things to do?

"Hey, Stacy!" A bright and perky voice answered on the other end. "It's Amber. How have you been?"

"Hey Amber," Stacy reluctantly replied. "I've been pretty good for the most part. Just enjoying my day off. You?"

"Oh, I have been catching up with friends. Danielle told me that she hasn't seen you in a few months."

"Well, I've been pretty busy. And, when I'm not busy, I'm too tired to want to go out and do anything."

"So," Amber said, humor in her voice, "what you're saying is, you're a hermit."

"Exactly," Stacy replied in an easy tone.

"Well, that sounds exciting," Amber retorted. "When was the last time you saw some of your friends besides at work?"

Stacy had to think about that for a moment. "I think it was…the last time I spent time with you," Stacy said as innocently as possible.

"Honey," Amber replied, dryly, "That was three weeks ago. You're telling me that you haven't seen anyone outside of work in three weeks?"

"I guess so."

"Stacy," Amber said, drawing her name out. "You need to hang out with people. Get out of your apartment for a while. It's not healthy. When was the last time you went on a date?"

Stacy let the silence answer that question.

"Oh," Amber said, reading the silence. "Oh, honey, I'm so sorry. I didn't mean to—"

"Its fine," Stacy said, trying to pull herself back together. "You didn't mean to. I know. Let's just say I haven't dated in a while."

"Stacy," Amber said in all seriousness, "You do realize the only way you will ever be happy again is to accept what has happened and move on? You need to start seeing other people."

"Thanks for the suggestion," Stacy replied, "but, no, I don't. I don't want to, and I certainly don't need to. I don't have time to date right now."

"Well, that's unfortunate, because you might need to make time." Amber said, letting the sarcasm back on.

"Why?" Stacy replied, the word being used as a clear warning.

"I got you a date for this evening."

"You did WHAT?" Stacy exploded, frustration choking out of her words.

"I got you a date," Amber said, this time much firmer. "Listen, it's been a year. Yes, Stacy, we all miss him. I can't begin to imagine what you went through. But, after the accident, you cut yourself off from everyone. We all miss the old Stacy. The only way you bring her back is to move on and finally get a date. Don't worry, just because you go on one lousy date doesn't mean you two are going to get married and have fat children together. It's just a fun activity that you are going to do with a member of the opposite sex that he will gladly pay for."

Stacy tried to bring her fury back down as she took deep breaths. Finally she said as calmly as she could, "Call it off."

"Sorry," Amber said, "I can't. This is for your own good. He's picking you up at seven."

Stacy closed her eyes and pinched the bridge of her nose. "At least tell me who it is."

"It's Phillip Miller. Do you remember him? He was in a few of our classes in sophomore year."

"Yeah," Stacy said. "I remember him. He was the one that was obsessed with ghosts and stuff. He was really awkward. You are setting me up with someone who's really awkward? How thoughtful."

"Oh, he's improved," Amber said, "He's actually kind of hot now. And, even if he is awkward, it will be good for you to at least have some human interaction."

"I hate you." Stacy said.

"I know." Amber replied. Then she hung up her phone.

Stacy flung herself backward, letting her head rest at the top of her couch and let out an exasperated breath. *Well, I better get ready.* She looked at her phone to see what time it was, then placed it on the couch next to her and thought, *I'll start getting ready in a bit.*

Chapter Three

Seven o'clock came way too quickly. She had just finished putting her hair up when she heard a knock on the door.

She dashed to the door, unlocked it and pulled it open. The man standing before her wasn't what she expected.

It was Phillip Miller. But, it wasn't the Phillip Miller that she had known from high school. Growing up had definitely improved him. He used to have long, greasy hair that would constantly get into his eye, causing him to do the "Phillip flip," as she and her friends used to call it. He also used to have patchy facial hair that was too long and smooth to be stubble, but too short to be called a beard. His glasses would always be slightly dirty and his clothing had carried a musty smell with them.

However, the Phillip Miller who stood in the hallway had short hair, which was parted to the side. He had thick dark stubble that covered the lower portion of his face. He wore a red tie with a light blue shirt that was just tight enough to show his pecs. The shirt was tucked into dark blue designer denim jeans. His engaging smile flaunted pearly white teeth. He had intense green eyes that she had never noticed before. She stared at those eyes for a bit longer and hoped he didn't notice.

"Hi, Stacy," Phillip said, making Stacy realize that she had said nothing to him.

Face red, she replied, "Hey, Phillip. Sorry, I've had an interesting day, so, I'm a bit tired." She smiled at him. He smiled back. Something about his smile made her woozy. It was such a charming, calm smile. Yet, she couldn't help but feel a chill run down her spine as she looked at it. *It's probably nothing,* she told herself. *This your first date in a while. You probably just have the jitters.*

"So, are you ready to go?" Phillip asked.

Stacy paused for a moment. That voice sounded so familiar to her somehow. Where had she heard it before?

"Stacy?" Phillip prompted.

Well, of course it sounds familiar, Stacy told herself. *You did kind of go to high school with him.* "Yeah," Stacy said, "I just have to get my purse. Hold on."

* * *

This car is really nice, Stacy thought. The seats were grey leather, the dashboard was shiny, and there was a pleasant smell in the air. It wasn't overpowering. In fact, it was quite the opposite. It just tickled her nose, daring her to sniff in deeper.

The streets were pretty empty for a Saturday night. There were some people jogging on the sidewalks and very few cars on the street. The pavement was damp enough to reflect the beam of Phillip's headlights, and it reflected the lights of the city that much more. *This could actually turn out to be a good date,* Stacy thought to herself as she and Phillip conversed.

"Oh, man," Phillip continued, "High school was the worst."

"You're telling me," Stacy let out with a giggle. "Do you remember that pink sweater I wore on picture day?"

"You mean the one with the stain on it?" Phillip asked with his lips quirked up in a half smile.

"Yes! No one told me, and I took my junior picture with this huge stain on my sweater. Worst yearbook picture ever!"

Laughing, Phillip said, "Well, at least that was only one day. My clothes were always nasty, and no one ever told me."

"Why were they nasty?" Stacy asked in a joking tone, although she was genuinely curious. She leaned closer and waited for him to speak.

"Well, we didn't have a washing machine at my house, and my mom never wanted to waste money on things that weren't important, like sanitation. She obviously forgot what high school was like. Clothes and smell are super important."

Stacy laughed a little as she said, "Yeah that sounds rough. But, you're much better now." She noticed that he made a quick smile back at her, and her heart skipped a beat. Sobering up, she looked out the window and asked, "So, do you still like all of those ghosts and things?"

Phillip shrugged. "Well, I would be lying if I didn't say they interested me. I really like paranormal stuff."

"Really?" Stacy said, nodding her head, "What makes them so interesting?"

There was a brief pause as Phillip looked around for the right words to say. "I don't know," he began. "I think the idea that something we can't explain living among us is really interesting. You know, all of these beings that people have sworn they've seen or felt. These creatures have had sightings, legends, and religions built around them for hundreds of years, yet the majority of the world doesn't believe they are cohabitating the earth with us. I mean, I like to think that there are mysteries out there that people still haven't seen or figured out yet. You know?" He glanced at her, and asked, "Does that sound crazy?"

"No, that makes complete sense," Stacy said. Leaning back against the seat, she thought about the possibility of things like that out there. She had never really done that before. She had always dismissed the supernatural. Admittedly, her dismissal was partly because she really didn't want to open herself up to the possibilities. It was hard enough living alone with the worry of human threats. If she added paranormal entities into the equation, she would never sleep at night. However, she couldn't help but admire his open mindedness.

"So," Stacy said, "You have books and stuff on them I'm guessing?"

"I actually have more books on those subjects than I should. I put some money into getting books, some of them really old, about a bunch of stuff. Ghosts, the fey, demons…"

"Demons? Like, with horns and a cape and whatnot?"

"Well, from what I've read, if they exist, they could probably take whatever form they wanted, as long as they are given enough power."

"Power?"

"Yeah. Demons alone don't have power, because they don't have bodies. They are spiritual by nature. So, someone has to give them power, whether it be through fear, anger, guilt, or signing their power away."

"Signing their power? Like, selling your soul to the devil?"

Phillip looked at her approvingly. "Exactly. However, I've read you don't just have to sell your soul. There are plenty of things you can do to get a favor done. Sacrifice, worship, things like that. All you need to do is summon it and work out a deal of some sort."

Stacy looked at Phillip and said, "Well, that's creepy."

"It is, isn't it?" Phillip agreed with a wink. "Let's talk about something else."

Stacy saw that he was about to say something, but then his eyes got wide with panic. With one hand, he patted his chest and pants, and then let out a curse under his breath.

"What?" Stacy asked. "What's wrong?"

"I'm so sorry. I left my wallet at home. I will take just a few minutes to drive back to my place, and then we'll be on our way. I hope you don't mind."

"It's fine," Stacy said with sympathy in her voice, "We all have those days."

Chapter Four

Phillip's house was a little one-story shack. The roof sagged in the middle and the porch leaned far to the right. The streetlamp on the sidewalk revealed the pillar on the porch speckled with white paint chipping off, and the house itself looked like there was never any paint on it; just light tan, shiny wood. There was a window next to the porch that looked like it hadn't been washed in quite some time. The damp grass around it needed to be mowed.

All in all Stacy thought to herself as she examined the property, *this does not look like a place I would enjoy living in.*

Stacy looked at Phillip and said, 'You live here?"

"Well, yes and no." He said, apologetically. "My mom used to live here. She left it for me in the will. I am looking for a place to live right now, but, in the meantime, I'm settling here for now and cleaning it up. I don't really like it, though. There are a lot of memories…"

His voice trailed off as his eyes darkened.

"It's okay," Stacy said as she put her hand on his. "We have all had tough times. I get it. You go in and look for what you need."

"Alright. I'll be back. I'm sure you'd understand if I asked you to wait here. The outside of my house is embarrassing enough."

"Its fine," Stacy confirmed.

As he left the car, Stacy pulled out her phone to pass the time. Phillip walked past her side of the car to walk into his house, and Stacy couldn't help but glance at him as he did. Those jeans really did look good on him…

"No." Stacy quietly scolded herself. "I can't. Not yet. I can't be with anybody. Just get through this date." She sighed as she scrolled through her various social media networks.

After five minutes, Stacy became a little concerned. She looked, hoping to see Phillip hurrying out of the door, but, he was not to be seen. *Okay*, she thought, *maybe he just misplaced his wallet or something. I can wait a bit longer. I'm sure he'll be out soon.*

But that didn't keep her from looking past his house into the black nothingness behind it. The lamplight did a marvelous job of emphasizing certain shadows and making the darkness appear so much darker. Her heart sped up while she imagined what could be waiting beyond the darkness, just out of sight. Someone? Something?

Damn she swore to herself. *I shouldn't have asked about ghost stuff. That was –*

A shadow fell over the car and vanished as something passed through the light of the lamp. She turned her head to see what it was, but found nothing.

Stacy leaned her back against the headrest and closed her eyes. *Come on, Phillip*, she silently pleaded. *Hurry up.*

The silence was broken by a light tap on the driver's side window. Stacy looked over hoping that Phillip had gotten around the car unseen. Chills crawled up her spine as she saw nothing but darkness out the window.

"Forget this," Stacy exclaimed as she unbuckled herself and kicked the door open. "I'm not having this tonight."

Stacy rushed to the door, never looking back to see what was behind her. She turned the doorknob, but the door was jammed. Panic coursed through her as she repeatedly rammed the door with her shoulder.

She paused for a moment, trying to swallow her panic and catch her breath when she heard hurried footsteps in the wet grass.

She didn't know whether or not the footsteps behind her were in her head, but they were getting closer. Letting out a strained yell, Stacy slammed her shoulder into the door one last time. The door gave way and let her inside. Slamming the door behind her, she shoved her back against it. Bending over and placing her hands on her knees, gasping gulps of air.

After a few moments, she took some time to examine what was around her. There was a hallway in front of her with an opening to her right. The hallway continued into another, smaller opening a few feet ahead of her. The only thing illuminating the house was the streetlamp outside working its way in.

Working up the courage, Stacy called, "Phillip! Hey, sorry that I came in. There was something outside and I have no idea what it was. It sounds pathetic, but, I got scared and came inside. I hope you're okay with that. Is everything okay?"

She waited to hear a response, but was only greeted by the faint echo of her own voice and an overwhelming silence.

Hesitantly, Stacy started walking down the long, dark hallway. She looked to her right and found the living room. There were two old and dusty couches placed next to each other, and a bookshelf behind the couches full of old books. A giant window faced the street. Narrow beams of light entered around pulled shades illuminating the room while still leaving shadows deep enough for something to hide in.

She turned away from the living room and continued down the narrow hallway. She nearly missed a doorway on her left just before the opening that led to a small kitchen. A pale blue light escaped from underneath the door and around the sides at the bottom.

"Phillip?" Stacy called again, fear creeping into her voice. "Phillip. Come on, where are you?"

Stacy started walking past the door, but something made her stop. She looked at the intimidatingly strong door. *I shouldn't go in*, she thought to herself. *That would be rude. But, he might be down there, and I don't like being here alone at all. Besides, if whatever is outside comes in, I'd rather have a giant door between us.*

The hallway seemed to absorb all sound except the beating of Stacy's heart as she slowly reached for the doorknob. She turned it, letting the weight of the door swing itself open into the entrance.

Stacy looked down to see steep wooden stairs illuminated by a soft pale light. The stairway was narrow and the walls made of cement.

As Stacy placed her foot on the first step, a groan of ancient disapproval sounded from the stair. Carefully, she walked down the rickety staircase and noticed the stairs were not as dusty as the rest of the house.

Finally, her foot found a solid, cemented floor that didn't moan under her weight. She looked around the room in wonder.

The room was tiny and the brown office chair that was against the desk took up about half of the floor space. There were scraps of paper pinned onto a corkboard. Some of the scraps had words scribbled on them. Others showed pictures of something that seemed to crawl out of a nightmare. She looked closely at one picture that had a circle with a star inside, and different symbols were placed around the five tips of the star. On the wall opposite the stairs, sitting on the desk was a tiny screen that emanated the pale light.

Her heart started pounding faster and she contemplated running away from the room, closing the door, and never thinking of it again. However, her curiosity trumped her better judgment as something close to the screen reflected light into her eye.

Stacy moved closer to the computer screen and started to reach for the tiny ring of metal on the surface of the desk under the monitor. However, she glanced at the picture on the monitor and a chill crawled down her spine as she realize what she was seeing.

The computer screen held the image of a room. A tiny bed with a door facing it. A light switch next to the door. She could see that the room was not very big, but it was very familiar.

Her heart dropped as she confirmed her fear. It was her room. The image on the computer was her room.

Pictures were scattered on the desk. She looked at one photo, and saw that it was of her at graduation. She saw her mom and dad holding a camera, ready to take a picture of Stacy holding her diploma from a distance. She looked at another picture, and saw herself years before that, eating in the cafeteria with some friends from a distance. The hairs on the back of her neck stood up as she looked at another picture, taken at her old house, through her window. In the picture, she was changing and her mouth was open, as if she was singing a song to herself. This one had a written message underneath, saying, "She has a beautiful voice that she hides in shame."

Stacy frantically skimmed each picture, all of them of her. Each of them, just close enough that if she would have turned her head she might have seen the photographer. A lump caught in her throat as she looked back at the screen. She leaned closer to it, examining it. *Please* Stacy begged in her mind. *Please let that be a picture.*

Her fears were realized when she looked closer through the doorframe and saw the curtain at the end of the hall moving. That image was no picture.

Her mind raced as she thought of her bedroom, trying to figure out where she was looking from. Where could this camera possibly be?

Biting back a scream, she looked at the monitor in horror. Pleading in her mind that it wasn't true, she shook in disbelief. The camera was on the bed, next to where her head usually was. Where she put it down, just after she had brought it close to her. It was her teddy bear.

"It is very impolite to sneak around someone's home uninvited," the soft voice behind her chided, no threat or malice detected within the words.

Chapter Five

Stacy slowly turned around to see Phillip standing behind her, staring at her with calm, cool eyes. He had neither happiness nor regret on his face, just a still resolve. The shadows cast by the screen made the hollows of his cheeks look endless, and shadow wrapped around his eyes, causing only a slight reflection of green to be seen. He stood straight, with his hands behind his back, looking at her with the dignity of a soldier.

Stacy stared at him, and put her back against the desk, as far as she could be from Phillip.

"Please," Phillip said, worry touching his voice. "Please, don't be like this. I didn't mean to scare you; I never meant to scare you." He reached his hand out and started slowly easing forward, like one might do with a scared animal. "Please, just hear me out," he continued, each sentence getting closer. "I just want to talk to you."

Stacy remained silent, fear making her unable to speak. Phillip continued getting closer, and Stacy had nowhere left to back up to.

She could soon feel his breath on her as he got closer. He slowly reached for her shoulders.

Stacy kneed him in the groin. As he went down, she kicked him again in the gut. He let out a startled cry and crumpled to the floor. She jumped around him and ran for the stairs.

"Stacy," Phillip groaned, disappointment touching his voice, like he was scolding a child. "Dammit, Stacy. Don't do this."

Stacy reached the first stair when she felt Phillip's hand around her ankle. He pulled it sharply, and she fell forward against the stairs. Stars flooded her vision as her forehead clipped the corner of a stair. She continued scrambling upward, lashing her caught leg out against her captor. His hold was strong, but as he shifted towards her, he inadvertently allowed her to get closer to the door.

A warm heavy liquid slid over her eyebrow as she glance up the stairs, looking at her escape. The door was just out of reach.

Suddenly, the grip changed and she was being pulled backwards. The door and her escape were getting further away. She tried to let out a cry for help, but her screams were stuck in her throat.

She felt another strong hand grip her thigh, pulling her downward. Desperate, she clung to the timeworn stairs. As she pulled in one direction and he pulled her the other, her nails gave way in blood and splinters as she lost more ground. *NO!* She screamed in her head. *No, no, no. Please, no.* The hand around her ankle let go, but then she felt an arm wrap around her hips.

"I didn't want to hurt you," Phillip panted out between breaths. "I just wanted you to love me. You have to love me. You're mine."

She kept fighting until her fingers were raw and bleeding. Phillip's body was on top of her legs, pining them down. In a final act of desperation, Stacy found a small area where the stairs and the cemented walls parted. *Please,* she pleaded in her mind. *Please, God, let this help me.* Sticking the fingers of her right hand in it, she tried pulling her upper body closer to the hole.

"Please, stop struggling," Phillip said, slight annoyance now becoming evident. "You are only making this worse."

She felt the grip on her thigh disappear, only to have it replaced by a stronger grip around her waist. The blood from her fingertips made the grip in the hole difficult to keep, and she readjusted, still trying to kick her legs. She found, however, that her legs were being held together by two larger legs. A loud pop followed by sharp pain came from Stacy's finger and she immediately pulled them out of the hole, losing more ground.

She wrapped her hands on the stairs underneath her and continued to move, trying get out of his grip. She tried to scream but, she could only let out soft grunt of pain and fear.

"No." Phillip begged, "Don't make me hurt you. I don't want to hurt you. Just stop struggling."

She felt his arm around her neck as she continued to fight against her oppressor. Her heart sped up as she realized she couldn't breathe.

She felt him pressed against her as everything started to fade. She could feel his heart racing against her back and his hot breath against her hair.

Stacy shivered in repulsion as she felt the heat of his face against hers. He whispered directly into her ear, "Stacy, I love you."

When she lost consciousness, she didn't see blackness. She saw a purple teddy bear with a stitched on smile that was keeping a secret from her. And, she heard the echo of a voice. The soft voice that she had heard so many times. The voice that seemed so familiar. The voice she had always wanted to assume was Brad's.

The smile on the purple teddy bear was not a smile at all. It was a snarl.

Chapter Six

Stacy woke up in a cold sweat gasping for air. She whipped her head around wildly, trying to see where she was, but all she discovered was darkness. A bead of sweat dropped into her eye and she went to wipe it off, only to discover that her arms were bound behind her. She tried to blink the sweat out of her eye, but it made the sweat only sting more.

Okay, Stacy thought, breathing deeply to clear her head. *Be calm, be calm. Be calm, Stacy. Now, where the hell are we?* She leaned back and moved her hips to discover the squeaking of an old wooden chair. She found that her legs were bound to the chair as well. A soft drip echoed every now and again from somewhere close by, and the scent of mildew, iron, and perspiration hung in the air. There was also a smell that Stacy didn't recognize. It was strong and similar to smoke, but different somehow.

She moved her arms and the wire stubbornly dug into her wrists. She tried again, this time twisting her arms in opposite directions. A sharp pain came from her wrist as blood trickled down to the tip of her pinky, and dribbled off. Before she was able to make another attempt, she was interrupted by a soft voice from the darkness.

"Alright, Stacy, that's enough. Please don't hurt yourself anymore. I want you to be as beautiful as you can be."

"GO TO HELL!" Stacey shouted.

The room suddenly exploded with light. Stacy jerked her head back and squinted her eyes. She looked up and saw several silhouettes stalking toward her in front of a lightbulb hanging on a chain. The lightbulb swayed ever so gently, causing the shadow in front of the silhouettes to dance on the ground.

Her eyes adjusted and she saw the walls around her were limestone. The room was spacious and empty and in the distance were plain wooden steps leading up to a trap door on the ceiling. The floor was clean and made of finished concrete. She saw that there was a chalk drawing around her set up as a circle with a five-pointed star on the inside. She was in the center of the star. A dense mist hung in the air and she could see smoke flowing out of metal bowls that were placed next to odd symbols, maybe an ancient language of some sort. She looked over and noticed an empty wooden chair close to hers. There was no only one silhouette and as it got closer, she recognized the smell and look of him. Phillip Miller.

"That's not very nice," Phillip said in a mocking tone. "And here I went through all this trouble decorating just for you."

"What the hell do you mean?" Stacy spat.

"Careful," Phillip warned, all joking over. "You forget which one of us is tied up. I don't want to hurt anymore, but I have a temper. I don't want to do something irrational, but..." a snarl touched his lips and his eyes met hers, "I'm only human."

"What do you want?" Stacy asked, keeping no resentment out of her voice.

Phillip strolled over to the empty chair and dragged it in front of Stacy's, the back of it facing her. "Quite simply, you." he answered as he straddled the chair. He crossed his arms over the top and casually rested his chin on them. He stared into Stacy's eyes with admiration and joy. A hint of a smile graced his lips. Then, with a quick inhale, he pulled his head back and said, "I bet you're absolutely confused, aren't you? How about this? I will answer a few questions for you. Does that sound good? After all, today is a good day. I'm happy for the first time in a long time."

"I've got no questions for you," Stacy growled. She was tired of listening to him, and she didn't want to reward him with the sound of his own voice echoing throughout the room.

"Oh, come on," Phillip teased, leaning closer and tipping his chair in her direction. "I know you're curious."

Stacy looked at the floor, turning away from him as much as she could. She realized that her chair was bolted to the floor.

Phillip, taking the hint, let out a huff of air. "Well," he said after a long silence, "I guess I will continue to admire you. I can do that." He stretched his hand close to her face and lightly caressed her cheek, down to her jaw, and to her neck. He then brought his hand back as he saw the gooseflesh crawl from where he touched. "I've wanted to admire you in person for such a long time," he breathed, closing his eyes. He inhaled and let out a soft sigh that made the hairs on the back of Stacy's neck rise.

Stacy saw him reaching for her again, so she finally asked, "Why?"

Phillip paused and smiled as he brought his hand back. "Why what?"

"Why did you kill him?"

Stacy felt a surge of triumph as she saw Phillip's smile vanish. Phillip rubbed his fingers around his chin and his eyebrows went up. "Who told you that? I didn't kill your boyfriend. He was speeding down the road on a foggy night. He was being reckless. All I did was provide a..." A smile touched his lips as he said, "worst case scenario."

"So, that's when you put that bear in his car." Stacy drilled, malice and rage bubbling over. "That's when you put that bear that you recorded your voice on in his damn car—" She broke off, and tears slid down her cheeks, cutting through the sweat and grime. She didn't want to cry in front of a scumbag like him but, but the emotions came bursting out through clenched teeth. "Damn you," she spat.

Phillip looked at her with concerned eyes. He tilted his head and stretched one of his hands to her chin. "Hey," he said, in a soft and understanding voice. "Shhh, hey, listen. I know. I know." Forcing her chin up so she would look at him, he wiped her tears with his thumb. "I didn't want to," Phillip said. "I never wanted to do any of these things. I never wanted to hurt you, and I never wanted to watch you cry. But, I had to. I know you'll understand. I had to get rid of him. He was holding you back. I couldn't let that happen. He was going to ruin everything and take you away. I couldn't let him do that to you. You don't belong to him. You belong to me."

Stacy pulled her head away and looked at the floor. Through eyes full of tears, she glared at Phillip. "Go to hell," she whispered.

"Well," Phillip said, sounding disappointed. He stood and began walking away. "That's unfortunate. I was hoping you would understand where I was coming from. I hoped that you could see that I couldn't let him give you…" Pausing, he shook his head and dismissed the thought. "Never mind. It's not important."

Raising her head, Stacy peered at Phillip. "What was he going to give me?"

"It's not important." Phillip repeated, pointing his finger down on each syllable for emphasis.

"No…" Stacy said, with realization. The tears stopped only to be replaced with a sick knot in her stomach. The room began to move as nausea overcame her. A ringing started in her head, and all she could do was concentrate on not throwing up.

She understood what Brad was going to give her. She realized what the metal shine in Phillip's room was. Why the present had to be different. Why Brad was so excited to see her that night. "It was…an engagement ring."

"No. No, no, NO!" Phillip whimpered. He raked his fingers through his hair and stomped his foot. "You weren't supposed to find out! You aren't supposed to know. You need to love me! Forget Brad! He's meaningless. No. NO!" He grabbed his chair and flung it across the room, breaking one of the legs and leaving marks on the limestone wall.

He took a calming breath. "It's okay." Phillip reassured himself, one hand on his hip and the other in his hair. "He won't mind. He can work around this. He's powerful. This will work."

Stacy watched in horror as Phillip trembled with fear. The smooth confidence was replaced with childlike terror, and beads of sweat fell onto his brow. He licked his lips self-consciously and his eyes began to water.

"This all can't be for nothing," he said, turning around and walking toward the stairs. "Please let him be okay."

"Who?" Stacy called.

Phillip turned around and pointed at Stacy. "NONE OF YOUR BUSINESS!" Suddenly, it looked like he realized who he had just shouted at, and took a deep breath. He smoothed his shirt out and slid his fingers through his hair as he said with restraint, "Enough questions for today."

As he put a hand on the trap door, Stacy said, "You might as well kill me."

Phillip stopped and stood still. Sorrow shone through his dark green eyes as he slowly turned his head toward Stacy.

"Why?" Phillip asked, concern written all over his face.

"You're sick and pathetic. I will never love you. You killed the only man I ever loved."

A dead silence crept into the room. Stacy braced herself for the worst. She wanted to die right then, because she didn't want him to have the satisfaction of taking her life. However, Phillip didn't react like she thought he would.

As Phillip stared at her, the deep frown was slowly replaced by a genuine smile, and soon that was overtaken by a snarl. "Oh, you will love me. You will have no choice. You'll forget about him. And, don't worry. I promise you, Stacy, after tonight, this will all be just a bad dream."

He turned his head and made his way up the stairs. Opening the trap door, he called, "Stacy, I love you."

The thud of the trap door echoed throughout the room.

Chapter Seven

Stacy woke up to someone gently shaking her. "Stacy? Honey? Are you okay?" The room was blurry and the voice muffled. Slowly, everything began to come into focus as the voice became clearer. "Stacy, wake up. Stacy? Are you okay, Stacy?" The soft voice became clear and the room lost its fog. Sitting up in her bed, she placed her palm on her head and tried to blink away the headache.

"Yeah, honey. I'm fine. Just a bad dream, that's all. Why?"

"You were screaming in your sleep again," her husband replied, concern etched into his features. "You've been having those dreams more often. Are you sure you don't want to see someone?"

"I'm fine," she said, shaking it off. "I've just been reading too many paranormal books lately. I'll be fine."

The ringing started as soon as she yawned. That was one feature of these kinds of dreams. They always left her scared. However, when she tried to remember them, she never could. Then, the ringing would start, convincing her to stay away from the dream.

Her husband got out of bed and walked over to the bathroom a few feet away from their bed. He opened the door and walked in. "So," he said, quizzically from the small room, "Did you have the nightmare about being kidnapped again?"

He got undressed and opened the shower curtain, stepping inside.

"Yeah," Stacy replied. "I can never remember the details. But, this time I remember a ritual. And a metal ring..."

The ringing in her head grew louder as she tried to claw at the nightmare. A ring...why did this ring have so much sadness attached to it? A cold piece of metal, with so much meaning around it. What was it trying to tell her? Why was she so sad? So scared? Who gave her the ring...

"Stacy."

The ringing abruptly stopped as her husband pulled her out of her thoughts. He was now out of the shower, and wearing a blue shirt with the top button undone, a red silk tie that hung loosely around his neck, black pants, black shoes, and his leather belt. He had his hand gently placed on her shoulder.

"Yeah, honey?" Stacy said, looking at him.

"Have you been listening to anything I said?"

"Oh…yeah, I think,"

He moved his head closer to hers and looked her in the eye. "Are you sure you're okay? I can stay home if you want me to."

"No," Stacy said grateful for his concern, but gently pushing him away. "I'll be fine. You go to work, and bring home that sweet bacon."

She lightly smacked his butt as he walked to the mirror near their bed.

"Alright," he said, smiling back at her. "If you insist."

He brought his fingers to the top button of his shirt and worked at buttoning it. "You remember that we are having dinner with Amber and her husband, right?"

He looked away from the button to look at her reflection in the mirror.

Stacy let out a groan. "Again? Didn't we see them a few weeks ago?"

Her husband let out a soft chuckle as he tightened his tie. "Funny how friends want to see other friends more than just once a month, isn't it?"

"That means that I actually have to clean the house a bit and make dinner, doesn't it? Man, having friends is rough." Stacy concluded wryly, lying back down on her pillow.

"Oh, come on," her husband said, walking back toward her. He sat on the edge of the bed and put his hand on the side of her face. Stacy looked into his eyes. He looked back into hers. "After all," her husband continued, a smile touching his lips, "she was the one that introduced us."

Stacy rolled her eyes. "You're right. I guess friends are good for some things. Now, seriously, Phillip, you need to get to work. You're going to be late. I put your lunch in the fridge. Grab a banana before you leave."

Phillip smiled and kissed her forehead. "Have I ever told you what a wonderful wife you are?"

Stacy blushed and smiled back, "Yeah, but I can always hear it again."

"You are an amazing wife. Stacy, I love you."

"I love you, too."

Phillip stood and grabbed his suit jacket and headed for the door. He paused as he was about to open the door, and turned to look at Stacy.

"Honey, I'm going to talk to someone about the dreams. You won't have them anymore. I promise. Okay?"

Stacy smiled at him, his concern warming her hear. "Okay."

Phillip opened the door and closed it behind him. Stacy listened as the front door closed followed by the sound of Phillip's car starting.

She was just about to get out of bed when she looked at the dresser that was opposite the bathroom. It was a medium height, plain wooden dresser, with her jewelry on top, right next to her purple teddy bear. She stared at it for a moment, paying no attention to the ringing that slowly started up again.

There was something about that teddy bear that seemed wrong. She would normally look at the teddy bear's sweet smile and be comforted. She loved to press its paw and hear Phillip say back, "Stacy, I love you."

Today, however, she got a chill from the teddy bear's fake smile, and dead eyes. Something was off, and the more she tried to figure out what it was, the louder the ringing got. She shook her head, dismissing the thought. *There's nothing wrong with him*, she concluded. *I'm just imagining things. He's not watching me.*

She walked over to her bathroom and began to remove her clothes to take a shower. She looked over her shoulder at the teddy bear's fake smile.

She slowly closed the door to the bathroom.

THE HOTEL CALIFORNIA

by

Donnie Light

I'd been driving through Hell for an hour before I began to reconsider the wisdom of my adventure and started to look for a place to get ice water.

Hell, in this case, meant somewhere in the Mohave Desert. My ill-considered adventure began with a spur-of-the-moment decision to buy a car in Vegas and drive back to LA and to the comforts of home for a few days. I had a week to myself before our next gig, and I looked forward to enjoying some downtime and getting my head right again.

My brand new '77 Corvette clipped along a dark desert highway at eighty, and I listened to the rumble of the big V-8 under the fiberglass hood. Damn, it felt good to be away from the guys for a little while. Cruising through the middle of nowhere, the wind whipped my long blond hair out behind my head like a stallion's mane at full gallop.

I looked up and saw the stars, millions of them, painted boldly on the moonless canvas above me. The lighter band of the Milky Way made me feel small for a few moments as I contemplated my life and where it had led me recently. And it was definitely *life* that led *me*, as I seemed to have no input.

My name is Adam Moss, (fans call me Hatchet), and I'm the drummer and primary songwriter for a rock band called The Fast Lane. That name still bugs me, as it was not the original name of the band, but the one the record company wanted us to use. No, let me rephrase that—*it was the name they insisted we use*—and that was that.

The band—me and three other guys I'd known since high school—was originally called Tulsa, because that's the closest big city to where we all grew up. But the record company always knows best (or so we were told) so the marketing division came up with the name The Fast Lane and made us sign on the dotted line. Seemed like a good idea at the time.

I had a handful of tapes in my duffel bag and I dragged out a couple. I thought music would take my mind off my problems for a while, and stop this constant voice in my head that questioned my decisions of late. Was I really considering giving it all up so soon after getting there?

The first tape I grabbed was ZZ Top. Man, those dudes from Texas knew how to rock the house, but I wasn't in the mood for them, so I considered a Stones tape for moment. They were my favorite band at the time, but the Stones just didn't fit my current melancholia. The next tape I found was one of our own, so I tossed it back. I'd heard those songs hundreds of times, and wanted to get away from The Fast Lane. One more grab and I came up with Bob Dylan, which I considered a perfect choice. I crammed the tape into the 'Vette's cassette slot and turned the volume up to where I could feel the bass in the back of the seat and could see the vibrations in the rearview mirror. It was time to find that ice water. My throat had become as dry as the endless sand and scrub that surrounded me, but I didn't see a light anywhere. All that lay before me was a black two-lane ribbon that seemed endless.

After Dylan's third song, I decided that I really needed quiet instead. Life in The Fast Lane had gotten into my head, like a headache that aspirin wouldn't touch.

We had signed with the record company two years before, and our first album did pretty well. Things were simpler back then, and being in the band had been a hoot. We didn't have much money, but we'd never had any before, either. We were just four boys from the low hills of Oklahoma, playing a gig now and again at the local honky-tonks and county fairs. We all had day jobs, and played in the band for kicks. Sure, we dreamed of hitting it big and playing in sold-out venues, but none of us expected it to really happen.

Then the second album came out and, to our surprise, we had a big hit on our hands. A song called *Mystery Momma* hit the charts and climbed into the top ten. We got play time on radio stations all across the country, and even some play in England too. Of course, it excited us knowing that we had a big hit, and that's when life really got interesting.

Sales shot skyward, and then that album produced another hit called *Livin' Loose.* About that time, we went on tour with our own warm up band.

The next few months passed in a blur. Sometimes I couldn't remember what state we were in, much less what town. Our old tour bus became our roadies' bus, and we got a new one with custom paint and chrome wheels. A semi-truck and a couple of vans filled with equipment rounded out the little Fast Lane caravan that rolled steadily all year long.

Jimmy, Robbie and Max all seemed to dig it, and who wouldn't? The money poured in, even though the bastards at the record company took the lion's share for themselves and robbed us blind. It was big money, too, but none of us really cared. We had plenty, and our manager got us anything we wanted. I sent lots of money back to my folks in Wright City, and they put it up for me. I didn't need much. Hell, the record company executives had us wearing worn-out jeans and threadbare tee shirts because marketing said that was cool and the fans would dig it. That's what life turned into for me and the boys; someone constantly telling us to be here, go there, do this, sign that, drink this and swallow these.

At some point, I realized I'd been hit by a stroke of blind luck. By all rights, I should have been working in Daddy's hardware store in Wright City. I would likely have married Brenda Jane and had a kid or two and maybe a small house somewhere.

What should have been and what actually was couldn't have been further apart. Brenda Jane wouldn't even speak to me, the big famous rock star, when I went home from time to time.

The last time I went home, Daddy took me into the store's back room, amid the boxes of nails and lengths of black pipe. He stared me right in the eye and said that I looked like I'd aged a decade in the past two years; that I was burnin' the candle at both ends. After telling me to be careful, he took out his pocket testament and read me a line of scripture. *'For what is a man profited, if he shall gain the whole world, and lose his own soul? Or what shall a man give in exchange for his soul?'*

That bugged me a little. I've always tried my best to do right, and I know Daddy had his reasons for reading that to me. To be honest, back then I sometimes felt like I had sold my soul to the devil, but I told Daddy that I heard and understood, and for him and Momma to not worry. I told him that I would get home more often, and that I'd get a haircut next time I was in town. He gave me a look like I was telling him a tall tale and that hurt me more than anything he could have said.

I brought my mind back to my Corvette and the desert night and realized I was doing over a hundred miles an hour. I took my foot off the gas and let the little silver sports car catch its breath. Up ahead in the distance, lights shimmered in the last of the heat rising off the hot desert floor. My head felt a bit foggy, and my eyes burned with a combination of weariness and confusion.

Closer to the lights, I realized it wasn't a truck stop, but a small collection of various buildings. The first sign read *La misión de las almas perdidas.* I guessed it was some historic Spanish mission. A souvenir trading post boasting authentic Indian jewelry sat dark, closed for the night, and beside that, the CB radio shop was closed as well. The largest building hosted a sign that read *Welcome to the Hotel*

California in Spanish style writing. The big hotel's Southwestern architecture boasted lots of complex corners and portales, balconies and walkways. The ground lights cast harsh, eerie shadows, making it difficult to tell how much detail hid in the darkness.

It was obviously a nice place. Exotic cars filled the parking lot. Even in the relative darkness I could tell the grounds were immaculate. Several stately palm trees dotted the visible property in front of the building.

I killed the Corvette's engine and sat for a moment, listening to the engine tick as it cooled. I watched the lighted entryway for movement and saw a couple enter the building through the main doors. It looked like an interesting place, so I entertained the thought of spending the night and finishing the trip the next morning. I have regretted that mistake every day since.

I snatched the duffel bag off the passenger seat and made my way to the front doors. The large lobby's shiny tile floors seemed to go on forever in every direction. Just to my left at the counter, a strange-looking man in a suit watched me approach. He was thin—far too thin to look healthy. He wore a cheesy narrow mustache over slim lips, and dark circles ringed his eyes. He smiled when our eyes met, and a gold-capped front tooth glinted in the light.

"Good evening, señor," he said. "Welcome to the Hotel California. Will you be joining us tonight?"

"Yes," I said, still unsure that I wanted to, but so tired that I needed to.

"And how many in your party?" he asked, gold tooth gleaming like a beacon.

"It's just me."

"Very well." He pulled some papers from below the counter, then efficiently filled in the lines, requesting information for each one. His writing was beautiful, full of graceful loops and precise angles. The ornate bracelet on his right wrist jangled as he wrote.

While he finished filling out the form, a beautiful woman walked up behind the counter. She wore a long black dress that emphasized her turquoise-colored eyes. Her black hair flowed over her bare shoulders like a dark stream over smooth stone. A large diamond pendant hung in the center of her cleavage, the diamond flanked on each side by three smaller stones. Sizeable rubies in gold mounts graced each earlobe.

Her eyes met mine and I could not look away.

"Do you need any help with luggage?" the man asked.

I held up my duffel bag. "Got it all right here."

The woman put an arm around the thin man and gave his shoulder a gentle squeeze. "I will show our guest to his room, Hernando." Her voice was as silky as her dress, and I found myself staring at her, admiring her striking presence.

She picked up a key off the counter, hung it back on the board, and took a different one. Then she curled a finger toward me. "Please follow me, señor." Her long nails were polished the same color as her turquoise eyes. She walked toward a corridor on the far side of the lobby and I followed.

As I fell into cadence with her elegant strides, I could not help but notice the sway of her hips and the way her silky gown clung to her perfect form. The scent she wore wafted discreetly across my path, enticing me.

She stopped at a darkened stairway, reached into an antique cupboard and withdrew a tall, peach-colored candle in a silver holder, the kind I had only seen in old movies. She struck a match, and the flare lit her beautiful face in such a way that I could no longer remain silent.

"May I ask your name?"

She glanced sidelong at me while she held the match to the wick, awaiting the flame to catch. She then shook out the match, and I watched the curl of smoke lift from its shriveled head.

"You may call me Maria." Her voice flowed from her like a finely tuned violin. I thought if I played music for the rest of my life I'd never hear anything so sweet again.

"Your room is at the top of the stairs," she said. "Come, I will show you the way."

There were no lights in the stairway, which I found a little odd, but as I looked over Maria's shoulder to the top of the stairs, I could see a faint glow above her.

"This is the oldest part of the hotel," she explained. "We have not updated it because some of our guests like the nostalgic feel of the days of old." She reached the landing, stepped aside and turned toward me. "I'm sure you will find the room to your liking. If you do not, you will tell me, sí?"

I nodded, only because the look on her face seemed to be waiting for an answer. My mind was totally wrapped in her mental embrace; her presence like a thick smoke that filled the hallway. I breathed her in, unable to resist smoke so intoxicating.

She swung open the door to a room, moved to an old wall light that hung inside the door, and turned a knob. Weak yellow light joined the candlelight, and together they danced on the papered walls.

"There is electricity in the rooms," she said in her elegant Spanish accent. "But the wiring is old and cannot power modern electronics." She set the candle on the old desk in one corner. "But you did not come here to watch the television, am I right?"

Those eyes had me again. My mind was surely not working right, but no drugs pumped through my system, I swear. Only her. TV was the furthest thing from my mind at that moment.

I nodded again as she took the candle from its holder and used it to light another on the nightstand beside the bed.

"You came here to clear your mind," she said, giving me that sidelong glance again. "This is the perfect room for that, señor." She put her candle back in the holder, picked it up, then walked toward the door. As she stood in the doorway, I heard a bell toll and remembered the mission across the road. The key to the room dangled from her fingertips.

I walked toward her and reached for the key. She placed it gently in my hand, then caressed the side of my face. Taking my chin in her hand, she turned my head one way, then the other, carefully studying something.

"What is your name, señor?"

"Adam." My voice seemed to come from somewhere else, as if I were hearing this exchange from a room down the hall.

"Ahhh... Adam. God's first man, sí?"

"Yes, I suppose," I heard myself answer.

"Well, Señor Adam," she said, still holding my chin, but now looking into my eyes. "By morning, you will shave, sí?"

My captive mind knew that shaving would be a bad thing for me, the drummer of a popular rock band. The guys would never let me live it down. It also struck me that asking me to shave was an odd and unusual thing to request of a guest.

"Sí," I replied when I found my voice. "I will shave." I got the response I wanted, because she smiled.

"Ahh...," she cooed, then stroked the side of my face again with a touch as soft as a lover's whisper. "I shall enjoy seeing your face, without the beard."

"Sí," I again replied, unable to do otherwise.

"And tomorrow, in the evening, we will dine together, you and I?"

"Yes, tomorrow evening," I said, *realizing* that I answered without thinking first.

She kissed her fingertips then placed them on the side of my face. "Tomorrow, my lips will touch your clean-shaven face."

"Yes." So mesmerized by her touch, I wanted it to be tomorrow evening right then.

"Very well, Señor Adam," she said with that sly smile of hers. "I will be waiting for you."

She then stepped into the hall and turned toward the stairs, but not before blessing me with one final glance over her bare shoulder. Then she was gone, the light of her candle fading as she descended the creaky wooden steps.

I stepped into the hallway and looked in her direction, wondering what I had just experienced. My Bad Sense told me that this could be Heaven, while my Good Sense reminded me that this could be Hell.

Then, from down the corridor, I heard Hernando's distant voice greeting another guest.

"Welcome to the Hotel California."

I heard the guest comment that it was such a lovely place, and then asked if they had any available rooms.

"Plenty of room at the Hotel California," Hernando replied.

I closed my door and looked around the room. This part of the hotel had been built around the turn of the century, based on the doorknobs, light fixtures and other hardware. I did, after all, grow up in a hardware store, and my daddy taught me well.

The bed looked like it came from that same period. Ornate brass headboard and footboard, polished to a brilliant sheen. Heavy velvet curtains (I could not tell the color in the dim light) hung at the sides of the single window, with elegant lace sheers beneath them. Paintings hung on two adjacent walls. Both were landscapes—one depicting a sunny meadow filled with wildflowers—the other showed dark clouds over a distant mountain range.

I sat down on the bed and fell onto my back, still wondering what had just happened to me. I wondered about Maria, and tried to determine exactly what about her had me acting like a boy in puberty.

Having been in a big-time rock band allowed me to meet my share of ladies, and I had certainly spent more than my share of nights in a hotel. Truth be known, I have spent a lot of time with a lot of women in a lot of hotels. But Maria and the Hotel California had given me a whole new take on both subjects.

Lying on my bed, deep in perplexing thought, I also felt restless and decided I'd rather take a walk as I thought about…it…her…

I grabbed a pack of smokes from my bag and headed for the lobby. Hernando nodded at me with a strange grin as I made my way out the doors. The night air had cooled considerably since I parked the Corvette earlier. I lit my smoke and took a deep drag, filling my lungs with poison while trying to clear my mind of Maria.

After pacing around the carport for a moment, I heard laughter from the side of the building. I made my way in the direction of the amusement and discovered a small courtyard. Miniature lights set in the ground between the ornamental plants and trees cast a soft, indirect illumination on a dozen people who mingled on a flagstone patio.

I watched from a distance as I smoked, noticing all of the people dressed nicely. Not formally dressed, but many of the men wore open-collared shirts under light jackets. The few women in attendance wore long gowns or dresses. I could also see many sparkling jewels and precious metals among both the men and women as they tipped their glasses and told their stories.

At one side of the patio, a bartender stood behind a table draped in white linen, mixing drinks and discreetly accepting tips. Bottles of various sizes and shapes covered the table.

One corner of the patio held a gazebo, painted white and covered in climbing vines that clung to the latticework. Then I saw her, seated in the gazebo, sipping from a goblet.

Our eyes met for an instant. She turned to the man she was talking to and must have excused herself, because she got up and began to walk toward me. I crushed out my cigarette as she sauntered my way, stopping briefly to speak to a man who also glanced in my direction. He appeared to be the oldest person there. His gray hair in a severe crew-cut matched his stocky, muscular build. He stood stiffly while Maria whispered something into his ear, then nodded and turned away.

"Señor Adam," she said as she approached. "Are you unable to sleep?"

I shook my head. "I'm tired, but not sleepy. I'm still unwinding from the drive."

She nodded and took a sip from her goblet. The wine in the glass was the darkest I had ever seen. It clung to her lips and reflected the soft light. Then she gave me a wry grin and narrowed those turquoise eyes.

"Perhaps a drink will help you to unwind, sí? You will come and join us for a while before you must sleep?"

"No, that's okay. I'm really not dressed for a party," I stammered, looking down at my faded jeans and black tee shirt.

"Oh, but I must insist." She took me by the hand and led me toward the gathering. I tried to resist, but the attempt was futile. I felt like a puppy in the talons of an imposing dragon.

We stopped when we reached the gray-haired man. "Captain Benson," she said. "Please meet Señor Adam, God's first man." Then she giggled and took a long drink of her wine.

Captain Benson turned to me, and nodded almost imperceptibly. Maria had called him 'Captain,' and he did have the air of a military man, standing at salute with arms flat to his sides.

"Our friend would like a drink, Captain," Maria said. "Would you, please?"

The captain gazed at me with gray eyes. "What's your pleasure, son?" he asked without any expression.

I thought for just a second, and as I was about to speak, Maria interrupted me.

"Tequila." She looked at me as if expecting me to agree, which I did.

I raised both palms upward at the waist. "Tequila it is."

Maria smiled. She again took me by the hand and led me to a wrought-iron bench at the edge of the courtyard. Waving a hand at the bench, she asked me to take a seat.

"The night is still young," she said. She took the final sip from her glass before walking away, and I noticed that a residue still clung thickly to the sides. At that point, I knew she was not drinking wine.

The captain returned in a moment with a short glass of tequila and handed it to me without a word. He left again, and took a position at the edge of the patio, seemingly awaiting his next order.

Alone on the bench, I felt very much out of place as I sipped the tequila and watched the people. The crowd consisted mostly of men. Except for the captain, they all seemed about my age, in their early to mid-twenties. I also noticed them all cleanly shaven, with moderate to shoulder-length hair.

Maria returned to the gazebo where she joined two other men and a woman at a small table in the center. She took a decanter and refilled her goblet, then took another deep drink.

I watched and listened for few more minutes until the effects of the tequila began to kick in, and my eyes grew heavy. I lit another smoke and drained my glass, ready to walk again and to try to figure out what I was doing and why I was still here.

As I lay on my bed that night, my body finally relaxed, but my mind churned with errant thoughts. Who was this Maria, and what interest did she have in me? What was this bit about me shaving my beard, and joining her for dinner? I had only intended to stay the night, which brought up the most troubling question of all. Why did I say yes to her request for dinner the next night?

Some part of me wanted more than anything to have dinner with Maria. I felt that if I didn't, I would regret it for the rest of my life. That feeling, strong in my mind, made me determined to have that dinner, and see what I could find out about the alluring Maria.

Yet, another part of my mind screamed that something was wrong. I felt like I could not say no to Maria, even if I had wanted to. It was as if she were a bad drug and I was a junkie, powerless to walk away. The whole situation somehow seemed right, and yet wrong at the same time.

I know I drifted off to sleep a few times that night because I dreamed of Maria. The fleeting, senseless dreams told no story and contained no dialog, just images of Maria and feelings of eagerness mixed with dread. I awoke on more than one occasion in a sweat, with my heart beating rapidly, although I could not remember anything except the images of Maria. At other times, (I'm not sure if I dreamed this or if I was just in a stupor) I awoke to the sound of Hernando greeting guests downstairs. *Welcome to the Hotel California.*

When I next awoke, the sun was shining in the window, casting crazy, slanted shadows toward the floor. I felt like hell physically, but mentally I was excited to see the new day. With no clock on the wall, nor an alarm clock on the nightstand, I dug my watch out of my bag and discovered it was ten in the morning. Being a big rock star meant that I often slept during the day and stayed awake all night, especially after a concert. After playing fast and hard for a couple of hours in front of thousands of screaming fans, it was hard to just turn it off when the concert ended. Being up at 10 a.m. still felt mighty early in my book.

I pulled on my Levis and went to the main desk in the lobby. A different man stood there, a bit younger than Hernando. He had slick black hair and a thin mustache that looked like it had been drawn on his upper lip. He was busy with some papers, so I waited silently. A name tag pinned to the front of his vest said *Hector*. A moment later, Hector glanced up and noticed me waiting.

"Señor?" he asked. "May I be of service?"

"Yes," I said, with the flair of an important guest. "I'm going to be staying for another night and I need some supplies. How far is it to the nearest town with some decent stores?"

"Well, señor, we do have supplies in the gift shop. What exactly are you looking for?"

"Clothes. I left with only what I have on and I have an important dinner tonight."

Hector gave me directions to a town thirty minutes away, and the name of the store that I should look for. I walked out to the Corvette and drove past twenty miles of scrub and cacti, until I saw buildings emerge from the waves of heat rising from the blacktop.

A little over two hours later, I parked in front of the Hotel California again. I had bought shaving supplies and new clothes, including a real kick-ass suit that I hoped would make an impression on Maria later that evening. I put the T-tops back on the 'Vette just to keep the blistering sun from cooking the black leather seats.

Back in my room, I set to getting rid of a four-inch beard. As I watched the remnants of my beard fall into the old sink, the guy in the mirror started to look more familiar. I saw that kid again, the one who only three years ago still worked in his dad's hardware store and played local gigs after closing time. That same innocent kid who had never seen people snort cocaine through a hundred-dollar bill or stick a needle in their arm in an attempt to feel better about themselves. He'd never seen the women who performed dirty deeds for a handful of pills and the chance to say they had slept with a rock star. That same baby-faced boy had fallen in love with Brenda Jane back in high school. The same kid that Brenda Jane had fallen out of love with soon after The Fast Lane became a big hit.

As my former face emerged from behind the beard, I realized that I loved that kid and had really missed him. It dawned on me that I had grown a beard to hide that face—perhaps from myself, but certainly from others. I know that must sound pretty messed up, but sometimes the truth hurts. I hid that kid away by covering him up in hopes that he wouldn't see all of the crap going on around me these days. I hoped he wouldn't see me do some things that I was not particularly proud of, and I hoped he still loved me, even just a little. But now that he was here, I wanted to get a message to him; *being rich and famous can be hazardous to your soul.*

Just as those thoughts came pouring forth, I heard the mission bells tolling again. It reminded me of being lonely, and I realized how much I missed Brenda Jane.

As I said earlier, there was no TV in my room. Not even a clock radio. There wasn't anything that made any noise. I was used to noise, and the silence started to drive me crazy. So while I put the razor to my face, I did what I used to do before The Fast Lane—I hummed my favorite tunes and made up a few of my own.

Just seeing that kid again made me a little happier, probably because it took me back a few years. Back to a happier time when I drove my daddy's old truck to school, and picked up Brenda Jane on the way. I had very little money then, so Brenda and I would go Dutch when we went to the Burger Barn on Friday nights after the game.

I remember smiling at that kid in the mirror, remembering that I was happier being broke and driving that old truck around. Out in the parking lot sat a brand-new Corvette, and I didn't even know how much it cost. I just told my business manager I wanted one, and he brought it to me a few hours later. I had gotten used to that but, like I said before, that kind of treatment could be hazardous to my soul.

Then I reflected on how confident that kid was, and how he had plans for his future, plans that excited him as he looked forward to the challenges he knew would come. Never had he dreamed of anything like The Fast Lane happening to him back in those days when a little dab of Brylcreem helped keep his blond hair in place while he played second base with gifted hands. He'd been confident when he collected soda bottles along the side of the road so he could buy that Schwinn Sting Ray with his own hard-earned money. And by God, that kid did just that, one glass penny at a time.

I enjoyed my quiet time after that and wanted to be sure to thank Maria for putting me in that room with no TV or radio. It was good to have to do my own thinking for a change and not let somebody else's thoughts invade my head and make my decisions. I actually picked up a paperback copy of Stephen King's *Carrie* from the gift shop and read a few chapters that afternoon in the quiet room. It turned out to be one of the best days I'd had in a long time. Just me, myself, and the kid.

At five o'clock that afternoon, I wandered down to the lobby and discovered Hernando back at the desk. He watched as I approached.

"Good evening, señor," he said. "Welcome to the Hotel California."

I reminded him that I was staying at the hotel, and a look of recognition came over his face. I had been a bearded hoodlum in jeans and tee-shirt when I checked in, and now I was clean shaven and wearing slacks and a polo shirt. I told him that Maria had invited me to dinner that evening, and I wondered if he knew where I could find her.

"Ahhh… Miss Maria will contact you, I am sure," he said.

"Okay, please tell her that I was looking for her."

"Sí, señor. I will give her the message."

I decided to explore the hotel, and found myself wandering down a wide corridor. Just a few steps from the lobby I found a bar called the 'Golden Sunset.' The front opened to the corridor, and several people sat at the bar and others at tables scattered about the room. I decided that a drink was in order, hoping it would help me feel more relaxed before my dinner with Maria.

I took a stool between two other men at the bar and ordered a tequila mockingbird. A woman worked the bar, and in her efficient manner, she had my drink in front of me in just a minute. The man to my left looked to be thirty or so, was dressed in a jacket and wore an expensive watch. He nursed his drink, and then looked down, deep in thought. The man to my right, about my age, seemed more energetic, and drank with vigor. He turned my way and gave a brief nod, then lifted his glass toward me. After a few seconds, I realized he meant to toast, so I raised my glass, and he touched his to mine.

"To the Hotel California," he said, then gulped down the remainder of his drink.

The man to my left heard the exchange, and mockingly raised his glass, toasting no one.

The vigorous drinker then got up, brushed the wrinkles from his slacks, and slapped a bill on the bar top. He walked away, clapping a man on the back who sat a few stools down as he left.

The man on my left looked up, watched him leave, and said, "He must be new around here." He then looked at me, took a sip of his drink, and said, "You must be new here, too. I haven't seen you before."

I didn't know exactly how to take that comment, except to think the man was drunker than he looked. *New around here?* I thought. *It's a hotel.* I took a sip while I thought it over, then answered the man.

"I just stopped in on a whim. I was too tired to make it back to LA last night."

He looked at me with a strange grin on his face, which I again attributed to him being drunk. He glanced at his Rolex. "Stopped for the night, huh? And yet, you're still here."

A moment of silence ensued as we both took another sip. He seemed to be in a bad mood, and I didn't want to get involved. I had enough trouble of my own; no need to share in his.

"Let me guess," the man said. "I'm betting that you have dinner with someone a little later. Am I right?"

Now I was surprised. I turned to him and that strange grin of his grew.

"Yeah, I thought so," he said. "You look like the type." With that, he finished his drink, and like the other man, laid a bill on the bar and left.

I chalked that conversation up as one that I wish I'd never had. It gave me the creeps the way he laid it out and the way he grinned. Looking back, I wish I had been a little brighter and had taken it as it was meant—as a warning.

The woman working the bar, whom I later found was named Lucinda, apparently heard the exchange. As she removed his glass and wiped the bar, she said, "I believe he has had too much to drink." She looked at me, waiting for a reaction.

"Sounds that way," I remember saying as I pondered the meaning of his words.

I had a sudden urge to go back to my room and chill out for a while until I made contact with Maria. I settled up at the bar and walked through the lobby.

The lobby, brilliantly lit, reflected the red-gold color of the descending sun coming through the front doors and windows. Sunset was still an hour away, but the shadows outside the door grew longer with each passing minute.

I began to wonder if I was being stood up by Maria. I had not heard from her, and had no way of contacting her. I decided that if she did not show up soon, I would make my way back to LA as I had originally planned.

When I got to my room, I noticed a note taped to the door. It informed me that Maria would meet me at the gazebo at eight o'clock, and that I should come prepared to go to dinner.

At least then I knew, even if I had to learn it from an anonymous note. The note, unsigned and not written in first-person, indicated to me that Maria had not written it. Just knowing that I would see her soon got my memories from the previous night flowing, and I paced the room, thinking of clever things to say to the mysterious beauty. My desire to impress her was profound, and I still did not know why.

By ten minutes of eight, my pulse rate was higher than normal and tiny beads of sweat broke out on my forehead. I tried to calm down, knowing that my nervousness was not only unusual, but concerning as well. I had only met this woman briefly the night before, so my brain said that if I never saw her again, I would have lost nothing. And yet, my heart beat furiously with the anticipation of seeing her and hearing that luxurious voice with the Mexican accent.

I took a deep breath, brushed my teeth, and headed for the gazebo. The sun had set, but the wispy clouds in the desert sky still reflected red light. The scene in the courtyard looked much as it did the night before. Young, well-dressed men populated the area amid a handful of bejeweled, beautiful women. All of them held a glass, and a few of them smoked. Music had been piped in from some unseen source, and a few couples danced to a classic instrumental.

I walked to the edge of the patio and saw Maria standing in the gazebo, talking to Captain Benson. She whispered something into his ear, and I saw him nod and turn away. Maria then turned toward me, as if she knew I was there, and began to walk in my direction.

Her gait was like no other I had ever seen. She seemed to float along, and yet the tilt of her hips as she swayed with each step was obvious. Wearing a low-cut purple gown trimmed in gold lace, she looked like a princess. As she approached, her eyes locked onto mine.

A large diamond adorned her neck, held in place not by a chain, but by a velvet string wrapped in gold accents. She extended a hand, which I took in mine. With her other hand, she stroked the side of my face and smiled. Like the night before, she took my chin in her hands and turned my head first one way, and then the other.

"Much better, sí?" She then moved into me, her chest against mine, and placed a soft kiss on my cheek.

A mild shock went through me, making it difficult to stand.

"Come," Maria said, pulling my hand. "Have a drink, and mingle with my friends. The captain is having our meal prepared, and soon we will dine together."

We walked across the patio to where the bartender readied drinks. Maria spoke to him, and then handed me a drink. Tequila.

We wandered toward the gazebo, which had small lights under the edges of the roof, casting a soft glow toward the interior. I made eye contact with several people as we walked, and each of them looked me over. I felt like I was attending a party where I was not welcome. The looks ranged from cold to curious, and some were downright hostile. I felt that I was doing something wrong. Perhaps I was not properly invited, or maybe, I was just not part of this crowd.

Maria spoke quietly with some of the others, mostly the few women present. I took a seat and pretended to be comfortable while sipping the tequila. Several times, when I spotted Maria, she and the person she was speaking with happened to be looking at me. It was almost as if she were introducing me without me even being there. I thought that strange, but just sat there and endured the sidelong glances and the plastic smiles.

Finally, Maria made her way back and took me by the hand. "Come," she said. "Our dinner is ready now." She led me to the nearest entrance to the hotel, and we made our way through a maze of corridors to a dining room. Thirty tables were set with fine linens and silverware. Only half were filled with diners taking a meal at this late hour. The people there ranged in age, some young and some well into their sixties or beyond. The maître d' led us to a table next to a large window looking out over the dark, wild land east of the hotel. I could make out some tall saguaro cacti silhouetted in the moonlight.

He seated Maria, and I took a chair opposite her.

"Adam," Maria said. "Please come and sit here next to me, sí?" She pulled out the chair beside her and motioned with a curled index finger.

I did as asked, and adjusted myself in my seat.

"Our meal has been prepared," Maria said, just as a waiter in black pants and white shirt arrived with a covered, silver tray. Behind him, another server arrived with a tray containing smaller plates and bowls, and she distributed them before us.

There were bowls of spiced chicken, beef, and pork, along with steamed tortillas and fresh vegetables. It smelled amazing.

Starved, I began to pick through the bowls, sampling a bit of it all. Maria barely ate anything, but asked many questions.

"So, Señor Adam, how do you spend your time?"

I told her about The Fast Lane and how that kept me busy.

She apologized for having never heard of us.

I told her that I wanted to spend a little more time at home and with my old friends, and how I missed my family in Oklahoma. I told her how crazy life had become in a famous rock band, and that I just wanted to slow down and enjoy life.

She looked at me with those turquoise eyes gleaming. "Then I am very glad you stopped at the Hotel California. Life is happy here, and we have much to enjoy, sí?"

"It's a lovely place, but it pales in comparison to your lovely face." After I said that, I really felt stupid. I didn't normally talk like that, and I couldn't figure out what had come over me. I felt like that high school kid I had uncovered earlier in the day.

Maria just smiled.

I picked at the food while Maria asked her questions. After an hour, I pushed my plate aside. I think I had told her more about myself than I had told anyone else in my life, and it felt good. Maria was a good listener, and she seemed to care about my answers, many of which I had never realized until that night.

"Come," Maria said as she stood. "I want some fun now, and I would like to be alone with you."

Her comment was not a request, nor was it disguised as one.

She took me by the hand and led me outside. We walked in the moonlight around one end of the hotel to a small parking lot. Coming to a Mercedes convertible, she motioned for me to get in the passenger side.

With Maria behind the wheel, the Mercedes pulled out and headed into the desert. She drove the car into the foothills of a nearby mountain range and navigated the twisting two-lane road at high speed. I slid from one side of the seat to the other as she downshifted and turned. I could hear the tires scream for mercy when she rounded the curves, laughing the whole time.

I tried to maintain a smile, as if I were enjoying the ride, and that's when I discovered that two parts of me acted independently. My mind begged me to get out of this car, and keep a healthy distance from this crazy woman. Another part of me suppressed those feelings, and wanted more than anything to be right there, right then, with that wonderfully dangerous creature. I imagined Good Sense on one shoulder, shouting warnings into my ear, while Bad Sense sat on the other, whispering that this would be fun. I listened to the whispers, and sat on those leather seats with a grin on my face, while hanging on with white knuckles.

Maria whipped the Benz into a scenic pull-off, skidded to a stop and killed the engine. I sat there, dazed for a moment, before realizing that I was indeed still drawing breath. Maria turned in her seat and put two fingers to the side of my neck.

"Your pulse is racing, Señor Adam!" She turned back in her seat, and looked out over the hood. The Mercedes sat five feet from a guardrail, high up on the mountainside. From that vantage point, I could see for miles over the desert floor, a scattering of lights far off in the distance.

Maria raised her right hand to eye level, and I looked at the rings on her fingers. She gracefully swayed them, watching the sparkles in the moonlight. She pointed with her other hand to the ring on her middle finger. I could not tell if the large stone was a diamond or sapphire in the bluish moonlight.

"This one is new to me," she said with a big smile. "It is beautiful, sí?"

"Very beautiful," I heard myself say.

"I have many pretty, pretty boys who bring me gifts from Tiffany's. My friends have very good taste, sí?"

She continued to gaze at the rings on each hand. Grinning broadly as she straightened some of them, her mind seemed twisted by their dazzle. Eventually, she placed her hands back in her lap and gazed up at the stars.

"It's peaceful, here, sí?" she asked.

"Yes," I said. My labored breathing and her soft, purring, voice were the only sounds.

"Peaceful is good," she said. "I sense that you do not have a lot of peaceful time in your life."

"My life is at the other end of that spectrum. I haven't had much peace in a long time."

Maria nodded and looked out over the mountainside. The moon lit her face, and everything around us looked to be some shade of blue.

"I have a question for you," she said, "but first, I must do something." She then leaned over, pulled my face to hers, and kissed me passionately. My body went weak, and I could feel the muscles in my arms twitch. The kiss seemed to go on and on, our lips pressed together with such force that mine seemed to go numb. But that kiss ended suddenly, when she bit my bottom lip—hard.

I felt her teeth pierce the skin, and then both Good Sense and Bad shouted in my mind. I pulled away with a horrified look on my face.

Maria sunk back into the leather seat and turned her face up toward the moon. Her eyes were closed, and she licked her lips as if she had just finished a piece of world-class chocolate. I said nothing, but my mind raced with chaotic thoughts. Images flashed in my mind, mostly of Maria, some of the hotel, and a few from my childhood. The last image to fade away was that of a rattlesnake, coiled to strike.

She then turned to me again and smiled. When she saw the look on my face, she laughed aloud.

"Señor Adam, have you ever been kissed so well?" I got that sidelong glance and sprightly smirk of hers.

"It was interesting. It ended much different than most."

She opened the console between the seats, pulled out a tissue and wiped my lip. "When I kiss a man for the first time, it is my intention that it never be forgotten." As she drew the tissue away, I noticed a dark spot of blood on it before she tossed it out the window.

"And now I have a question for you, Adam, but I do not want the answer right now. You will give it to me later, sí?"

"Okay."

"If you could be any way you want, what would be the word for that?"

I must have looked at her dumbly, because she rephrased the question.

"If you had to think of one word that would describe how you want to be in your life, what word would that be?"

I started to ask her to clarify, but as soon as I spoke, she put her index finger to my lips and held them closed.

"Not now, Adam, but soon, I will ask you for that word. Just one, simple word."

I nodded and leaned back in my seat.

"And now, before we return to the hotel, I have something to tell you that might help you find your word. In many ancient cultures," she said, "the victorious warriors drank the blood of their fallen enemies. Do you know of this, Adam?

"I think I've heard something about that. I'm not really much on history."

"It is true," she said. "And in some cultures, the warriors would eat the heart of their foes. Have you heard of this? Before I could answer, Maria continued. "It was believed that if they drank the blood or ate the flesh, the warrior would gain the power of his enemy, and would become like *two* men."

I sat there dumbly, wondering where this conversation was going next.

"So think about this, Adam. If you could slay your enemy and drink his blood, what power would you gain from him?"

She reached for the key and the Mercedes roared to life.

"Just think about that as you think of your word."

Maria drove us back to the hotel at a much calmer pace. During the ride, I wondered just what I had gotten myself into, and if there was still time to bail out. I knew that something was wrong, but I felt helpless to stop it. The last twenty-four hours seemed like a dream turning into a nightmare.

Maria parked the Benz in the same place and took me by the hand.

"Please join me again in the courtyard," Maria said playfully, tugging me along. "We are living it up at the Hotel California, and we have much left to do."

I had given up on trying to make sense of anything Maria said. It all sounded so bizarre, so cryptic. *We have much left to do.* I wondered what she meant.

We walked back to the courtyard, and there on the patio, numerous people milled about. They sipped drinks and chatted, just as they had before. The bartender was busy, and classical Spanish guitar music played softly in the background.

Maria asked me to sit on the bench, and moments later, she brought me a drink.

"Think of your word now," she said. "Choose wisely, Adam, and your life will be changed."

I took the glass from her and raised it to my lips, not recognizing the drink's strong, unusual aroma. It went down smoothly, trailing a length of heat down my chest.

Remembering what Maria asked me to do, I began thinking about the word she wanted me to find. While I had no idea as to what this was all about, it did get me to thinking about the happy boy I had once been, and the rich, famous, yet miserable man I had become. It seemed funny to think back to when we first got the band together, and how excited we were to play our music. We had no money then, and we all had big dreams of fancy cars and fast women, and our faces on the front of Rolling Stone.

Now that I had all of that, it seemed ironic to want to go back to when being broke was so much damn fun. Then a word came to me, and I began to ponder it. I tasted it and turned it over in my mouth. Yes, it seemed to meet Maria's request for one word that stated how I wanted to be. In fact, that one word, I then realized, was truly the only way a person should consider being.

Satisfied with my choice, I walked into the crowd, looking for Maria, but did not see her. As I walked to the far side of the patio, I noticed the man I spoke to in the bar hours earlier, the one with the nice Rolex. He and a fellow in a red blazer stood away from the crowd, speaking in hushed tones. The man's eyes shifted nervously as he spoke to the other who had his back to me. As I got closer, the man with the Rolex became silent, and I saw him touch the other on the shoulder. The man in the blazer turned and looked at me, swirled the scant amount of liquid in his glass, then walked toward the bartender.

The Rolex guy nodded at me, and I did the same in return. I walked closer, and he looked at me cautiously. I extended my hand.

"I'm Adam," I said. The man hesitated, but finally reached for my hand and shook it.

"I'm Blake."

"From our earlier conversation, I take it you've been here many times before."

"Yes, too many times. Far too many times." He took a long gulp from his glass. "But I think this will be my last visit. One way, or another, it will be my last."

I looked at the people in the center of the courtyard, many of whom now danced to the music.

Blake tilted his glass toward the group. "Wine, women, and song. Some dance to remember, some dance to forget."

I raised an eyebrow at that comment. "Remember what?" I asked. "Forget what?"

"Life before the Hotel California. They all look happy, right?"

"Everyone but you. And maybe your friend who just walked away. He didn't look too happy, either."

Blake looked at me funny. "Just wait. You will soon understand what I'm talking about. And when you do, when you become one of them," he nodded at the crowd, "just remember to bring your alibis."

With that, he walked away. Perhaps he went to look for his friend, or perhaps he just wanted to be alone with his disturbed thoughts.

I wondered why people around there seemed to speak in riddles. It was definitely the strangest place I'd ever been, and I'd seen some pretty strange places. Then I wondered if it was just me. Something had come over me since I'd first set eyes on this place, of that I was certain. Was it because of the place...or Maria... or a combination of the two? To this day, I'm still not sure.

When I turned away from the departing Blake, I came face-to-face with Maria who had come up behind me. I wondered if Blake walked away because of her.

"Adam," she said slyly. "Do you have your word now?"

"Yes," I replied, wondering just what kind of game this was. I knew I'd had a few too many drinks, but I didn't feel drunk. And yet, I did feel rather strange, like I was watching a movie—starring me—filmed from the first-person perspective. I didn't feel in control of myself, and old Good Sense really started to howl.

"Very good," Maria replied. "It's a good word, sí?"

"It's a very good word. The best one I could think of."

"I see. Then there is one final step that I will ask of you, and your life will be forever changed."

"For the better, I hope," I said without thinking.

"Sí," she answered, and kissed me again on the lips. "The captain will prepare a special wine for you. Please find him and tell him your word, and he will bring the wine for you when the time is right. After you find him and tell him your word, please come to the gazebo and I will take you to a very special place."

I stood as if I were in a trance as she traced the long nail of her index finger down the side of my jaw, then down my neck. When she walked away, I set out to find the captain and tell him my word.

Strange as it seemed, Bad Sense was rather excited to see where this was all going.

I found the captain standing at attention near the bar. He watched me as I approached, but never greeted me when I stopped in front of him.

"Captain," I said. "Please bring me my wine."

"What's your word, son?"

"Blissful," I answered. I could think of no way that I would rather be than blissful.

The captain stared straight ahead, but he said, "We haven't had that spirit here since nineteen sixty nine. Do you have another word?"

That caught me off guard. I didn't plan for a backup word. I tried to think of another word that meant the same thing as blissful, but none of them had the same strength. *Happy* was not the same as *blissful*, nor was *joyful*. *Blissful* was like a word-island, and no other word fit the idea I had in my mind. I ran a few more words through, like *euphoric* and *ecstatic*, but they also did not match the feeling that I got for *blissful*. Then, another idea came to me, inspired by the innocent boy I had uncovered earlier in the day.

"Confident," I said.

The captain nodded, but did not turn or look at me, much less congratulate me on my word.

"I'll prepare your wine, son, and bring it to the feast." He turned and walked away.

Feast? I thought. I'd had dinner only a couple of hours before, and didn't want to have a feast. My curiosity grew to an all-time high. Maria had promised my life would change, and I wondered what that had to do with this special wine, and the word. *Confident*, I had said. I could never have guessed how important that word would turn out to be.

I found Maria in the gazebo. She took me by the hand and led me into the hotel. We navigated several long corridors, and somewhere in the heart of the hotel, Maria stopped in front of a large pair of old, heavy, wooden doors. She inserted a key, and pushed the doors open.

Inside was one of the most lavish suites I had ever seen. Off to the left, a large pedestal bed that looked like a giant wineglass dominated the area. Instead of glass, the bed consisted of white mortar or cement. Satin sheets and pillows covered the inside of the bed, and mirrors covered the ceiling over it. In the other direction, I saw a sitting room with ornate furniture. A small kitchen area was in the far corner, and a hallway led off to parts unseen in another corner.

Maria led me to the strange bed. Next to it on a small table sat an ice bucket holding a bottle. Maria took the bottle and asked me to open it.

As I did, she pulled two goblets from under the table and asked me to pour. I filled the goblets with a pink liquid.

"Champagne, to celebrate," Maria said, lifting her glass to meet mine.

"What are we celebrating?"

"The beginning of the rest of your life," she answered with a giggle that made her even more irresistible.

I sipped the sweetest champagne I had ever tasted, and I had never been fond of the stuff before that night. Everything at the Hotel California seemed to be sweeter than out in the real world. I caught that thought as it crossed my mind, and figured that I no longer thought of this place as real.

"It's good," I said.

After a few sips in silence, Maria put her glass down and slipped onto the satin sheets. She patted the space next to her, and her eyes told me to join her.

I turned my back to the bed, let myself slip over the hard edge and onto the softness beyond. She moved next to me and cradled my head in her arms. At that moment, I couldn't think of a place I'd rather have been. Her arms felt cool to the sides of my face, but in a way that touched me like a fresh, night breeze. I could hear her deep, even breathing as she stroked my cheek.

"The captain told me your word," Maria said. "I must say, it is not a word that most men choose."

"It wasn't my first choice, but it seemed to fit in with what I've been thinking about lately."

Maria continued to stroke my face, and then adjusted herself on the bed so that she placed a couple of fingers from each hand at my temples and began to massage them. I felt a mild electric current passing through my head, and after a moment, I just melted into the bed and let Maria overwhelm me.

"We have captured the spirit of many great men," she said. "Most of my pretty boys will choose words like *powerful, courageous,* or *brave* to enhance the warrior within them. Many will waste their gift and choose *famous* or *wealthy*, not realizing that those are just side effects of other great qualities. A few choose spirits simply for themselves, like *artistic* and *intelligent*."

I got lost in her words, but Good Sense whispered in my ear. *Captured the spirit?* It tried to raise an alarm.

Bad Sense made a better comment, simply whispering *enjoy the moment.*

"But you, Señor Adam, you chose *confident.* "

She continued to massage my temples, and by then my body felt like a mass of jell-o, becoming one with the softness of the bed and absorbed in her words.

"It's an interesting choice," she then said. "And time will tell if that word works out for you."

My eyes were closed while she spoke those last words, but I sensed Maria bending down, and I soon felt her lips pressed against mine. I realized I could not move. Paralysis had come over me, and I panicked. Adrenaline pumped furiously through my veins, but try as I might, I could not even twitch a muscle. Good Sense screamed out, *you've been hyp-no-tized!*

I could hear every breath Maria took in, and I swear I could hear the blink of her eyes. My own pulse pounded a rapid cadence in my now hyper-sensitive ears, and yet I could also hear the ticking of some faraway clock.

"Señor Adam," Maria said. "Do not be afraid. Relax and simply listen to me now."

It didn't appear that I had any choice, so I willed myself to relax and could hear my pulse slow.

"We shall have a ceremony soon," Maria said. "We call this ceremony *The Feast*. My sisters and I will be there, as will a few of my friends, like you," she added. "You will receive your wine, and you will drink. When you have finished, you will have ingested the spirit of another, making you very special and very fortunate, indeed." She paused for a moment while she rubbed my temples. "It will also make you very *delicious*." She tapped my lips with her fingers.

Even with my eyes closed, I could see her evil little smirk in my mind.

With my head spinning, I began to ponder her words. Bad Sense grew uncommonly quiet, but Good Sense bellowed loud and clear, *she's got you now, you fool! You are now her slave! I told you this wasn't right!*

"After you drink your wine, you will be initiated," she said. "You will become part of our family here at the Hotel California, and you will come back to visit many times. Each time, you will bring me a gift, sí? And each time, I will give you a gift as well."

I could feel her moving, and again she placed a passionate kiss upon my paralyzed lips. Even with the fear I now felt, I ached to respond and kiss her back.

"One final thing," Maria said in a business-like voice. "You will never speak of this place to another, ever. If you try, you will not be able to. So please save yourself the pain, and do not even try."

I then felt one of her fingers making a small circle on my forehead.

"Señor Adam," she called in a sing-song voice. "It is time that we go to the ceremony."

I found myself staring into my own eyes reflected from the mirrored ceiling above me. The look on my boyish face, dead and dull, lacked any emotion. Muscles began to twitch in my hands, and soon I could raise my arms. Maria slid from the bed and reached for my hand.

"Come," she said. "It is time for *The Feast*."

I tested my voice. "Maria?"

Her delicate eyebrow rose.

"Am I a prisoner here?"

She shot her eyes downward. "We are all just prisoners here," she said. "Of our own device."

I finally gained control of my legs, and followed Maria like a good little slave. Though aware of my surroundings, I was powerless to control my own behavior. As Maria and I walked down dark corridors, it was like watching a movie in my head. I knew she had some sort of power over me, and even though I struggled against it, I was like the fly in the spider's web—struggling in futility.

We went down at least two flights of stairs, and through dark and narrow corridors. Maria paused in front of another pair of old, wooden doors.

"Welcome to my private chambers," she said. "You will come here again many times, but the first time is the most special." I got that sexy sidelong glance and naughty smile from her before she pushed open the doors.

Before I entered the room lit only by candles, various aromas hit me at the doorway. Smoke, in a variety of flavors, and incense were the most obvious. I saw a long, narrow table covered in red linen and set with silver goblets. A dozen chairs lined one side of this table, filled with young, clean-shaven men. Five chairs were centered on the other side, and four lovely ladies in gowns sat there, all of whom I recognized from the courtyard gatherings. The only two empty chairs sat on either side.

The people seated looked up as Maria led me into the room. They spoke in hushed tones and many whispered directly into the ears of the ones seated next to them. I was seated at the chair centered on the side with all men, and Maria made her way around the far end of the table to her seat on the other side. Maria stood behind her empty chair, which to me looked more like a throne. She took her silver goblet into both hands, then raised it, turning first to her right, then to her left.

"Welcome to The Feast," she said. Everyone raised their goblets, so I did the same. She touched the rim of her goblet to the rim of the goblet of the lady next to her, and the gentle ring of silver on silver spread round the table.

Nobody smiled during this toast, but held an emotionless demeanor. On my left sat Blake, the man I had met earlier on the patio, and to my right sat his friend who I had yet to meet. A bead of sweat ran down the side of Blake's face, and his friend stared down at his goblet.

I looked at my goblet, half full with a dark, viscous liquid. Good Sense shouted into my ear. *Blood! You know that's blood!*

Maria took her seat and then bowed her head as if in prayer.

Blake held both hands under the table, working at something. He looked nervous, and moved like a tightly wound spring.

I saw Maria staring at me. The eyes of a demon tore through to my soul, bright red, and glistening in the candlelight. I looked to the ladies on either side of Maria, whose eyes had also changed. Fear gripped my heart, causing it to pause. I felt my head swim in a sudden dizziness. My mind wanted to scream, but paralysis caught hold of me again, and I could not move.

A flash of motion caught my attention when Blake got up from his seat and lunged across the table at Maria. I saw a flash of steel, and then saw Maria fall back into her seat, with the hilt of a knife protruding from her upper chest. Her head shot back and she howled in pain. The man on my right followed Blake's lead and also lunged with a knife. This one caught Maria near the base of the throat. The man climbed on the table and pushed the knife even harder, knocking over my goblet in the process.

I maintained enough awareness to see the other women jump from their chairs, hissing like angry cats while bearing enormous fangs. Their fingernails became sharp talons, and their eyes burned with fury. One grabbed Blake's friend, burying a set of claws into his throat and pulling a handful of flesh away. The man buckled onto the table, his throat a bubbling mass of blood and torn flesh.

Blake fell back, knocking over his chair. Two of the demon ladies leapt upon him in seconds, but I did not see what happened to him. My eyes went back to Maria, who I thought was surely dead. She sat in her chair with a scowl on her face and pulled the knife from her neck. Surprisingly, very little blood came from the wound. Maria reached for the other knife, and slowly pulled it from her chest.

Chaos erupted all around me. I heard Blake scream before I realized I'd regained most of my senses. I was no longer in that fog Maria created around me. Both Good Sense and Bad urged me in the same direction. I looked at the silver goblet before me, tilted on its side, the dark red contents soaking into the tablecloth. The goblet reflected my own face in a distorted fashion, but I recognized the kid and prayed his confidence could get us out of this mess. I realized I didn't need any special wine to find that confidence; I'd had it all along, buried somewhere within me. Now was the time to dig it out and put it to good use.

I rolled to the side as one of the demons leapt past me, grabbed a man by the collar and pushed him to the floor. On hands and knees under the table, I saw one of the knives that Maria had removed from her body, so I grabbed it and shuffled to the back of the room. The women were like sharks in a feeding frenzy, their faces smeared with blood. The hideous sounds they emitted did not sound human.

I turned to get my bearings when something hit me from behind, knocking me harshly into the wall. I dropped to my knees, losing the knife. When I turned, I saw a man's bloody body had been tossed my way, and that was what had knocked me down.

Someone had opened the doors to the chamber, and I clambered over bodies, both moving and still, until I reached them. Still weak, my nervousness caused my legs to rebel. People moved all about the room, but nobody tried to stop me as I headed for the exit.

I turned in the dark corridors and ran, seeking any stairway that led upward. I could not tell how long it took me to find my way back to the main level, but soon the relative brightness of the lobby greeted me, which was thankfully empty at this time of night. Empty, except for Hernando.

I saw him at the same time he saw me, and he came out from behind the counter with a strange, wild grin on his face. Grabbing me by the lapels, he slammed me up against the wall. He looked into my horrified face and put his close enough to mine that I could smell the mint he had recently eaten.

"Relax, señor," he said with a grim smile. "We are programmed to receive."

I grabbed his arms and tried to break his grip, but he held me firm.

"You can check out any time you like," he said, "but you can never leave!"

I twisted and fought, but Hernando proved far more powerful than I thought. Or, perhaps I was just that weak after what I had seen. Hernando still held me against the wall when he next spoke.

"The Hotel California is in you now. Even if you leave this place, the place will never leave you. You will be back!"

I brought my hands up as he stared into my eyes, then brought them down on his wrists with all the energy I had. I heard my jacket tear and I twisted free of his grip and ran for the exit.

Hernando laughed madly as I ran out into the cool night. He must have run to the door behind me, because I heard him clearly when he shouted, "You belong to us now, señor!"

When I found the keys to the 'Vette, he stood outside, waving. A woman appeared and stood beside Hernando. Although I could not see well, I knew it was Maria, and I swear that she blew me a kiss as I scrambled to leave.

Seconds later, with my hands shaking, I had the V-8 growling and the tires screaming as I left the parking lot and shot out onto the highway. I had no idea which direction I headed, but I pushed the Corvette for all it was worth and the desert landscape flew past me in a blur.

My mind churned images like a kaleidoscope until I saw the pinkness of the sunrise in my rearview mirror. I saw a sign proclaiming that Los Angeles lay another 40 miles ahead of me, and I began to think more rationally once again. I entered the city limits as the sun crested the horizon behind me. I had never been more grateful to see the sunlight and watch the shadows disappear.

* * *

The story I just told you happened more than thirty years ago. I have never told anyone about it before, but not because I haven't tried. If I try to talk about my experience at The Hotel California, I get a sudden, crushing headache in the center of my forehead. The pain gets so bad that I can no longer talk. So the story has gone untold until now, when I realized that I could write about it without the tremendous pain.

I managed to fulfill my contract with the record company, and The Fast Lane made one more hit record before I called it quits and went back to Oklahoma.

During that time, I wrote letters to Brenda Jane, and told her what I had been going through and what a fool I had been. I told her how I longed for a normal life again, and just one more Saturday night at the Burger Barn, listening to the jukebox—with her. After the third such letter, Brenda Jane began writing back.

We eventually patched things up and tied the knot twenty-seven years ago. We have three grown kids and the first grandbaby on the way.

Daddy passed away a few years back, so I run the hardware store now, along with my son Blake. He knows the difference between a blind hinge and a butt hinge, and can tell you what kind of caulk to use in a bathroom and what kind to use around windows. Customers like him too.

I also opened a car dealership with some of the money I made from The Fast Lane, but I have people who run that for me, because I'd rather be in the hardware store; less paperwork.

Hernando was wrong when he said that I'd come back to the Hotel California. But he was also right in a way. While I have never been back to that area of the country again, I visit the hotel quite often in my dreams, and of course, that includes reliving my short time with Maria.

I can still see her face as plain as the night she bit my lip. The dreams always start out pleasant, but before the dream ends, I see those demon eyes and wake up in a cold sweat.

It's not as bad as it used to be. Brenda Jane wakes me up two or three times a year now, jostling me out of the nightmare and comforting me when I come to, breathing hard and shaking like a cold pup. I know it could have been worse. I often wonder where I would be now if Blake and his nameless friend had not done what they did. I wonder what would have happened to me if I had drunk my wine, and if I had been with Maria again. Good Sense still tells me I'm far better off the way things are, but Bad Sense tickles my brain with thoughts about Maria, and lying in her pedestal bed.

In general, life is good. With or without the wine, I have become the confident and fortunate man who I wished to be those many years ago.

THE END

AUTHORS

About the Authors

Ophelia Julien

Ophelia Julien grew up in a haunted house on the near north side of Chicago, a circumstance that has given a decided slant to her work since she first began writing stories somewhere around third grade. *Dead of Summer*, her first published work, appeared in 1990. *Saving Jake* was released in 2002. She writes for Young Adult/New Adult readers, but recently her audience began expanding with her Bridgeton Park Cemetery Series. *Haunted*, the first book in the series debuted in 2012 and was followed by book two, *Dead Voices* in 2014. In addition, she has a nonfiction title, *Ghosts of Lake Michigan*, available through Quixote Press, and a short e-story, *Hunting Spirits*. She is currently working on book three for the Bridgeton Park Cemetery Series.

Ms. Julien loves ghost stories, gets recharged by watching paranormal reality TV shows, and takes every ghost tour she can find, especially when traveling. Should you ever meet her, feel free to discuss the paranormal or swap a ghost story with her. She firmly believes that *everyone* has a ghost story.

Website:

http://opheliajulien.com

Blog: Ubiquitous Ghosts on BlogSpot

http://opheliajulien.blogspot.com/

Facebook and Twitter

Andrea Jones

Andrea Jones, author of "Smooth Criminal," is inspired by edgy works of music, and also by literary classics. Jones' first novel, *Hook & Jill* (Reginetta Press), is a serious parody of J.M. Barrie's Peter Pan story, and intended for adult readers.

Hook & Jill won five literary awards, among them the Gold Award for Adult Fiction and Literature in the 2010 Mom's Choice Awards®, and Best New Fiction in the 2010 International Book Awards.

Other Oceans: Book Two of the Hook & Jill Saga netted seven more awards. Jones plans five books for the series. Her short story, "Deeper Creatures," appears in *The Sea* (Crossroad Press). Jones is the editor of classic restoration projects: J.M. Barrie's *Peter and Wendy: the Restored Text*; and *Prince of Thieves* and *Robin Hood the Outlaw* by Alexandre Dumas (Reginetta Press).

Graduated from the University of Illinois at Urbana-Champaign, Jones studied Oral Interpretation of Literature, with a Literature minor. In her career in television production, she worked for CBS, PBS, and corporate studios.

Andrea Jones is known around the world as Capitana Red-Hand of the international pirate brotherhood, Under the Black Flag. She is a member of the Brethren of the Great Lakes. Jones' home port is near Chicago.

David McAfee

David McAfee is the author of the UK Bestseller, *33 A.D.*, as well as its two sequels. He has written over a dozen novels, both under his own name and as a ghostwriter, and has contributed numerous short stories to various horror collections like this one. In addition to horror, he has also penned a nonfiction account about being a stay at home parent, a scary prospect in and of itself. He currently resides in Tennessee with his wife and children.

He can be reliably found on Facebook, or less reliably via his oft-neglected blog:

mcafeeland.wordpress.com

Rumor has it he has a Twitter account as well, though reliable information on this cannot be found.

Donnie Light

Donnie Light lives in rural Northern Illinois. He has a background in engineering and information technology.

Growing up, Donnie read every action-adventure and horror story he could get his hands on. Since he wrote his first novel, *Dark Justice* in 1992, he has strived to deliver fast-paced scary stories to his readers.

He co-wrote *The Ripper Trilogy* with author Shawn Weaver, which consists of Book One: *Ripper's Row*, Book Two, *Ripper's Revenge*, and Book Three, *Ripper's Wrath*.

He currently has another exciting novel in editing, expected to be released early in 2016.

Website:

http://donnielight.com

Email:

donnie.light@gmail.com

He is also on Facebook and occasionally on Twitter.

Connor Millard

[In the interest of public memetic safety, this bio has been redacted. And in actuality, this redaction should itself be redacted. We apologize for any unwanted contact with transconceptual entities. The following information, however, is safe:]

Blog:

http://theverydefinitionofprocrastination.blogspot.com

Email:

connor.e.millard@gmail.com

Ann Fields

Ann began her writing career in the romance genre. She published four romance novels and one novella under the pen name of Anna Larence before she encountered her first ghost. That one brush with the supernatural shifted her focus from love and happily ever after to love and life in the after. In her novel, *Fuller's Curse* and her short stories featured in *Voices from the Block* and *The Writer's Block*: *A Legacy of African-American Literature*, she explores life in all its many dimensions.

Website:

www.annfields.com

Twitter:

https://twitter.com/ann_fields

Facebook:

https://www.facebook.com/AnnFieldsAuthor

Niki Danforth

Niki Danforth, daughter of a Cold War covert intelligence officer, has the thriller/adventure gene in her DNA. After a career in New York television, including as a director for *Lifestyles of the Rich and Famous*, this empty-nester recreated herself as an author of suspenseful mysteries. Introducing a feisty, sexy, mid-life heroine in *Stunner: A Ronnie Lake Mystery*, Danforth has given her budding detective a new whodunit to solve in *Delilah: A Ronnie Lake Cold Case*. Danforth is currently at work on A Ronnie Lake Murder Mystery. The author, who recently completed *A Wild Ride: The Adventures of Misty & Moxie Wyoming*, a children's magical mystery novel, lives in New Jersey with her husband and two drama-queen dogs.

Website:

http://nikidanforth.com

Email:

nikidanforth5@gmail.com

Facebook:

https://www.facebook.com/NikiDanforthAuthor

Twitter:

https://twitter.com/NikiDanforth

Terri Reid

Terri is the creator of the *Mary O'Reilly Paranormal Mysteries*. An indie author, Reid published her first book *"Loose Ends – A Mary O'Reilly Paranormal Mystery"* in August 2010. By the end of 2013, *"Loose Ends"* had sold over 200,000 copies. She now has thirteen other books in the Mary O'Reilly Series and has enjoyed Best-Seller, Top Rated and Hot New Release status for all of them in the Mystery, Paranormal Romance, Horror, Cozy, or Women Sleuths categories. Her books have been translated into Spanish, Portuguese and German and are also now also available in audio versions.

Reid has been quoted in a number of books about the self-publishing industry including *"Let's Get Digital Edition One and Edition Two"* by David Gaughran and *"Interviews with Indie Authors: Top Tips from Successful Self-Published Authors"* by Claire and Tim Ridgway. She was honored to have some of her works included in A. J. Abbiati's book *"The NORTAV Method for Writers – The Secrets to Constructing Prose Like the Pros."*

Reid is from Northwest Illinois, near the town of Freeport, the home of her fictional characters. Her background is in marketing and public relations. She is married, the mother of seven children and the grandmother of sixteen adorable grandchildren.

Website:

http://terrireid.com/

Sharon Love Cook

Sharon Love Cook began her writing career at age 17 as a correspondent for the *Cape Ann Summer Sun*, a seasonal supplement to the *Gloucester Daily Times (Mass.)*. She covered the beach colony where she lived. She also provided a cartoon each week, the first time her 'toons appeared in print. Not much happened during those summers in the mid '60s. Her copy tended to be about the Red Cross swim classes, the restoration of the wooden steps leading to the beach and the jellyfish invasions. On one occasion a teenage resident received a visit from her Japanese pen pal. This blew the jellyfish story right off the page.

She is the author of the Granite Cove Mysteries and is working on #3: *Laugh 'til You Die*. In it, Rose McNichols, Cook's protagonist, does stand-up comedy at nursing homes, something Cook herself has done—and doesn't recommend.

She lives with her husband and small herd of cats in Beverly Farms, on Boston's North Shore. Contact her at sharonlovecook(at)comcast.net, or sharonlovecook.com. Check out Granite Cove, where the only things open at midnight are the sea clams:

Website:

sharonlovecook.com

Email:

sharonlovecook@comcast.net

A.T. Reid

A.T. Reid is an award-winning novice author from Northwest Illinois. Reid also enjoys screenplay writing and acting, including work in short films that have made their way to film festivals. He has also been the writer and director of an award-winning short film.

Reid considers himself a geek and would be in heaven if Firefly could somehow drop into an Avengers movie. His geekiness extends to his writing mode as he enjoys experimenting with cross-genre subjects.

Reid is currently working on a series of short stories based in the world of Teraven. They will be available through Amazon.

Email:

a.t.reid007@gmail.com

Made in the USA
Middletown, DE
29 October 2016